STRONG POISON

'Bunter,' said Lord Peter, looking up from this letter,
'I *knew* there was something fishy about that will.'

'Yes, my lord.'

'There is something about wills which brings out
the worst side of human nature. People who under
ordinary circumstances are perfectly upright and
amiable, go as curtly as corkscrews and foam at the
mouth whenever they hear the words "I devise and
bequeath". That reminds me, a spot of champagne
in a silver tankard is no bad thing to celebrate on.
Get up a bottle of the Pommery and tell Chief
Inspector Parker I should be glad of a word with
him. And bring me those notes of Mr Arbuthnot's.
And oh, Bunter!'

'My lord?'

'Get Mr Crofts on the phone and give him my
compliments, and say I have found the criminal and
the motive and hope presently to produce proof of
the way the crime was done, if he will see that the
case is put off for a week or so.'

'Very good, my lord.'

'All the same, Bunter, I really don't know how it
was done.'

'That will undoubtedly suggest itself before long,
my lord.'

'Oh, yes,' said Wimsey airily. 'Of course. Of
course. I'm not worrying about a trifle like that.'

**Also by the same author,
and published by
Hodder and Stoughton Paperbacks**

About the Author

Born in Oxford in 1893, Dorothy Leigh Sayers was later to become a classical scholar and honours graduate in modern languages. Between 1921 and 1932 she was employed as a copywriter in an advertising agency.

But in 1923 she put into print a character who was to become one of the most popular fictional heroes of the century – Lord Peter Wimsey, man-about-town and amateur sleuth, who features in a dozen novels and numerous short stories. Several of the novels have been adapted for radio and television.

She died in 1957, leaving the final canto of the COMEDY – 'Paradiso' – unfinished. It was later completed by her friend, Dr Barbara Reynolds.

Strong Poison

Dorothy L. Sayers

CORONET BOOKS
Hodder and Stoughton

First published by Victor Gollancz
Ltd., 1930

First published as a Four Square edi-
tion 1960
NEL edition 1968
New NEL edition 1970
New edition 1975
New reset edition 1977
Coronet Crime edition 1989

Second impression 1990

Printed and bound in Great Britain for
Hodder and Stoughton Paperbacks, a
division of Hodder and Stoughton
Ltd., Mill Road, Dunton Green,
Sevenoaks, Kent TN13 2YA (Editorial
Office: 47 Bedford Square, London
WC1B 3DP) by Clays Ltd, St Ives plc.

ISBN 0-340-50227-4

Chapter I

THERE were crimson roses on the bench; they looked like splashes of blood.

The judge was an old man; so old, he seemed to have out-lived time and change and death. His parrot-face and parrot-voice were dry, like his old, heavily-veined hands. His scarlet robe clashed harsh with the crimson of the roses. He had sat for three days in the stuffy court, but he showed no sign of fatigue.

He did not look at the prisoner as he gathered his notes into a neat sheaf and turned to address the jury, but the prisoner looked at him. Her eyes, like dark smudges under the heavy square brows, seemed equally without fear and without hope. They waited.

'Members of the jury – '

The patient old eyes seemed to sum them up and take stock of their united intelligence. Three respectable tradesmen – a tall, argumentative one, a stout, embarrassed one with a droop-ing moustache, and an unhappy one with a bad cold; a director of a large company, anxious not to waste valuable time; a publi-can, incongruously cheerful; two youngish men of the artisan class; a nondescript, elderly man, of educated appearance, who might have been anything; an artist with a red beard disguising a weak chin; three women – an elderly spinster, a stout capable woman who kept a sweet-shop, and a harassed wife and mother whose thoughts seemed to be continually straying to her aban-doned hearth.

'Members of the jury – you have listened with great patience and attention to the evidence in this very distressing case, and it is now my duty to sum up the facts and arguments which have been put before you by the learned Attorney-General and by the learned counsel for the defence, and to put them in order as clearly as possible, so as to help you in forming your decision.

'But first of all, perhaps I ought to say a few words with regard to that decision itself. You know, I am sure, that it is a great principle of English law that every accused person is held to be innocent unless and until he is proved otherwise. It is not necessary for him, or her, to prove innocence; it is, in the modern slang phrase, "up to" the Crown to prove guilt, and unless you are quite satisfied that the Crown has done this beyond all reasonable doubt, it is your duty to return a verdict of "Not guilty". That does not necessarily mean that the prisoner has established her innocence by proof; it simply means that the Crown has failed to produce in your minds an undoubted conviction of her guilt.'

Salcombe Hardy, lifting his drowned-violet eyes for a moment from his reporter's note-book, scribbled two words on a slip of paper and pushed them over to Waffles Newton. 'Judge hostile.' Waffles nodded. They were old hounds on this blood-trail.

The judge creaked on.

'You may perhaps wish to hear from me exactly what is meant by those words "reasonable doubt". They mean, just so much doubt as you might have in everyday life about an ordinary matter of business. This is a case of murder, and it might be natural for you to think that, in such a case, the words mean more than this. But that is not so. They do not mean that you must cast about for fantastical solutions of what seems to you plain and simple. They do not mean those nightmare doubts which sometimes torment us at four o'clock in the morning when we have not slept very well. They mean that the proof must be such as you would accept about a plain matter of buying and selling, or some such commonplace transaction. You must not strain your belief in favour of the prisoner any more, of course, than you must accept proof of her guilt without the most careful scrutiny.

'Having said just these few words, so that you may not feel too much overwhelmed by the heavy responsibility laid upon you by your duty to the State, I will now begin at the beginning and try to place the story that we have heard, as clearly as possible before you.

'The case for the Crown is that the prisoner, Harriet Vane,

6

murdered Philip Boyes by poisoning him with arsenic. I need not detain you by going through the proofs offered by Sir James Lubbock and the other doctors who have given evidence as to the cause of death. The Crown say he died of arsenical poisoning, and the defence do not dispute it. The evidence is, therefore, that the death was due to arsenic, and you must accept that as a fact. The only question that remains for you is whether, in fact, that arsenic was deliberately administered by the prisoner with intent to murder.

'The deceased, Philip Boyes, was, as you have heard, a writer. He was thirty-six years old, and he had published five novels and a large number of essays and articles. All these literary works were of what is sometimes called an "advanced" type. They preached doctrines which may seem to some of us immoral or seditious, such as atheism, and anarchy, and what is known as "free love". His private life appears to have been conducted for some time at least, in accordance with these doctrines.

'At any rate, at some time in the year 1927 he became acquainted with Harriet Vane. They met in some of those artistic and literary circles where "advanced" topics are discussed, and after a time they became very friendly. The prisoner is also a novelist by profession, and it is very important to remember that she is a writer of so-called "mystery" or "detective" stories, such as deal with various ingenious methods of committing murder and other crimes.

'You have heard the prisoner in the witness-box, and you have heard the various people who came forward to give evidence as to her character. You have been told that she is a young woman of great ability, brought up on strictly religious principles, who, through no fault of her own, was left, at the age of twenty-three, to make her own way in the world. Since that time – and she is now twenty-nine years old – she has worked industriously to keep herself, and it is very much to her credit that she has, by her own exertions, made herself independent in a legitimate way, owing nothing to anybody and accepting help from no one.

'She has told us herself, with great candour, how she became deeply attached to Philip Boyes, and how, for a considerable time, she held out against his persuasions to live with him in an

7

irregular manner. There was, in fact, no reason at all why he should not have married her honourably; but apparently he represented himself as being conscientiously opposed to any formal marriage. You have the evidence of Sybil Marriott and Eiluned Price that the prisoner was made very unhappy by this attitude which he chose to take up, and you have heard also that he was a very handsome and attractive man, whom any woman might have found it difficult to resist.

'At any rate, in March of 1928, the prisoner, worn out, as she tells us, by his unceasing importunities, gave in, and consented to live on terms of intimacy with him, outside the bonds of marriage.

'Now you may feel, and quite properly, that this was a very wrong thing to do. You may, after making all allowances for this young woman's unprotected position, still feel that she was a person of unstable moral character. You will not be led away by the false glamour which certain writers contrive to throw about "free love" into thinking that this was anything but an ordinary, vulgar act of misbehaviour. Sir Impey Biggs, very rightly using all his great eloquence on behalf of his client, has painted this action of Harriet Vane's in very rosy colours; he has spoken of unselfish sacrifice and self-immolation, and has reminded you that, in such a situation, the woman always has to pay more heavily than the man. You will not, I am sure, pay too much attention to this. You know quite well the difference between right and wrong in such matters, and you may think that, if Harriet Vane had not become to a certain extent corrupted by the unwholesome influences among which she lived, she would have shown a truer heroism by dismissing Philip Boyes from her society.

'But, on the other hand, you must be careful not to attach the wrong kind of importance to this lapse. It is one thing for a man or woman to live an immoral life, and quite another thing to commit murder. You may perhaps think that one step into the path of the wrong-doing makes the next one easier, but you must not give too much weight to that consideration. You are entitled to take it into account, but you must not be too much prejudiced.'

The judge paused for a moment, and Freddy Arbuthnot jerked an elbow into the ribs of Lord Peter Wimsey, who appeared to be a prey to gloom.

'I should jolly well hope not. Damn it, if every little game led to murder, they'd be hanging half of us for doin' in the other half.'

'And which half would *you* be in?' inquired his lordship, fixing him for a moment with a cold eye and then returning his glance to the dock.

'Victim,' said the Hon. Freddy, 'victim. Me for the corpse in the library.'

'Philip Boyes and the prisoner lived together in this fashion,' went on the judge, 'for nearly a year. Various friends have testified that they appeared to live on terms of the greatest mutual affection. Miss Price said that, although Harriet Vane obviously felt her unfortunate position very acutely – cutting herself off from her family friends and refusing to thrust herself into company where her social outlawry might cause embarrassment and so on – yet she was extremely loyal to her lover and expressed herself proud and happy to be his companion.

'Nevertheless, in February 1929 there was a quarrel, and the couple separated. It is not denied that the quarrel took place. Mr and Mrs Dyer, who occupy the flat immediately above Philip Boyes's, say that they heard loud talking in angry voices, the man swearing and the woman crying, and that the next day Harriet Vane packed up all her things and left the house for good. The curious feature in the case, and one which you must consider very carefully, is the reason assigned for the quarrel. As to this, the only evidence we have is the prisoner's own. According to Miss Marriott, with whom Harriet Vane took refuge after the separation, the prisoner steadily refused to give any information on the subject, saying only that she had been painfully deceived by Boyes and never wished to hear his name spoken again.

'Now it might be supposed from this that Boyes had given the prisoner cause for grievance against him, by unfaithfulness, or unkindness, or simply by a continued refusal to regularise the situation in the eyes of the world. But the prisoner absolutely denies this. According to her statement – and on this point her evidence is confirmed by a letter which Philip Boyes wrote to his father – Boyes did at length offer her legal marriage, and this was the cause of the quarrel. You may think this a very

9

remarkable statement to make, but that is the prisoner's evidence on oath.

'It would be natural for you to think that this proposal of marriage takes away any suggestion that the prisoner had a cause of grievance against Boyes. Anyone would say that, under such circumstances, she could have no motive for wishing to murder this young man, but rather the contrary. Still, there is the fact of the quarrel, and the prisoner herself states that this honourable, though belated, proposal was unwelcome to her. She does not say – as she might very reasonably say, and as her counsel has most forcefully and impressively said for her – that this marriage-offer completely does away with any pretext for enmity on her part towards Philip Boyes. Sir Impey Biggs says so, but that is not what the prisoner says. She says – and you must try to put yourselves in her place and understand her point of view if you can – that she was angry with Boyes because, after persuading her against her will to adopt his principles of conduct, he then renounced those principles and so, as she says, "made a fool of her".

'Well, that is for you to consider: whether the offer which was in fact made could reasonably be construed into a motive for murder. I must impress upon you that no other motive has been suggested in evidence.'

At this point the elderly spinster on the jury was seen to be making a note – a vigorous note, to judge from the action of her pencil on the paper. Lord Peter Wimsey shook his head slowly two or three times and muttered something under his breath.

'After this,' said the judge, 'nothing particular seems to have happened to these two people for three months or so, except that Harriet Vane left Miss Marriott's house and took a small flat of her own in Doughty Street, while Philip Boyes, on the contrary, finding his solitary life depressing, accepted the invitation of his cousin, Mr Norman Urquhart, to stay at the latter's house in Woburn Square. Although living in the same quarter of London, Boyes and the accused do not seem to have met very often after the separation. Once or twice there was an accidental encounter at the house of a friend. The dates of these occasions cannot be ascertained with any certainty – they were informal parties – but there is some evidence that there was a

10

meeting towards the end of March, another in the second week in April, and a third some time in May. These times are worth noting, though, as the exact day is left doubtful, you must not attach too much importance to them.

'However, we now come to a date of the very greatest importance. On April 10th, a young woman, who has been identified as Harriet Vane, entered the chemist's shop kept by Mr Brown in Southampton Row, and purchased two ounces of commercial arsenic, saying that she needed it to destroy rats. She signed the poison-book in the name of Mary Slater, and the handwriting has been identified as that of the prisoner. Moreover, the prisoner herself admits having made this purchase, for certain reasons of her own. For this reason it is comparatively unimportant – but you may think it worth noting – that the housekeeper of the flats where Harriet Vane lives has come here and told you that there are no rats on the premises, and never have been in the whole time of her residence there.

'On May 5th we have another purchase of arsenic. The prisoner, as she herself states, this time procured a tin of arsenical weedkiller, of the same brand that was mentioned in the Kidwelly poisoning case. This time she gave the name of Edith Waters. There is no garden attached to the flats where she lives, nor could there be any conceivable use for weedkiller on the premises.

'On various occasions also, during the period from the middle of March to the beginning of May, the prisoner purchased other poisons, including prussic acid (ostensibly for photographic purposes) and strychnine. There was also an attempt to obtain aconitine, which was not successful. A different shop was approached and a different name given in each case. The arsenic is the only poison which directly concerns this case, but these other purchases are of some importance, as throwing light on the prisoner's activities at this time.

'The prisoner has given an explanation of these purchases which you must consider for what it is worth. She says that she was engaged at that time in writing a novel about poisoning, and that she brought the drugs in order to prove by experiment how easy it was for an ordinary person to get hold of deadly poisons. In proof of this, her publisher, Mr Trufoot, has produced the manuscript of the book. You have had it in your hands, and you will be given it again, if you like, when I have finished my summing-up, to look at in your own room. Passages were read out to you, showing that the subject of the book was murder by arsenic, and there is a description in it of a young woman going to a chemist's shop and buying a considerable quantity of this deadly substance. And I must mention here what I should have mentioned before, namely, that the arsenic purchased from Mr Brown was the ordinary commercial arsenic, which is coloured with charcoal or indigo, as the law requires, in order that it may not be mistaken for sugar or any other innocent substance.'

Salcombe Hardy groaned: 'How long, O Lord, how long shall we have to listen to all this tripe about commercial arsenic? Murderers learn it now at their mother's knee.'

'I particularly want you to remember those dates – I will give them to you again – the 10th of April and the 5th of May.' (The jury wrote them down. Lord Peter Wimsey murmured: 'They all wrote down on their slates, "She doesn't believe there's an atom of meaning in it." ' The Hon. Freddy said, 'What? what?' and the judge turned over another page of his notes.)

'About this time, Philip Boyes began to suffer from renewed attacks of gastric trouble to which he had been subject from time to time during his life. You have read the evidence of Dr Green, who attended him for something of the sort during his University career. That is some time ago, but there is also Dr Weare, who in 1925 prescribed for a similar attack. Not grave illnesses, but painful and exhausting, with sickness and so on and aching in the limbs. Plenty of people have such troubles from time to time. Still, there is a coincidence of dates here which may be significant. We get these attacks – noted in Dr Weare's case-book – one on March 31st, one on April 15th, and one on May 12th. Three sets of coincidences – as you may perhaps think them to be – Harriet Vane and Philip Boyes meet "towards the end of March", and he has an attack of gastritis on March 31st; on April 10th, Harriet Vane purchases two ounces of arsenic – they meet again "in the second week in April", and on April 15th he has another attack; on May 5th there is the purchase of weedkiller – "some time in May" there is another meeting, and on May 12th he is taken ill for the third time. You may think that is rather curious, but you must not

12

forget that the Crown have failed to prove any purchase of arsenic before the meeting in March. You must bear that in mind when considering this point.

'After the third attack – the one in May – the doctor advises Boyes to go away for a change, and he selects the north-west corner of Wales. He goes to Harlech, and spends a very pleasant time there and is much better. But he has a friend to accompany him, Mr Ryland Vaughan, whom you have seen, and this friend says that "Philip was not happy". In fact, Mr Vaughan formed the opinion that he was fretting after Harriet Vane. His bodily health improved, but he grew mentally depressed. And so on June 16th we find him writing a letter to Miss Vane. Now that is an important letter, so I will read it to you once more:

'"DEAR HARRIET, Life is an utter mess-up. I can't stick it out here any longer. I've decided to cut adrift and take a trip out West. But before I go, I want to see you once again and find out if it isn't possible to put things straight again. You must do as you like, of course, but I still cannot understand the attitude you take up. If I can't make you see the thing in the right perspective this time I'll chuck it for good. I shall be in town on the 20th. Let me have a line to say when I can come round.

"Yours,
"P."

'Now that, as you have realised, is a most ambiguous letter. Sir Impey Biggs, with arguments of great weight, has suggested that by expressions "cut adrift and take a trip out West", "I can't stick it out here", and "chuck it for good", the writer was expressing his intention to make away with himself if he could not effect a reconciliation with the accused. He points out that "to go west" is a well-known metaphor for dying, and that, of course, may be convincing to you. But Mr Urquhart, when examined on the subject by the Attorney-General, said that he supposed the letter to refer to a project, which he himself had suggested to the deceased, of taking a voyage across the Atlantic to Barbados, by way of change of scene. And the learned Attorney-General makes this other point that when the writer says "I can't stick it out *here* any longer", he means here in Britain, or perhaps merely "here in Harlech", and that if the phrase had reference to suicide it would read simply "I can't stick it out any longer".

'No doubt you have formed your own opinion on this point. It is important to note that the deceased asks for an appointment on the 20th. The reply to this letter is before us; it reads:

'"DEAR PHIL, You can come round at 9.30 on the 20th if you like but you certainly will not make me change my mind."

'And it is signed simply "M". A very cold letter, you may think – almost hostile in tone. And yet the appointment is made for 9.30.

'I shall not have to keep your attention very much longer, but I do ask for it at this point, specially – though you have been attending most patiently and industriously all the time – because we now come to the actual day of death itself.'

The old man clasped his hands one over the other upon the sheaf of notes and leaned a little forward. He had it all in his head, though he had known nothing of it until the last three days. He had not reached the time to babble of green fields and childhood ways; he still had firm hold of the present; he held it pinned down flat under his wrinkled fingers with their grey, chalky nails.

'Philip Boyes and Mr Vaughan came back to town together on the evening of the 19th, and there would seem to be no doubt at all that Boyes was then in the best of health. Boyes spent the night with Mr Vaughan and they breakfasted together in the usual way upon bacon and eggs, toast, marmalade, and coffee. At 11 o'clock Boyes had a Guinness, observing that, according to the advertisements, it was "Good for you". At 1 o'clock he ate a hearty lunch at his club, and in the afternoon he played several sets at tennis with Mr Vaughan and some other friends. During the game the remark was made by one of the players that Harlech had done Boyes good, and he replied that he was feeling fitter than he had done for many months.

'After half-past seven he went round to have dinner with his cousin, Mr Norman Urquhart. Nothing at all unusual in his manner or appearance was noticed, either by Mr Urquhart or by the maid who waited at table. Dinner was served at 8 o'clock exactly, and I think it would be a good thing if you were to write down that time (if you have not already done so) and also the list of things eaten and drunk.

'The two cousins dined alone together, and first, by way of cocktail, each had a glass of sherry. The wine was a fine Oleroso of 1847, and the maid decanted it from a fresh bottle and poured it into the glasses as they sat in the library. Mr Urquhart retains the dignified old-fashioned custom of having the maid in attendance throughout the meal, so that we have here the advantage of two witnesses during this part of the evening. You saw the maid, Hannah Westlock, in the box, and I think you will say she gave the impression of being a sensible and observant witness.

'Well, there was the sherry. Then came a cup of cold bouillon, served by Hannah Westlock from the tureen on the sideboard. It was very strong, good soup, set to a clear jelly. Both men had some, and after dinner, the bouillon was finished by the cook and Miss Westlock in the kitchen.

'After the soup came a piece of turbot with sauce. The portions were again carved at the sideboard, the sauce-boat was handed to each in turn, and the dish was then sent out to be finished in the kitchen.

'Then came a *poulet en casserole* – that is, chicken cut up and stewed slowly with vegetables in a fireproof cooking utensil. Both men had some of this, and the maids finished the dish.

'The final course was a sweet omelette, which was made at the table in a chafing-dish by Philip Boyes himself. Both Mr Urquhart and his cousin were very particular about eating an omelette the moment it came from the pan – and a very good rule it is, and I advise you all to treat omelettes in the same way and never allow them to stand, or they will get tough. Four eggs were brought to the table in the shells, and Mr Urquhart broke them one by one into a bowl, adding sugar from a sifter. Then he handed the bowl to Mr Boyes, saying: "You're the real dab at omelettes, Philip – I'll leave this to you." Philip Boyes then beat the eggs and sugar together, cooked the omelette in the chafing-dish, filled it with hot jam, which was brought in by Hannah Westlock, and then himself divided it into two portions, giving one to Mr Urquhart and taking the remainder himself.

'I have been a little careful to remind you of all these things,

15

to show that we have good proof that every dish served at dinner was partaken of by two people at least, and in most cases by four. The omelette – the only dish which did not go out to the kitchen – was prepared by Philip Boyes himself and shared by his cousin. Neither Mr Urquhart, Miss Westlock, nor the cook, Mrs Pettican, felt any ill-effects from this meal.

'I should mention also that there was one article of diet which was partaken of by Philip Boyes alone, and that was a bottle of Burgundy. It was a fine old Corton, and was brought to table in its original bottle. Mr Urquhart drew the cork and then handed the bottle intact to Philip Boyes, saying that he himself would not take any – he had been advised not to drink at meal-times. Philip Boyes drank two glassfuls and the remainder of the bottle was fortunately preserved. As you have already heard, the wine was later analysed and found to be quite harmless.

'This brings us to 9 o'clock. After dinner, coffee is offered, but Boyes excuses himself on the ground that he does not care for Turkish coffee, and moreover will probably be given coffee by Harriet Vane. At 9.15 Boyes leaves Mr Urquhart's apartment house in Woburn Square, and is driven in a taxi to the house where Miss Vane has her flat, No. 100 Doughty Street – a distance of about half a mile. We have it from Harriet Vane herself, from Mrs Bright, a resident in the ground floor flat, and from Police Constable D. 1234, who was passing along the street at the time, that he was standing on the doorstep, ringing the prisoner's bell, at twenty-five minutes past nine. She was on the look-out for him and let him in immediately.

'Now, as the interview was naturally a private one, we have no account of it to go upon but that of the prisoner. She has told us that as soon as he came in she offered him "a cup of coffee which was standing ready upon the gas-ring". Now, when the learned Attorney-General heard the prisoner say that, he immediately asked what the coffee was standing ready in. The prisoner, apparently not quite understanding the purport of the question, replied "in the fender, to keep hot". When the question was repeated more clearly, she explained that the coffee was made in a saucepan, and that it was this which was placed on the gas-ring in the fender. The Attorney-General then drew the prisoner's attention to her previous statement to the police, in which this expression appeared: "I had a cup of coffee ready for him on his arrival". You will see at once the importance of this. If the cups were prepared and poured out separately before the arrival of the deceased, there was every opportunity to place poison in one of the cups beforehand and offer the prepared cup to Philip Boyes; but if the coffee was poured out from the saucepan in the deceased's presence, the opportunity would be rather less, though of course the thing might easily be done while Boyes's attention was momentarily distracted. The prisoner explained that in her statement she used the phrase "a cup of coffee" merely as denoting "a certain quantity of coffee". You yourselves will be able to judge whether that is a usual and natural form of expression. The deceased is said by her to have taken no milk or sugar in his coffee, and you have the testimony of Mr Urquhart and Mr Vaughan that it was his usual habit to drink his after-dinner coffee black and un-sweetened.

'According to the prisoner's evidence, the interview was not a satisfactory one. Reproaches were uttered on both sides, and at 10 o'clock or thereabouts the deceased expressed his intention of leaving her. She says that he appeared uneasy, and remarked that he was not feeling well, adding that her behaviour had greatly upset him.

'At ten minutes past ten – and I want you to note these times very carefully – the taxi-driver Burke, who was standing on the rank in Guildford Street, was approached by Philip Boyes and told to take him to Woburn Square. He says that Boyes spoke in a hurried and abrupt tone, like that of a person in distress of mind or body. When the taxi stopped before Mr Urquhart's house, Boyes did not get out, and Burke opened the door to see what was the matter. He found the deceased huddled in a corner with his hand pressed over his stomach and his face pale and covered with perspiration. He asked him whether he was ill, and the deceased replied: "Yes, rotten." Burke helped him out and rang the bell, supporting him with one arm as they stood on the doorstep. Hannah Westlock opened the door. Philip Boyes seemed hardly able to walk; his body was bent almost double, and he sank groaning into a hall-chair and asked for brandy. She brought him a stiff brandy-and-soda from the dining-room, and, after drinking this, Boyes recovered sufficiently to take

17

money from his pocket and pay for the taxi.

'As he still seemed very ill, Hannah Westlock summoned Mr Urquhart from the library. He said to Boyes, "Hullo, old man – what's the matter with you?" Boyes replied, "God knows! I feel awful. It can't have been the chicken." Mr Urquhart said he hoped not, he hadn't noticed anything wrong with it, and Boyes answered, No, he supposed it was one of his usual attacks, but he'd never felt anything like this before. He was taken upstairs to bed, and Dr Grainger was summoned by telephone, as being the nearest physician available.

'Before the doctor's arrival, the patient vomited violently, and thereafter continued to vomit persistently. Dr Grainger diagnosed the trouble as acute gastritis. There was a high temperature and rapid pulse, and the patient's abdomen was acutely painful to pressure, but the doctor found nothing indicative of any trouble in the nature of appendicitis or peritonitis. He therefore went back to his surgery, and made up a soothing medicine to control the vomiting – a mixture of bicarbonate of potash, tincture of oranges, and chloroform – no other drugs.

'Next day the vomiting still persisted, and Dr Weare was called in to consult with Dr Grainger, as he was well acquainted with the patient's constitution.'

Here the judge paused and glanced at the clock.

'Time is getting on, and as the medical evidence has still to be passed in review, I will adjourn the Court now for lunch.'

'He would,' said the Hon. Freddy, 'just at the beastliest moment when everybody's appetite is thoroughly taken away. Come on, Wimsey, let's go and fold a chop into the system, shall we? – Hullo!'

Wimsey had pushed past without heeding him, and was making his way down into the body of the court, where Sir Impey Biggs stood conferring with his juniors.

'Seems to be a bit of a stew,' said Mr Arbuthnot, meditatively. 'Gone to put an alternative theory of some kind, I expect. Wonder why I came to this bally show. Tedious, don't you know, and the girl's not even pretty. Don't think I'll come back after grub.'

He struggled out, and found himself face to face with the Dowager Duchess of Denver.

'Come and have lunch, Duchess,' said Freddy, hopefully. He liked the Dowager.

'I'm waiting for Peter, thanks, Freddy. Such an interesting case and interesting people, too, don't you think, though what the jury make of it I don't know, with faces like hams most of them, except the artist, who wouldn't have any features at all if it wasn't for that dreadful tie and his beard, looking like Christ, only not really Christ but one of those Italian ones in a pink frock and a blue top thing. Isn't that Peter's Miss Climpson on the jury, how does she get there, I wonder?'

'He's put her into a house somewhere round about, I fancy,' said Freddy, 'with a typewriting office to look after and live over the shop and run those comic charity stunts of his. Funny old soul, isn't she? Stepped out of a magazine of the nineties. But she seems to suit his work all right and all that.'

'Yes – such a good thing too, answering all those shady advertisements and then getting the people shown up so courageous too, some of them the horridest oily people, and murderers I shouldn't wonder with automatic thingummies and life-preservers in every pocket, and very likely a gas-oven full of bones like Landru, so clever wasn't he? And really *such* women – born murderesses as somebody says quite pig-faced but not of course deserving it and possibly the photographs don't do them justice, poor things.'

The Duchess was even more rambling than usual, thought Freddy, and as she spoke her eyes wandered to her son with a kind of anxiety unusual in her.

'Top-hole to see old Wimsey back, isn't it?' he said, with simple kindliness. 'Wonderful how keen he is on this sort of thing, don't you know. Rampages off the minute he gets home like the jolly old war-horse sniffing the T.N.T. Regularly up to the eyes in it.'

'Well, it's one of Chief Inspector Parker's cases, and they're such great friends, you know, quite like David and Beersheba – or do I mean Daniel?'

Wimsey joined them at this complicated moment, and tucked his mother's arm affectionately in his own.

'Frightfully sorry to keep you waiting, Mater, but I had to say a word to Biggy. He's having a rotten time, and that old Jeffreys of a judge looks as though he was getting measured for the black cap. I'm going home to burn my books. Dangerous to know too much about poisons, don't you think? Be thou as chaste as ice, as pure as snow, thou shalt not escape the Old Bailey.'

'The young woman doesn't seem to have tried that recipe, does she?' remarked Freddy.

'You ought to be on the jury,' retorted Wimsey, with unusual acidity, 'I bet that's what they're all saying at this moment. I'm convinced that that foreman is a teetotaller – I saw ginger-beer going into the juryroom, and I only hope it explodes and blows his inside through the top of his skull.'

'All right, all right,' returned Mr Arbuthnot, soothingly; 'what you want is a drink.'

Chapter II

THE scramble for places subsided; the jury returned; the prisoner reappeared in the dock suddenly, like a jack-in-the-box; the judge resumed his seat. Some petals had spilt from the red roses. The old voice took up its tale where it had left off.

'Members of the jury – there is no need, I think, for me to recall the course of Philip Boyes's illness in great detail. The nurse was called in on June 21st, and during that day the doctors visited the patient three times. His condition grew steadily worse. There was persistent vomiting and diarrhoea, and he could not keep any food or medicine down at all. On the day after, the 22nd, he was worse still – in great pain, the pulse growing weaker, and the skin about the mouth getting dry and peeling off. The doctors gave him every attention, but could do nothing for him. His father was summoned, and when he arrived he found his son conscious, but unable to lift himself. He was able to speak, however, and in the presence of his father and Nurse Williams he made the remark, "I'm going out, Dad, and I'm glad to be through with it. Harriet'll be rid of me now – I didn't know she hated me quite so much." Now that was a very remarkable speech, and we have heard two very different interpretations put upon it. It is for you to say whether, in your opinion, he meant: "She has succeeded in getting rid of me; I didn't know she hated me enough to poison me," or whether he meant, "When I realised she hated me so much, I decided I did not want to live any longer" – or whether, perhaps, he meant neither of these things. When people are very ill, they sometimes get fantastic ideas, and sometimes they wander in their minds; perhaps you may feel that it is not profitable to take too much for granted. Still, those words are part of the evidence, and you are entitled to take them into account.

'During the night he became gradually weaker and lost consciousness, and at 3 o'clock in the morning he died, without ever regaining it. That was on the 23rd of June.

'Now, up to this time, no suspicion of any kind had been aroused. Both Dr Grainger and Dr Weare formed the opinion that the cause of death was acute gastritis, and we need not blame them for coming to this conclusion, because it was quite consistent both with the symptoms of the illness and with the past history of the patient. A death-certificate was given in the usual way, and the funeral took place on the 28th.

'Well, then something happened which frequently does happen in cases of this kind, and that is that somebody begins to talk. It was Nurse Williams who talked in this particular case, and while you will probably think that this was a very wrong and a very indiscreet thing for a nurse to do, yet, as it turns out, it was a good thing that she did. Of course, she ought to have told Dr Weare or Dr Grainger of her suspicions at the time, but she did not do this, and we may at least feel glad to know that, in the doctors' opinions, even if she had done so, and if they had discovered that the illness was caused by arsenic, they would not have been able to do anything more to save the life of this unfortunate man. At any rate, what happened was that Nurse Williams was sent, during the last week of June, to nurse another patient of Dr Weare's, who happened to belong to the same literary set in Bloomsbury as Philip Boyes and Harriet Vane, and while she was there, she spoke about Philip Boyes, and said that, in her opinion, the illness looked very much like poisoning, and she even mentioned the word arsenic. Well, you know how a thing like that gets about. One person tells another, and it is discussed at tea-parties or what are known, I believe, as cocktail parties, and very soon a story gets spread about, and people mention names and take sides. Miss Marriott and Miss Price were told about it, and it also got to the ears of Mr Vaughan. Now Mr Vaughan had been greatly distressed and surprised by Philip Boyes's death, especially as he had been with him in Wales, and knew how much he had improved in health while on his holiday, and he also felt strongly that Harriet Vane had behaved badly about the love-affair. Mr Vaughan felt that some action ought to be taken about the matter, and went to Mr Urquhart and put the story before him. Now Mr Urquhart is a solicitor, and is therefore inclined to take a cautious view of rumours and suspicions, and he warned Mr Vaughan that it was not wise to go about making accusations against people, for fear of an action for libel. At the same time, he naturally felt uneasy that such a thing should be said about a relation who had died in his house. He took the course – the very sensible course – of consulting Dr Weare and suggesting that, if he was quite certain that the illness was due to gastritis and nothing else, he should take steps to rebuke Nurse Williams and put an end to the talk. Dr Weare was naturally very much surprised and upset to hear what was being said, but, since the suggestion had been made, he could not deny that – taking the symptoms only into account – there was just the bare possibility of something of the sort, because, as you have already heard in the medical evidence, the symptoms of arsenical poisoning and of acute gastritis are really indistinguishable.

'When this was communicated to Mr Vaughan, he was confirmed in his suspicions, and wrote to the elder Mr Boyes suggesting an inquiry. Mr Boyes was naturally very much shocked, and said at once that the matter should be taken up. He had known of the liaison with Harriet Vane, and had noticed that she did not come to inquire after Philip Boyes, nor attend the funeral, and this had struck him as heartless behaviour. In the end, the police were communicated with and an exhumation order obtained.

'You have heard the result of the analysis made by Sir James Lubbock and Mr Stephen Fordyce. There was a great deal of discussion about methods of analysis and the way that arsenic behaves in the body and so on, but I think we need not trouble too much about those fine details. The chief points in the evidence seemed to me to be these, which you may note down if you care to do so.

'The analysts took certains organs of the body – the stomach, intestines, kidneys, liver and so on – and analysed portions of these and found that they all contained arsenic. They were able to weigh the quantity of arsenic found in these various portions, and they calculated from that the quantity of arsenic present in the whole body. Then they had to allow so much for the amount of arsenic eliminated from the body by the vomiting and diarrhoea and also through the kidneys, because the kidneys play a very large part in the elimination of this particular poison. After making allowance for all these things, they formed the opinion that a large and fatal dose of arsenic – four or five grains, perhaps – had been taken about three days before the death.

'I do not know whether you quite followed all the technical arguments about this. I will try to tell you the chief points as I understood them. The nature of arsenic is to pass through the body very quickly, especially if it is taken with food or immediately following a meal, because the arsenic irritates the lining of the internal organs and speeds up the process of elimination. The action would be quicker if the arsenic were taken in liquid than if it were taken in the form of a powder. Where arsenic was taken with, or immediately on top of, a meal, nearly the whole of it would be evacuated within twenty-four hours after the onset of the illness. So you see that, although the actual quantities found in the body may seem to you and me very small indeed, the mere fact that they were found there at all, after three days of persistent vomiting and diarrhoea and so on, points to a large dose having been taken at some time.

'Now there was a great deal of discussion about the time at which the symptoms first set in. It is suggested by the defence that Philip Boyes may have taken the arsenic himself at some time between leaving Harriet Vane's flat and hailing the taxi in Guildford Street; and they bring forward books which show that in many cases the onset of symptoms takes place in a very short time after taking the arsenic – a quarter of an hour, I think, was the shortest time mentioned where the arsenic was taken in liquid form. Now the prisoner's statement – and we have no other – is that Philip Boyes left her at 10 o'clock, and at ten minutes past he was in Guilford Street. He was then looking ill. It would not take many minutes to drive to Woburn Square at that hour of the night, and by the time he got there, he was already in acute pain and hardly able to stand. Now Guildford Street is a very short way from Doughty Street – perhaps three minutes' walk – and you must ask yourselves, if the prisoner's statement is correct, what he did with those ten minutes. Did he occupy himself in going to some quiet spot and taking a dose of arsenic, which he must in that case have brought with him in anticipation of an unfavourable interview with the prisoner? And I may remind you here that the defence have brought no evidence to show that Philip Boyes ever bought any arsenic, or had access to any arsenic. That is not to say he could not have obtained it – the purchases made by Harriet Vane show that the law about the sale of poisons is not always as effective as one would like it to be – but the fact remains that the defence have not been able to show that the deceased ever had arsenic in his possession. And while we are on this subject, I will mention that, curiously enough, the analysts could find no traces of the charcoal, or indigo, with which commercial arsenic is supposed to be mixed. Whether it was bought by the prisoner or by the deceased himself, you would expect to find traces of the colouring matter. But you may think it likely that all such traces would be removed from the body by the vomiting and purging which took place.

'As regards the suggestion of suicide, you will have to ask yourselves about those ten minutes – whether Boyes was taking a dose of arsenic, or whether, as is also possible, he felt unwell and sat down somewhere to recover himself, or whether, perhaps, he was merely roaming about in the vague way we sometimes do when we are feeling upset and unhappy. Or you may think that the prisoner was mistaken, or not speaking the truth, about the time he left the flat.

'You have also the prisoner's statement that Boyes mentioned, before he left her, that he was feeling unwell. If you think this had anything to do with the arsenic, it of course disposes of the suggestion that he took the poison after leaving the flat.

'Then, when one looks into it, one finds that this question about the onset of symptoms is left very vague. Various doctors came here and told you about their own experiences and the cases quoted by medical authorities in books, and you will have noticed that there is no certainty at all about the time when the symptoms may be expected to appear. Sometimes it is a quarter of an hour or half an hour, sometimes two hours, sometimes as much as five or six, and, I believe, in one case as much as seven hours after taking the poison.'

Here the Attorney-General rose respectfully and said: 'In that case, me lud, I think I am right in saying that the poison was taken on an empty stomach.'

'Thank you, I am much obliged to you for the reminder. That was a case in which the poison was taken on an empty stomach. I only mention these cases to show that we are dealing with a very uncertain phenomenon, and that is why I was particular to remind you of all the occasions on which Philip Boyes took food during the day – the 20th of June – since there is always the possibility that you may have to take them into consideration.'

'A beast, but a just beast,' murmured Lord Peter Wimsey.

'I have purposely left out of consideration until now another point which arose out of the analysis, and that is the presence of arsenic in the hair. The deceased had curly hair, which he wore rather long; the front portion, when straightened out, measured about six or seven inches in places. Now, in this hair arsenic was found, at the end closest to the head. It did not extend to the tips of the longest hair, but it was found near the roots, and Sir James Lubbock says that the quantity was greater than could be accounted for in any natural way. Occasionally, quite normal people are found to have minute traces of arsenic in the hair and skin and so on, but not to the amount found here. That is Sir James's opinion.

'Now you have been told – and the medical witnesses all agree in this – that if a person takes arsenic, a certain proportion of it will be deposited in the skin, nails, and hair. It will be deposited in the root of the hair, and as the hair grows, the arsenic will be carried along with the growth of the hair, so that you get a rough idea, from seeing the position of the arsenic in the hair, how long the administration of arsenic has been going on. There was a good deal of discussion about this, but I think there was a fairly general agreement that, if you took a dose of arsenic, you might expect to find traces of it in the hair, close to the scalp, after about ten weeks. Hair grows at the rate of about six inches in a year, and the arsenic will grow out with it till it reaches the far end and is cut off. I am sure that the ladies on the jury will understand this very well, because I believe that the same thing occurs in the case of what is termed a "permanent wave". The wave is made in a certain portion of the hair, and after a time it grows out, and the hair near the scalp comes up straight and has to be waved again. You can tell by the position of the wave how long ago the waving was done. In the same way, if a finger-nail is bruised, the discoloration will gradually grow up the nail until it reaches the point where you can cut it off with the scissors.

'Now it has been said that the presence of arsenic in and about the roots of Philip Boyes's hair indicates that he must have taken arsenic three months at least before his death. You will consider what importance is to be attached to this in view of the prisoner's purchases of arsenic in April and May, and of the deceased's attacks of sickness in March, April, and May. The quarrel with the prisoner took place in February; he was ill in March and he died in June. There are five months between the quarrel and the death, and four months between the first illness and the death, and you may think that there is some significance in these dates.

'We now come to the inquiries made by the police. When suspicion was aroused, detectives investigated Harriet Vane's movements and subsequently went to her flat to take a statement from her. When they told her that Boyes was found to have died of arsenic poisoning, she appeared very much surprised, and said, "Arsenic? What an extraordinary thing!" And then she laughed, and said, "Why, I am writing a book all about arsenic poisoning." They asked her about the purchases of arsenic and other poisons which she had made, and she admitted them quite readily and at once gave the same explanation that she gave here in court. They asked what she had done with the poisons and she replied that she had burnt them because they were dangerous things to have about. The flat was searched, but no poisons of any kind were found, except such things as aspirin and a few ordinary medicines of that kind. She absolutely denied having administered arsenic or any kind of poison to Philip Boyes. She was asked whether the arsenic could possibly have got into the coffee by accident, and replied that that was quite impossible, as she had destroyed all the poisons before the end of May.'

Here Sir Impey Biggs interposed and begged with submission to suggest that his lordship should remind the jury of the evidence given by Mr Challoner.

'Certainly, Sir Impey, I am obliged to you. You remember that Mr Challoner is Harriet Vane's literary agent. He came here to tell us that he had discussed with her as long ago as last December the subject of her forthcoming book, and she then told him that it was to be about poisons, and very probably about arsenic. So you may think it is a point in the prisoner's favour that this intention of studying the purchase and administration of arsenic was already in her mind some time before the quarrel with Philip Boyes took place. She evidently gave considerable thought to the subject, for there were a number of books on her shelves dealing with forensic medicine and toxicology, and also the reports of several famous poison trials, including the Madeleine Smith case, the Seddon case, and the Armstrong case – all of which were cases of arsenical poisoning.

'Well, I think that is the case as it is presented to you. This woman is charged with having murdered her former lover by arsenic. He undoubtedly did take arsenic, and if you are satisfied that she gave it to him, with intent to injure or kill him, and that he died of it, then it is your duty to find her guilty of murder.

'Sir Impey Biggs, in his able and eloquent speech, has put it to you that she had very little motive for such a murder, but I am bound to tell you that murders are very often committed for what seem to be the most inadequate motives – if, indeed, any motive can be called adequate for such a crime. Especially where the parties are husband and wife, or have lived together as husband and wife, there are likely to be passionate feelings which may tend to crimes of violence in persons with inadequate moral standards and unbalanced mind.

'The prisoner had the means – the arsenic, she had the expert knowledge, and she had the opportunity to administer it. The defence say that this is not enough. They say the Crown must go further and prove that the poison could not have been taken in any other way – by accident, or with suicidal intent. That is for you to judge. If you feel that there is any reasonable doubt that the prisoner gave this poison to Philip Boyes deliberately, you must bring her in "Not guilty" of murder. You are not bound to decide how it was given, if it was not given by her. Consider the circumstances of the case as a whole, and say what conclusion you have come to.'

Chapter III

'THEY won't be long, I shouldn't think,' said Waffles Newton; 'it's pretty damned obvious. Look old man, I'm going to push my stuff in. Will you let me know what happens?'

'Sure,' said Salcombe Hardy, 'if you don't mind dropping mine in at your place as you go. You couldn't send me a drink by phone, could you? My mouth's like the bottom of a parrot's cage.' He looked at his watch. 'We shall miss the 6.30 edition, I'm afraid, unless they hurry up. The old man is careful, but he's damned slow.'

'They can't in decency not make a pretence of consulting about it,' said Newton. 'I give them twenty minutes. They'll want a smoke. So do I. I'll be back at ten to, in case.'

He wriggled his way out. Cuthbert Logan, who reported for a morning paper, and was a man of more leisure, settled down to write up a word-picture of the trial. He was a phlegmatic and sober person, and could write as comfortably in court as anywhere else. He liked to be on the spot when things happened, and to note down glances, tones of voices, colour effects, and so forth. His copy was always entertaining, and sometimes even distinguished.

Freddy Arbuthnot, who had not, after all, gone home after lunch, thought it was time to do so now. He fidgeted, and Wimsey frowned at him. The Dowager Duchess made her way along the benches and squeezed in next to Lord Peter. Sir Impey Biggs, having watched over his client's interests to the last, disappeared, chatting cheerfully to the Attorney-General, and followed by the smaller legal fry. The dock was deserted. On the bench the red roses stood solitary, their petals dropping.

Chief Inspector Parker, disengaging himself from a group of friends, came slowly up through the crowd and greeted the

Dowager. 'And what do you think of it, Peter?' he added, turning to Wimsey. 'Rather neatly got up, eh?'

'Charles,' said Wimsey, 'you ought not to be allowed out without me. You've made a mistake, old man.'

'Made a mistake?'

'She didn't do it.'

'Oh, come!'

'She did not do it. It's very convincing and water-tight, but it's all wrong.'

'You don't really think that.'

'I do.'

Parker looked distressed. He had confidence in Wimsey's judgement, and, in spite of his own interior certainty, he felt shaken.

'My dear man, where's the flaw in it?'

'There isn't one. It's damnably knife-proof. There's nothing wrong about it at all, except that the girl's innocent.'

'You're turning into a common or garden psychologist,' said Parker, with an uneasy laugh, 'isn't he, Duchess?'

'I wish I had known that girl,' replied the Dowager, in her usual indirect manner, 'so interesting and a really remarkable face, though perhaps not strictly good-looking, and all the more interesting for that, because good-looking people are so often cows. I have been reading one of her books, really quite good and so well-written, and I didn't guess the murderer till page 200, rather clever, because I usually do it about page 15. So very curious to write books about crimes and then be accused of a crime one's self, some people might say it was judgement. I wonder whether, if she didn't do it, she has spotted the murderer herself? I don't suppose detective writers detect much in real life, do they, except Edgar Wallace, of course, who always seems to be everywhere and dear Conan Doyle and the black man what was his name and of course the Slater person, such a scandal, though now I come to think of it that was in Scotland where they have such very odd laws about everything particularly getting married. Well I suppose we shall soon know now, not the truth, necessarily, but what the jury have made of it.'

'Yes; they are being rather longer than I expected. But, I say, Wimsey, I wish you'd tell me –'

'Too late, too late, you cannot enter now. I have locked my heart in a silver box and pinned it wi' a golden pin. Nobody's opinion matters now, except the jury's. I expect Miss Climpson is telling 'em all about it. When once she starts she doesn't stop for an hour or two.'

'Well, they've been half an hour now,' said Parker.

'Still waiting?' said Salcombe Hardy, returning to the press-table.

'Yes – so this is what you call twenty minutes! Three-quarters of an hour, I make it.'

'They've been out an hour and a half,' said a girl to her fiancé, just behind Wimsey. 'What can they be discussing?'

'Perhaps they don't think she did it after all.'

'What nonsense! Of course she did it. You could see it by her face. Hard, that's what I call it, and she never once cried or anything.'

'Oh, I dunno,' said the young man.

'You don't mean to say you admired her, Frank?'

'Oh, well, I dunno. But she didn't look to me like a murderess.'

'And how do you know what a murderess looks like? Have you ever met one?'

'Well, I've seen them at Madame Tussaud's.'

'Oh, waxworks. Everybody looks like a murderer in a wax-works.'

'Well, p'raps they do. Have a choc.'

'Two hours and a quarter,' said Waffles Newton, impatiently. 'They must have gone to sleep. Have to be a special edition. What happens if they are all night about it?'

'We sit here all night, that's all.'

'Well, it's my turn for a drink. Let me know, will you?'

'Right-ho!'

'I've been talking to one of the ushers,' said the Man Who Knows the Ropes, importantly to a friend. 'The judge has just sent round to the jury to ask if he can help them in any way.'

'Has he? And what did they say?'

'I don't know.'

'They've been out three hours and a half now,' whispered the girl behind Wimsey. 'I'm getting fearfully hungry.'

'Are you, darling? Shall we go?'

'No – I want to hear the verdict. We've waited so long now, we may as well stop on.'

'Well, I'll go out and get some sandwiches.'

'Oh, that would be nice. But don't be long, because I'm sure I shall get hysterics when I hear the sentence.'

'I'll be as quick as ever I can. Be glad you're not the jury – they're not allowed anything at all.'

'What, nothing to eat or drink?'

'Not a thing. I don't think they're supposed to have light or fire either.'

'Poor things! But it's central-heated, isn't it?'

'It's hot enough here, anyway. I'll be glad of a breath of fresh air.

Five hours.

'There's a terrific crowd in the street,' said the Man Who Knows the Ropes, returning from a reconnaissance. 'Some people started booing the prisoner and a bunch of men attacked them, and one fellow has been carried off in an ambulance.'

'Really, how amusing! Look! There's Mr Urquhart; he's come back. I'm so sorry for him, aren't you? It must be horrid having somebody die in your house.'

'He's talking to the Attorney-General. They've all had a proper dinner, of course.'

'The Attorney-General isn't as handsome as Sir Impey Biggs. Is it true he keeps canaries?'

'The Attorney-General?'

'No, Sir Impey.'

'Yes, quite true. He takes prizes with them.'

'What a funny idea!'

'Bear up, Freddy,' said Lord Peter Wimsey. 'I perceive movements. They are coming, my own, my sweet, were it never so airy a tread.'

The Court rose to its feet. The judge took his seat. The prisoner, very white in the electricity, reappeared in the dock. The door leading to the jury-room opened.

'Look at their faces,' said the fiancée. 'They say if it's going to be "Guilty" they never look at the prisoner. Oh, Archie, hold my hand!'

The Clerk of Assizes addressed the jury in tones in which formality struggled with reproach.

'Members of the jury, have you all agreed upon your verdict?'

The foreman rose with an injured and irritable countenance.

'I am sorry to say that we find it impossible to come to an agreement.'

A prolonged gasp and murmur went round the court. The judge leaned forward, very courteous and not in the least fatigued.

'Do you think that with a little more time you may be able to reach an agreement?'

'I'm afraid not, my lord.' The foreman glanced savagely at one corner of the jury-box, where the elderly spinster sat with her head bowed and her hands tightly clasped. 'I see no prospect at all of our ever agreeing.'

'Can I assist you in any way?'

'No, thank you, my lord. We quite understand the evidence, but we cannot agree about it.'

'That is unfortunate. I think perhaps you had better try again, and then, if you are still unable to come to a decision, you must come back and tell me. In the meantime, if my knowledge of the law can be of any assistance to you, it is, of course, quite at your disposal.'

The jury stumbled sullenly away. The judge trailed his scarlet robes out at the back of the bench. The murmur of conversation rose and swelled into a loud rumble.

'By Jove,' said Freddy Arbuthnot, 'I believe it's your Miss Climpson that's holdin' the jolly old show up, Wimsey. Did you see how the foreman glared at her?'

'Good egg,' said Wimsey. 'Oh, excellent, excellent egg! She has a fearfully tough conscience – she may stick it out yet.'

'I believe you've been corrupting the jury, Wimsey. Did you signal to her or something?'

'I didn't,' said Wimsey. 'Believe me or believe me not, I refrained from so much as a lifted eyebrow.'

'And he himself has said it,' muttered Freddy, 'and it's

greatly to his credit. But it's damned hard on people who want their dinners.'

Six hours. Six hours and a half.

'At last!'

As the jury filed back for the second time, they showed signs of wear and tear. The harassed woman had been crying and was still choking into her handkerchief. The man with the bad cold looked nearly dead. The artist's hair was rumpled into an untidy bush. The company director and the foreman looked as though they would have liked to strangle somebody, and the elderly spinster had her eyes shut and her lips moving as though she were praying.

'Members of the jury, are you agreed upon your verdict?'

'No; we are quite sure that it is impossible for us ever to agree.'

'You are quite sure?' said the judge. 'I do not wish to hurry you in any way. I am quite prepared to wait here as long as ever you like.'

The snarl of the company director was audible even in the gallery. The foreman controlled himself, and replied in a voice ragged with temper and exhaustion: 'We shall never agree, my lord – not if we was to stay here till Doomsday.'

'That is very unfortunate,' said the judge, 'but in that case, of course, there is nothing for it but to discharge you and order a fresh trial. I feel sure that you have all done your best and that you have brought all the resources of your intelligence and conscience to bear on this matter to which you have listened with so much patient and zealous attention. You are discharged, and you are entitled to be excused from all further jury service for the next twelve years.'

Almost before the further formalities were completed, and while the Judge's robes still flared in the dark little doorway, Wimsey had scrambled down into the well of the court. He caught the defending counsel by the gown.

'Biggy – well done! You've got another chance. Let me in on this and we'll pull it off.'

'You think so, Wimsey? I don't mind confessing that we've

done better than I ever expected.'

'We'll do better still next time. I say, Biggy, swear me in as a clerk or something. I want to interview her.'

'Who, my client?'

'Yes. I've got a hunch about this case. We've got to get her off, and I know it can be done.'

'Well, come and see me tomorrow. I must go and speak to her now. I'll be in my chambers at ten. Good-night.'

Wimsey darted off and rushed round to the sidedoor, from which the jury were emerging. Last of them all, her hat askew and her mackintosh dragged awkwardly round her shoulders, came the elderly spinster. Wimsey dashed up to her and seized her hand.

'Miss Climpson!'

'Oh, Lord Peter. Oh, dear! What a dreadful day it has been. Do you know, it was me that caused the trouble, mostly, though two of them most bravely backed me up, and oh, Lord Peter, I hope I haven't done wrong, but I couldn't, no, I *couldn't* in conscience say she had done it when I was sure she hadn't, could I? Oh, dear, oh, dear!'

'You're absolutely right. She didn't do it, and thank God you stood up to them and gave her another chance. I'm going to prove she didn't do it. And I'm going to take you out to dinner, and – I say, Miss Climpson!'

'Yes?'

'I hope you won't mind, because I haven't shaved since this morning, but I'm going to take you round the next quiet corner and kiss you.'

Chapter IV

THE following day was a Sunday, but Sir Impey Briggs cancelled an engagement to play golf (with the less regret as it was pouring cats and dogs) and held an extraordinary council of war.

'Well, now, Wimsey,' said the advocate, 'what is your idea about this? May I introduce Mr Crofts, of Crofts & Cooper, solicitors for the defence.'

'My idea is that Miss Vane didn't do it,' said Wimsey. 'I dare say that's an idea which has already occurred to you, but, with the weight of my great mind behind it, no doubt it strikes the imagination more forcibly.'

Mr Crofts, not being quite clear whether this was funny or fatuous, smiled deferentially.

'Quite so,' said Sir Impey, 'but I should be interested to know how many of the jury saw it in that light.'

'Well, I can tell you that, at least, because I know one of them. One woman and half a woman and about three-quarters of a man.'

'Meaning precisely?'

'Well, the woman I know stuck out for it that Miss Vane wasn't that sort of person. They bullied her a good deal, of course, because she couldn't lay a finger on any real weakness in the chain of evidence, but she said the prisoner's demeanour was part of the evidence and that she was entitled to take that into consideration. Fortunately, she is a tough, thin, elderly woman with a sound digestion and a militant High-Church conscience of remarkable staying-power, and her wind is excellent. She let 'em all gallop themselves dead, and then said she still didn't believe it and wasn't going to say she did.'

'Very useful,' said Sir Impey. 'A person who can believe all the articles of the Christian faith is not going to boggle over a trifle of adverse evidence. But we can never hope for a whole jury-box full of ecclesiastical die-hards. How about the other woman and the man?'

'Well, the woman was rather unexpected. She was the stout, prosperous party who keeps a sweet-shop. She said she didn't think the case was proved, and that it was perfectly possible that Boyes had taken the stuff himself, or that his cousin had given it to him. She was influenced, rather oddly, by the fact that she had attended one or two arsenic trials, and had not been satisfied by the verdict in some other cases – notably the Seddon trial. She has no opinion of men in general (she has buried her third) and she disbelieves all expert evidence on principle. She said that, personally, she thought Miss Vane might have done it, but she wouldn't really hang a dog on medical evidence. At first she was ready to vote with the majority, but she took a dislike to the foreman, who tried to bear her down by his male authority, and eventually she said she was going to back up my friend Miss Climpson.'

Sir Impey laughed.

'Very interesting. I wish we always got this inside information about juries. We sweat like hell to prepare evidence, and then one person makes up her mind on what isn't really evidence at all, and another supports her on the ground that evidence can't be relied on. How about the man?'

'The man was the artist, and the only person who really understood the kind of life these people were leading. He believed your client's version of the quarrel, and said that, if the girl really felt like that about the man, the last thing she would want to do would be to kill him. She'd rather stand back and watch his ache, like the man with the hollow tooth in the comic song. He was also able to believe the whole story about purchasing the poisons, which to the others, of course, seemed extremely feeble. He also said that Boyes, from what he had heard, was a conceited prig, and that anybody who disposed of him was doing a public service. He had had the misfortune to read some of his books, and considered the man an excrescence and a public nuisance. Actually he thought it more than likely that he had committed suicide, and if anybody was prepared to take that point of view he was ready to second it. He also

37

alarmed the jury by saying that he was accustomed to late hours and a stale atmosphere, and had not the slightest objection to sitting up all night. Miss Climpson also said that, in a righteous cause, a little personal discomfort was a trifle, and added that her religion had trained her to fasting. At that point, the third woman had hysterics and another man, who had an important deal to put through next day, lost his temper, so, to prevent bodily violence, the foreman said he thought they had better agree to disagree. So that's how it was.'

'Well, they've given us another chance,' said Mr Crofts, 'so it's all to the good. It can't come on now till the next sessions, which gives us about a month, and we'll probably get Bancroft next time, who's not such a severe judge as Crossley. The thing is, can we do anything to improve the look of our case?'

'I'm going to have a strenuous go at it,' said Wimsey. 'There must *be* evidence somewhere, you know. I know you've all worked like beavers, but I'm going to work like a king beaver. And I've got one big advantage over the rest of you.'

'More brains?' suggested Sir Impey, grinning.

'No – I should hate to suggest that, Biggy. But I do believe in Miss Vane's innocence.'

'Damn it, Wimsey, didn't my eloquent speeches convince you that I was a whole-hearted believer?'

'Of course they did. I nearly shed tears. Here's old Biggy, I said to myself, going to retire from the Bar and cut his throat if this verdict goes against him, because he won't believe in British justice any more. No – it's your triumph at having secured a disagreement that gives you away, old horse. More than you expected. You said so. By the way, if it's not a rude question, who's paying you, Biggy?'

'Crofts & Cooper,' said Sir Impey, slyly.

'They're in the thing for their health, I take it?'

'No, Lord Peter. As a matter of fact, the costs in this case are being borne by Miss Vane's publishers and by a – well, a certain newspaper, which is running her new book as a serial. They expect a scoop as the result of all this. But, frankly, I don't quite know what they'll say to the expense of a fresh trial. *I'm* expecting to hear from them this morning.'

'The vultures,' said Wimsey. 'Well, they'd better carry on,

but tell 'em I'll see they're guaranteed. Don't bring my name in, though.'

'This is very generous –'

'Not at all. I wouldn't lose the fun of all this for the world. Sort of case I fairly wallow in. But in return you must do something for me. I want to see Miss Vane. You must get me passed in as part of your outfit, so that I can hear her version of the story in reasonable privacy. Get me?'

'I expect that can be done,' said Sir Impey. 'In the meantime you have nothing to suggest?'

'Haven't had time yet. But I'll fish out something, don't you worry. I've already started to undermine the confidence of the police. Chief Inspector Parker has gone home to twine willow-wreaths for his own tombstone.'

'You'll be careful,' said Sir Impey. 'Anything we can discover will come in much more effectively if the prosecution don't know of it beforehand.'

'I'll walk as on egg-shells. But if I find the real murderer (if any), you won't object to my having him or her arrested, I take it?'

'No; I won't object to that. The police may. Well, gentlemen, if there's nothing further at the moment, we'd better adjourn the meeting. You'll get Lord Peter the facilities he wants, Mr Crofts?'

Mr Crofts exerted himself with energy, and on the following morning Lord Peter presented himself at the gates of Holloway Gaol, with his credentials.

'Oh, yes, my lord. You are to be treated on the same footing as the prisoner's solicitor. Yes, we have had a separate communication from the police, and that will be quite all right, my lord. The warder will take you down, and explain the regulations to you.'

Wimsey was conducted through a number of bare corridors to a small room with a glass door. There was a long deal table in it and a couple of repellent chairs, one at either end of the table.

'Here you are, my lord. You sit at one end and the prisoner at the other, and you must be careful not to move from your seats, nor to pass any object over the table. I shall be outside

39

and see you through the glass, my lord, but I shan't be able to overhear nothing. If you will take a seat, they'll bring the prisoner in, my lord.'

Wimsey sat down and waited, a prey to curious sensations. Presently there was a noise of footsteps, and the prisoner was brought in, attended by a female wardress. She took the chair opposite to Wimsey, the wardress withdrew, and the door was shut. Wimsey, who had risen, cleared his throat.

'Good morning, Miss Vane,' he said, unimpressively.

The prisoner looked at him.

'Please sit down,' she said, in the curious, deep voice which had attracted him in court. 'You are Lord Peter Wimsey, I believe, and have come from Mr Crofts.'

'Yes,' said Wimsey. Her steady gaze was unnerving him. 'Yes. I – er – I heard the case and all that, and – er – I thought there might be something I could do, don't you know.'

'That was very good of you,' said the prisoner.

'Not at all, not at all, dash it! I mean to say, I rather enjoy investigating things, if you know what I mean.'

'I know. Being a writer of detective stories, I have naturally studied your career with interest.'

She smiled suddenly at him and his heart turned to water.

'Well, that's rather a good thing in a way, because you'll understand that I'm not really such an ass as I'm looking at present.'

That made her laugh.

'You're not looking an ass – at least, not more so than any gentleman should under the circumstances. The background doesn't altogether suit your style, but you are a very refreshing sight. And I'm really very grateful to you, though I'm afraid I'm rather a hopeless case.'

'Don't say that. It can't be hopeless, unless you actually did it, and I know you didn't.'

'Well, I didn't, as a matter of fact. But I feel it's like one book I wrote, in which I invented such a perfectly watertight crime that I couldn't devise any way for my detective to prove it, and had to fall back on the murderer's confession.'

'If necessary, we'll do the same. You don't happen to know who the murderer is, I suppose?'

'I don't think there is one. I really believe Philip took the

40

stuff himself. He was rather a defeatist sort of person, you know.'

'I suppose he took your separation pretty hard?'

'Well, I daresay it was partly that. But I think it was more that he didn't feel he was sufficiently appreciated. He was apt to think that people were in league to spoil his chances.'

'And were they?'

'No, I don't think so. But I do think he offended a great many people. He was rather apt to demand things as a right – and that annoys people, you know.'

'Yes, I see. Did he get on all right with his cousin?'

'Oh, yes; though of course he always said it was no more than Mr Urquhart's duty to look after him. Mr Urquhart is fairly well off, as he has quite a big professional connection, but Philip really had no claim on him, as it wasn't family money or anything. His idea was that great artists deserved to be boarded and lodged at the expense of the ordinary man.'

Wimsey was fairly well acquainted with this variety of the artistic temperament. He was struck, however, by the tone of the reply, which was tinged, he thought with bitterness and even some contempt. He put his next question with some hesitation.

'Forgive my asking, but – you were very fond of Philip Boyes?'

'I must have been, mustn't I – under the circumstances?'

'Not necessarily,' said Wimsey, boldly; 'you might have been sorry for him – or bewitched by him – or even badgered to death by him.'

'All those things.'

Wimsey considered for a moment.

'Were you friends?'

'No.' The word broke out with a kind of repressed savagery that startled him. 'Philip wasn't the sort of man to make a friend of a woman. He wanted devotion. I gave him that. I did, you know. But I couldn't stand being made a fool of. I couldn't stand being put on probation like an office-boy, to see if I was good enough to be condescended to. I quite thought he was honest when he said he didn't believe in marriage – and then it turned out that it was a test, to see whether my devotion was

41

abject enough. Well, it wasn't. I didn't like having matrimony offered as a bad-conduct prize.'

'I don't blame you,' said Wimsey.

'Don't you?'

'No. It sounds to me as if the fellow was a prig – not to say a bit of a cad. Like that horrid man who pretended to be a landscape-painter and then embarrassed the unfortunate young woman with the burden of an honour unto which she was not born. I've no doubt he made himself perfectly intolerable about it, with his ancient oaks and family plate, and the curtseying tenantry and all the rest of it.'

Harriet Vane laughed once more.

'Yes – it's ridiculous – but humiliating too. Well, there it is. I thought Philip had made both himself and me ridiculous, and the minute I saw that – well, the whole thing simply shut down – flop!'

She sketched a gesture of finality.

'I quite see that,' said Wimsey. 'Such a Victorian attitude, too, for a man with advanced ideas. He for God only, she for God in him, and so on. Well, I'm glad you feel like that about it.'

'Are you? It's not going to be exactly helpful in the present crisis.'

'No; I was looking beyond that. What I mean to say is, when all this is over, I want to marry you, if you can put up with me and all that.'

Harriet Vane, who had been smiling at him, frowned, and an indefinable expression of distaste came into her eyes.

'Oh, are you another of them? That makes forty-seven.'

'Forty-seven what?' asked Wimsey, much taken aback.

'Proposals. They come in by every post. I suppose there are a lot of imbeciles who want to marry anybody who's at all notorious.'

'Oh,' said Wimsey. 'Dear me, that makes it very awkward. As a matter of fact, you know, I don't need any notoriety. I can get into the papers off my own bat. It's no treat to me. Perhaps I'd better not mention it again.'

His voice sounded hurt, and the girl eyed him rather remorsefully.

'I'm sorry – but one gets rather a bruised sort of feeling in my position. There have been so many beastlinesses.'

'I know,' said Lord Peter. 'It was stupid of me –'

'No, I think it was stupid of me. But why – ?'

'Why? Oh, well – I thought you'd be rather an attractive person to marry. That's all. I mean, I sort of took a fancy to you. I can't tell you why. There's no rule about it, you know.'

'I see. Well, it's very nice of you.'

'I wish you wouldn't sound as if you thought it was rather funny. I know I've got a silly face, but I can't help that. As a matter of fact, I'd like somebody I could talk sensibly to, who would make life interesting. And I could give you a lot of plots for your books, if that's any inducement.'

'But you wouldn't want a wife who wrote books, would you?'

'But I should; it would be great fun. So much more interesting than the ordinary kind that is only keen on clothes and people. Though, of course, clothes and people are all right too, in moderation. I don't mean to say I object to clothes.'

'And how about the old oaks and the family plate?'

'Oh, you wouldn't be bothered with them. My brother does all that. I collect first editions and incunabula, which is a little tedious of me, but you wouldn't need to bother with them either unless you liked.'

'I don't mean that. What would your father think about it?'

'Oh, my mother's the only one that counts, and she likes you very much from what she's seen of you.'

'So you had me inspected?'

'No – dash it all, I seem to be saying all the wrong things today. I was absolutely stunned that first day in court, and I rushed off to my mater, who's an absolute dear, and the kind of person who really understands things, and I said, "Look here! here's the absolutely one and only woman, and she's being put through a simply ghastly awful business and for God's sake come and hold my hand!" You simply don't know how foul it was.'

'That does sound rather rotten. I'm sorry I was brutal. But, by the way, you're bearing in mind, aren't you, that I've had a lover?'

'Oh, yes. So have I, if it comes to that. In fact, several. It's the sort of thing that might happen to anybody. I can produce quite good testimonials. I'm told I make love rather nicely –

43

only I'm at a disadvantage at the moment. One can't be very convincing at the other end of a table with a bloke looking in at the door.'

'I will take your word for it. But, "however entrancing it is to wander unchecked through a garden of bright images, are we not enticing your mind from another subject of almost equal importance?" It seems probable –'

'And if you can quote *Kai Lung*, we should certainly get on together.'

'It seems very probable that I shall not survive to make the experiment.'

'Don't be so damned discouraging,' said Wimsey. 'I have already carefully explained to you that this time *I* am investigating this business. Anybody would think you had no confidence in me.'

'People have been wrongly condemned before now.'

'Exactly; simply because I wasn't there.'

'I never thought of that.'

'Think of it now. You will find it very beautiful and inspiring. It might even help to distinguish me from the other forty-six, if you should happen to mislay my features or anything. Oh, by the way – I don't positively repel you or anything like that, do I? Because, if I do, I'll take my name off the waiting-list at once.'

'No,' said Harriet Vane, kindly and a little sadly. 'No, you don't repel me.'

'I don't remind you of white slugs or make you go goose-flesh all over?'

'Certainly not.'

'I'm glad of that. Any minor alterations, like parting the old mane, or growing a toothbrush, or cashiering the eye-glass, you know, I should be happy to undertake, if it suited your ideas.'

'Don't,' said Miss Vane, 'please don't alter yourself in any particular.'

'You really mean that?' Wimsey flushed a little. 'I hope it doesn't mean that nothing I could do would make me even passable? I'll come in a different set of garments each time, so as to give you a good all-round idea of the subject. Bunter – my man, you know – will see to that. He has excellent taste in ties, and socks, and things like that. Well, I suppose I ought to be going. You – er – you'll think it over, won't you, if you have a

44

minute to spare? There's no hurry. Only don't hesitate to say if you think you couldn't stick it at any price. I'm not trying to blackmail you into matrimony, you know. I mean, I should investigate this for the fun of the thing, whatever happened, don't you see.'

'It's very good of you –'

'No, no, not at all. It's my hobby. Not proposing to people, I don't mean, but investigating things. Well, cheer-frightfully-ho and all that. And I'll call again, if I may.'

'I will give the footman orders to admit you,' said the prisoner, gravely; 'you will always find me at home.'

Wimsey walked down the dingy street with a feeling of being almost light-headed.

'I do believe I'll pull it off – she's sore, of course – no wonder, after that rotten brute – but she doesn't feel repelled – one couldn't cope with being repulsive – her skin is like honey – she ought to wear deep red – and old garnets – and lots of rings, rather old-fashioned ones – I could take a house, of course? – poor kid, I would damn well work to make it up to her – she's got a sense of humour too – brains – one wouldn't be dull – one would wake up and there'd be a whole day for jolly things to happen in – and then one would come home and go to bed – that would be jolly, too – and while she was writing, I could go out and mess round, so we shouldn't either of us be dull – I wonder if Bunter was right about this suit – it's a little dark, I always think, but the line is good –'

He paused before a shop window to get a surreptitious view of his own reflection. A large coloured window-bill caught his eye:

GREAT SPECIAL OFFER
ONE MONTH ONLY

'Oh, God!' he said, softly, sobered at once. 'One month – four weeks – thirty-one days. There isn't much time. And I don't know where to begin.'

Chapter V

'WELL, now,' said Wimsey, 'why do people kill people?'

He was sitting in Miss Katharine Climpson's private office. The establishment was ostensibly a typing bureau, and indeed there were three efficient female typists who did very excellent work for authors and men of science from time to time. Apparently the business was a large and flourishing one, for work frequently had to be refused on the ground that the staff was working at full pressure. But on other floors of the building there were other activities. All the employees were women – mostly elderly, but a few still young and attractive – and if the private register in the steel safe had been consulted, it would have been seen that all these women were of the class unkindly known as 'superfluous'. There were spinsters with small fixed incomes, or no incomes at all; widows without family; women deserted by peripatetic husbands and living on a restricted alimony, who, previous to their engagement by Miss Climpson, had had no resources but bridge and boarding-house gossip. There were retired and disappointed school-teachers; out-of-work actresses; courageous people who had failed with hat shops and tea parlours; and even a few Bright Young Things, for whom the cocktail party and the nightclub had grown boring. These women seemed to spend most of their time in answering advertisements. Unmarried gentlemen who desired to meet ladies possessed of competences with a view to matrimony; sprightly sexagenarians, who wanted housekeepers for remote country districts; ingenious gentlemen with financial schemes, on the look-out for capital; literary gentlemen, anxious for female collaborators; plausible gentlemen about to engage talent for production in the provinces: benevolent gentlemen, who could tell people how to make money in their spare time – gentlemen such as these were very liable to receive applications from members of Miss Climpson's staff. It may have been coincidence that these gentlemen so very often had the misfortune to appear shortly afterwards before the magistrate on charges of fraud, blackmail, or attempted procuration, but it is a fact that Miss Climpson's office boasted a private telephone line to Scotland Yard, and that few of her ladies were quite so unprotected as they appeared. It is also a fact that the money which paid for the rent and upkeep of the premises might, by zealous inquirers, have been traced to Lord Peter Wimsey's banking account. His lordship was somewhat reticent about this venture of his, but occasionally, when closeted with Chief Inspector Parker or other intimate friends, referred to it as 'My Cattery'.

Miss Climpson poured out a cup of tea before replying. She wore a quantity of little bangles on her spare, lace-covered wrists, and they clinked aggressively with every movement.

'I really don't know,' she said, apparently taking the problem as a psychological one, 'it is so *dangerous*, as well as so terribly *wicked*, one wonders that anybody has the *effrontery* to undertake it. And very often they gain so *little* by it.'

'That's what I mean,' said Wimsey, 'what do they set out to gain? Of course, some people seem to do it for the fun of the thing, like the German female, what's her name, who enjoyed seeing people die.'

'Such a *strange* taste,' said Miss Climpson. 'No sugar, I think? – You know, dear Lord Peter, it has been my melancholy duty to attend *many* death-beds, and though a number of them – such as my dear father's – were *most* Christian and beautiful, I could not call them *fun*. People have very different ideas of fun, of course, and personally I have never greatly cared for George Robey, though Charlie Chaplin always makes me laugh – still, you know, there are *disagreeable details* attending *any* death-bed which one would think could hardly be to anybody's taste, however depraved.'

'I quite agree with you,' said Wimsey. 'But it must be fun, in one sense, to feel that you can control the issues of life and death, don't you know.'

'That is an *infringement* upon the prerogative of the Creator,' said Miss Climpson.

'But rather jolly to know yourself divine, so to speak. Up above the world so high, like a tea-tray in the sky. I admit the fascination. But for practical purposes that theory is the devil – I beg your pardon, Miss Climpson, respect for sacred personages – I mean, it's unsatisfactory, because it would suit one person just as well as another. If I've got to find a homicidal maniac, I may as well cut my throat at once.'

'Don't say *that*,' pleaded Miss Climpson, 'even in jest. Your work here – so good, so valuable – would be worth living for in spite of the *saddest* personal disappointments. And I have known jokes of that kind turn out very badly, in the most surprising ways. There was a young man we used to know, who was given to talking in a sadly *random* way – a long time ago, dear Lord Peter, while you were still in the nursery, but young men were wild, even then, whatever they say now about the eighties – and he said one day to my poor, dear mother, "Mrs Climpson, if I don't make a good bag today, I shall shoot myself" (for he was very fond of sport), and he went out with his gun and as he was getting over a stile, he caught the trigger in the hedge and the gun went off and blew his head to pieces. I was quite a girl, and it upset me *dreadfully*, because he was a very handsome young man, with whiskers which we all admired very much, though today they would be smiled at, and they were burnt *right off* him with the explosion, and a shocking hole in the side of his head, so they said, for of course I was not allowed to see him.'

'Poor chap,' said his lordship. 'Well, let's dismiss homicidal mania from our minds for the moment. What else do people kill people for?'

'There is – passion,' said Miss Climpson, with a slight initial hesitation at the word, 'for I should not like to call it *love*, when it is so unregulated.'

'That is the explanation put forward by the prosecution,' said Wimsey. 'I don't accept it.'

'Certainly not. But – it might be possible, might it not, that there was some other unfortunate young woman who was attached to this Mr Boyes, and felt vindictively towards him?'

'Yes, or a man who was jealous. But the time is the difficulty. You've got to have some plausible pretext for giving a bloke arsenic. You can't just catch him standing on a doorstep, and

48

say, "Here, have a drink of this," can you?'

'But there were ten minutes unaccounted for,' said Miss Climpson, shrewdly. 'Might he not have entered some public house for refreshment, and there met an enemy?'

'By Jove, that's a possibility.' Wimsey made a note, and shook his head dubiously. 'But it's rather a coincidence. Unless there was a previous appointment to meet there. Still, it's worth looking into. At any rate, it's obvious that Mr Urquhart's house and Miss Vane's flat were not the only conceivable places where Boyes might have eaten or drunk between 7 and 10.10 that evening. Very well: under the head "Passion" we find: (1) Miss Vane (ruled out *ex hypothesi*); (2) jealous lovers; (3) ditto rival. Place, public house (query). Now we go on to the next motive, and that's Money. A very good motive for murdering anybody who has any, but a poor one in Boyes's case. Still, let us say, Money. I can think of three sub-headings for that: (1) robbery from the person (very improbable); (2) insurance; (3) inheritance.'

'What a clear mind you have,' said Miss Climpson.

'When I die you will find "Efficiency" written on my heart. I don't know what money Boyes had on him, but I shouldn't think it was much. Urquhart and Vaughan might know; still, it's not very important, because arsenic isn't a sensible drug to use on anyone you want to rob. It takes a long time, comparatively, to begin business, and it doesn't make the victim helpless enough. Unless we suppose the taxi driver drugged and robbed him, there was no one who could possibly profit by such a silly crime.'

Miss Climpson agreed, and buttered a second tea-cake.

'Then, insurance. Now we come to the region of the possible. Was Boyes insured? It doesn't seem to have occurred to anybody to find out. Probably he wasn't. Literary blokes have very little forethought, and are careless about trifles like premiums. But one ought to know. Who might have an insurable interest? His father, his cousin (possibly), other relations (if any), his children (if any) and – I suppose – Miss Vane, if he took out the policy while he was living with her. Also anybody who may have lent him money on the strength of such insurance. Plenty of possibilities there. I'm feeling better already, Miss Climpson, fitter and brighter in every way. Either I'm getting a line on the

49

thing, or else it's your tea. That's a good, stout-looking pot. Has it got any more in it?'

'Yes, indeed,' said Miss Climpson, eagerly. 'My dear father used to say I was a great hand at getting the *utmost* out of a teapot. The secret is to *fill* up as you *go* and never empty the pot completely.'

'Inheritance,' pursued Lord Peter. 'Had he anything to leave? Not much, I shouldn't think. I'd better hop round and see his publisher. Or had he lately come into anything? His father or cousin would know. The father is a parson – "slashing trade, that" as the naughty bully says to the new boy in one of Dean Farrar's books. He has a threadbare look. I shouldn't think there was much money in the family. Still, you never know. Somebody might have left Boyes a fortune for his *beaux yeux* or out of admiration for his books. If so, to whom did Boyes leave it? Query: did he make a will? But surely the defence must have thought of these things. I am getting depressed again.'

'Have a sandwich,' said Mrs Climpson.

'Thank you,' said Wimsey, 'or some hay. There is nothing like it when you are feeling faint, as the White King truly remarked. Well, that more or less disposes of the money motive. There remains Blackmail.'

Miss Climpson, whose professional connection with 'The Cattery' had taught her something about blackmail, assented with a sigh.

'Who was this fellow Boyes?' inquired Wimsey rhetorically. 'I know nothing about him. He may have been a blackguard of the deepest dye. He may have known unmentionable things about all his friends. Why not? Or he may have been writing a book to show somebody up, so that he had to be suppressed at all costs. Dash it all, his cousin's a solicitor. Suppose he has been embezzling trust deeds or something, and Boyes was threatening to split on him? He'd been living in Urquhart's house, and had every opportunity for finding out. Urquhart drops some arsenic into the soup and – Ah! there's the snag. He puts arsenic into the soup and eats it himself. That's awkward. I'm afraid Hannah Westlock's evidence rather knocks that on the head. We shall have to fall back on the mysterious stranger in the pub.'

He considered a little, and then said:

'And there's suicide, of course, which is what I'm really rather inclined to believe in. Arsenic is tom-fool stuff to commit suicide with, but it has been done. There was the Duc de Praslin, for instance – if his *was* suicide. Only, where's the bottle?'

'The bottle?'

'Well, he must have carried it in something. It might be in a paper, if he took the powdered form, though that would be awkward. Did anybody look for a bottle or paper?'

'Where would they look for it?' asked Miss Climpson.

'That's the rub. If it wasn't on him, it would be anywhere round about Doughty Street, and it's going to be a job looking for a bottle or paper that was chucked away six months ago. I do loathe suicides – they're so difficult to prove. Oh, well, faint heart never won so much as a scrap of paper. Now look here, Miss Climpson. We've got about a month to work this out in. The Michaelmas Term ends on the 21st; this is the 15th. They can't very well bring it up before then, and the Hilary Term starts on January 12th. They'll probably take it early, unless we can show reason for delay. Four weeks to get fresh evidence. Will you reserve the best efforts of yourself and the staff? I don't know yet what I shall want, but I shall probably want something done.'

'Of course I will, Lord Peter. You know that it is only *too* great a pleasure to do *anything* for you – even if the whole office were not your own property, which it is. Only let me know, at *any* minute of the night or day, and I will do my *very* best to help you.'

Wimsey thanked her, made a few inquiries about the work of the bureau, and departed. He hailed a taxi and was immediately driven to Scotland Yard.

* * *

Chief Detective-Inspector Parker was, as usual, delighted to see Lord Peter, but there was a worried expression on his plain though pleasant face as he greeted his visitor.

'What is it, Peter? The Vane case again?'

'Yes. You've come a mucker over this, old man, you really have.'

'Well, I don't know. It looked pretty straightforward to us.'

'Charles, acushla, distrust the straightforward case, the man who looks you straight in the eyes, and the tip straight from the horse's mouth. Only the most guileful deceiver can afford to be so aggressively straight. Even the path of the light is curved – or so they tell us. For God's sake, old man, do what you can to put the thing right before next assizes. If you don't, I'll never forgive you. Damn it, you don't *want* to hang the wrong person, do you? – especially a woman and all that.'

'Have a fag,' said Parker. 'You're looking quite wild about the eyes. What have you been doing to yourself? I'm sorry if we've got the wrong pig by the ear, but it's the defence's business to point out where we're wrong, and I can't say they put up a very convincing show.'

'No, confound them. Biggy did his best, but that fool and beast Crofts gave him no materials at all. Blast his ugly eyes! I know the brute thinks she did it. I hope he will fry in hell and be served up with cayenne pepper on a red-hot dish!'

'What eloquence!' said Parker, unimpressed. 'Anybody would think you'd gone goopy over the girl.'

'That's a damned friendly way to talk,' said Wimsey, bitterly. 'When you went off the deep end about my sister, I may have been unsympathetic – I daresay I was – but I swear I didn't dance on your tenderest feelings, and call your manly devotion "going goopy over a girl". I don't know where you pick up such expressions, as the clergyman's wife said to the parrot. "Goopy", indeed! I never heard anything so vulgar.'

'Good Lord,' exclaimed Parker, 'you don't seriously say – '

'Oh, no!' retorted Wimsey, bitterly. 'I'm not expected to be serious. A buffoon, that's what I am. I now know exactly what Jack Point feels like. I used to think the *Yeoman* sentimental tosh, but it is all too true. Would you like to see me dance in motley?'

'I'm sorry,' said Parker, taking his cue rather from the tone than the words. 'If it's like that, I'm damned sorry, old man. But what can I do?'

'Now you're talking. Look here – the most likely thing is that this unsavoury blighter Boyes committed suicide. The unspeakable defence haven't been able to trace any arsenic to his possession – but then they probably couldn't trace a herd of black cattle over a snow-bound field in broad noonday with a microscope. I want you people to take it up.'

'Boyes – query arsenic,' said Parker, making a note on a pad. 'Anything else?'

'Yes. Find out if Boyes visited any pub in the neighbourhood of Doughty Street between, say, 9.50 and 10.10 on the night of June 20th – if he met anybody, and what he took to drink.'

'It shall be done. Boyes – query pub.' Parker made another note. 'Yes?'

'Thirdly, if any bottle or paper that might have contained arsenic was picked up in that district.'

'Oh, indeed? And would you like me to trace the bus ticket dropped by Mrs Brown outside Selfridge's in the last Christmas rush? No use making it too easy.'

'A bottle is more likely than a paper,' went on Wimsey, ignoring him, 'because I think the arsenic must have been taken in liquid form to work so quickly.'

Parker made no further protest, but noted down 'Boyes – Doughty Street – query bottle', and paused expectantly.

'Yes?'

'That's all for the moment. By the way, I should try the garden in Mecklenburgh Square. A thing might lie quite a long time under those bushes.'

'Very well. I'll do my best. And if you find out anything which really proves that we've been on the wrong track, you'll let us know, won't you? We don't want to make large and ignominious public mistakes.'

'Well – I've just earnestly promised the defence that I'll do no such thing. But if I spot the criminal, I'll let you arrest him.'

'Thanks for small mercies. Well, good luck! Funny for you and me to be on opposite sides, isn't it?'

'Very,' said Wimsey. 'I'm sorry about it, but it's your own fault.'

'You shouldn't have been out of England. By the way – '

'Yes?'

'You realise that probably all our young friend did during those missing ten minutes was to stand about in Theobalds Road or somewhere, looking for a stray taxi?'

'Oh, shut up!' said Wimsey, crossly, and went out.

Chapter VI

THE next day dawned bright and fair, and Wimsey felt a certain exhilaration as he purred down to Tweedling Parva. 'Mrs Merdle', the car, so called because, like that celebrated lady, she was averse to 'row', was sparking merrily on all twelve cylinders, and there was a touch of frost in the air. These things conduce to high spirits.

Wimsey reached his destination about 10 o'clock, and was directed to the vicarage, one of those large, rambling, and unnecessary structures which swallow the incumbent's income during his life and land his survivors with a heavy bill for dilapidations as soon as he is dead.

The Rev. Arthur Boyes was at home, and would be happy to see Lord Peter Wimsey.

The clergyman was a tall, faded man, with lines of worry deeply engraved upon his face, and mild blue eyes a little bewildered by the disappointing difficulty of things in general. His black coat was old, and hung in depressed folds from his stooping, narrow shoulders. He gave Wimsey a thin hand and begged him to be seated.

Lord Peter found it a little difficult to explain his errand. His name evidently aroused no associations in the mind of this gentle and unworldly parson. He decided not to mention his hobby of criminal investigation, but to represent himself, with equal truth, as a friend of the prisoner's. That might be painful, but it would be at least intelligible. Accordingly, he began, with some hesitation:

'I'm fearfully sorry to trouble you, especially as it's all so very distressin' and all that, but it's about the death of your son, and the trial and so on. Please don't think I'm wanting to make an interfering nuisance of myself, but I'm deeply interested – personally interested. You see, I know Miss Vane – I – in fact I like her very much, don't you know, and I can't help thinking there's a mistake somewhere and – and I should like to get it put right if possible.'

'Oh – oh, yes!' said Mr Boyes. He carefully polished a pair of pince-nez and balanced them on his nose, where they sat crookedly. He peered at Wimsey and seemed not to dislike what he saw, for he went on:

'Poor misguided girl! I assure you, I have no vindictive feelings – that is to say, nobody would be more happy than myself to know that she was innocent of this dreadful thing. Indeed, Lord Peter, even if she were guilty, it would give me great pain to see her suffer the penalty. Whatever we do, we cannot bring back the dead to life, and one would infinitely prefer to leave all vengeance in the hand of Him to whom it belongs. Certainly, nothing could be more terrible than to take the life of an innocent person. It would haunt me to the end of my days if I thought there were the least likelihood of it. And I confess that, when I saw Miss Vane in court, I had grievous doubts whether the police had done rightly in accusing her.'

'Thank you,' said Wimsey, 'it is very kind of you to say that. It makes the job much easier. Excuse me, you say "when you saw her in court". You hadn't met her previously?'

'No. I knew, of course, that my unhappy son had formed an illicit connection with a young woman, but I could not bring myself to see her – and indeed, I believe that she, with very proper feeling, refused to allow Philip to bring her into contact with any of his relations. Lord Peter, you are a younger man than I am, you belong to my son's generation, and you will perhaps understand that – though he was not bad, not depraved, I will never think that – yet somehow there was not that full confidence between us which there should be between father and son. No doubt I was much to blame. If only his mother had lived – '

'My dear sir,' mumbled Wimsey, 'I perfectly understand. It often happens. In fact, it's continually happening. The post-war generation and so on. Lots of people go off the rails a bit – no real harm in 'em at all. Just can't see eye to eye with the older people. It generally wears off in time. Nobody really to blame. Wild oats and – er – all that sort of thing.'

'I could not approve,' said Mr Boyes, sadly, 'of ideas so opposed to religion and morality – perhaps I spoke my mind too openly. If I had sympathised more –'

'It can't be done,' said Wimsey. 'People have to work it out for themselves. And, when they write books and so on, and get into that set of people, they tend to express themselves rather noisily, if you see what I mean.'

'Maybe, maybe. But I reproach myself. Still, this does not help you at all. Forgive me. If there is any mistake, and the jury were evidently not satisfied, we must use all our endeavours to put it right. How can I assist?'

'Well, first of all,' said Wimsey, 'and I'm afraid this is rather a hateful question, did your son ever say anything, or write anything to you which might lead you to think that he – was tired of his life or anything of that kind? I'm sorry.'

'No, no – not at all. I was, of course, asked the same question by the police and by the counsel for the defence. I can truly say that such an idea never occurred to me. There was nothing at all to suggest it.'

'Not even when he parted company with Miss Vane?'

'Not even then. In fact, I gathered that he was rather more angry than despondent. I must say that it was a surprise to me to hear that, after all that had passed between them, she was unwilling to marry him. I still fail to comprehend it. Her refusal must have come as a great shock to him. He wrote so cheerfully to me about it beforehand. Perhaps you remember the letter?' He fumbled in an untidy drawer. 'I have it here, if you would like to look at it.'

'If you would just read the passage, sir,' suggested Wimsey.

'Yes, oh, certainly. Let me see. Yes. "Your morality will be pleased to hear, Dad, that I have determined to regularise the situation, as the good people say." He had a careless way of speaking and writing sometimes, poor boy, which doesn't do justice to his good heart. Dear me. Yes. "My young woman is a good little soul, and I have made up my mind to do the thing properly. She really deserves it, and I hope that when everything is made respectable, you will extend your paternal recognition to her. I won't ask you to officiate – as you know, the registrar's office is more in my line, and though she was brought up in the odour of sanctity, like myself, I don't think she will

56

insist on the 'Voice that Breathed o'er Eden'. I will let you know when it's to be, so that you can come and give us your blessing (*qua* father if not *qua* parson) if you should feel so disposed." You see, Lord Peter, he quite meant to do the right thing, and I was touched that he should wish for my presence.'

'Quite so,' said Lord Peter, and thought. 'If only that young man were alive, how dearly I should love to kick his bottom for him.'

'Well, then there is another letter, saying that the marriage had fallen through. Here it is. "Dear Dad, Sorry, I'm afraid your congratulations must be returned with thanks. The wedding is off, and the bride has run away. There's no need to go into the story. Harriet has succeeded in making a fool of herself and me, so there's no more to be said." Then later I heard that he had not been feeling well – but all that you know already.'

'Did he suggest any reason for these illnesses of his?'

'Oh, no – we took it for granted that it was a recurrence of the old gastric trouble. He was never a very robust lad. He wrote in very hopeful mood from Harlech, saying that he was much better, and mentioning his plan of a voyage to Barbados.'

'He did?'

'Yes. I thought it would do him a great deal of good, and take his mind off other things. He spoke of it only as a vague project, not as though anything were settled.'

'Did he say anything more about Miss Vane?'

'He never mentioned her name to me again until he lay dying.'

'Yes – and what did you think of what he said then?'

'I didn't know what to think. We had no idea of any poisoning then, naturally, and I fancied it must refer to the quarrel between them that had caused the separation.'

'I see. Well now, Mr Boyes. Supposing it was not self-destruction – '

'I really do not think it could have been.'

'Now is there anybody else at all who could have an interest in his death?'

'Who could there be?'

'No – no other woman, for instance?'

'I never heard of any. And I think I should have done. He was not secretive about these things, Lord Peter. He was remarkably open and straightforward.'

'Yes,' commented Wimsey internally, 'liked to swagger about it, I suppose. Anything to give pain. Damn the fellow.' Aloud he merely said: 'There are other possibilities. Did he, for instance, make a will?'

'He did. Not that he had much to leave, poor boy. His books were very cleverly written – he had a fine intellect, Lord Peter – but they did not bring him in any great sums of money. I helped him with a little allowance, and he managed on that and on what he made from his articles in the periodicals.'

'He left his copyrights to somebody, though, I take it?'

'Yes. He wished to leave them to me, but I was obliged to tell him that I could not accept the bequest. You see, I did not approve of his opinions, and I should not have thought it right to profit by them. No; he left them to his friend Mr Vaughan.'

'Oh! – may I ask when this will was made?'

'It is dated at the period of his visit to Wales. I believe that before that he had made one leaving everything to Miss Vane.'

'Indeed!' said Wimsey. 'I suppose she knew about it.' His mind reviewed a number of contradictory possibilities, and he added: 'But it would not amount to an important sum, in any case?'

'Oh, no. If my son made fifty pounds a year by his books, that was the utmost. Though they tell me,' added the old gentleman, with a sad smile, 'that, after this, his new book will do better.'

'Very likely,' said Wimsey. 'Provided you get into the papers, the delightful reading public don't mind what it's for. Still – Well, that's that. I gather he would have no private money to leave?'

'Nothing whatever. There has never been any money in our family, Lord Peter, nor yet in my wife's. We're quite the proverbial Church mice.' He smiled faintly at this little clerical jest. 'Except, I suppose, for Cremorna Garden.'

'For – I beg your pardon?'

'My wife's aunt, the notorious Cremorna Garden of the sixties.'

'Good Lord, yes – the actress?'

'Yes. But she, of course, was never, never mentioned. One did not inquire into the way she got her money. No worse than others, I daresay – but in those days we were very easily shocked. We have seen and heard nothing of her for well over fifty years. I believe she is quite childish now.'

'By Jove! I'd no idea she was still alive!'

'Yes, I believe she is, though she must be well over ninety. Certainly Philip never had any money from her.'

'Well, that rules money out. Was your son's life insured, by any chance?'

'Not that I ever heard of. We found no policy among his papers, and, so far as I know, nobody has made any claim.'

'He left no debts?'

'Only trifling ones – tradesmen's accounts and so on. Perhaps fifty pounds' worth altogether.'

'Thank you so much,' said Wimsey, rising; 'that has cleared the ground a good deal.'

'I am afraid it has not got you much further.'

'It tells me where to look, at any rate,' said Wimsey, 'and that all saves time, you know. It's frightfully decent of you to be bothered with me.'

'Not at all. Ask me anything you want to know. Nobody would be more glad than myself to see that unfortunate young woman cleared.'

Wimsey again thanked him and took his leave. He was a mile up the road before a regretful thought overtook him. He turned Mrs Merdle's bonnet round, skimmed back to the church, stuffed a handful of Treasury notes with some difficulty into the mouth of a box labelled 'Church Expenses', and resumed his way back to town.

*　　*　　*

As he manoeuvred the car through the City, a thought struck him, and, instead of heading for Piccadilly, where he lived, he turned off into a street south of the Strand, in which was situated the establishment of Messrs Grimsby & Cole, who published the works of Mr Philip Boyes. After a little delay, he was shown into Mr Cole's office.

Mr Cole was a stout and cheerful person, and was much interested to hear that the notorious Lord Peter Wimsey was concerning himself with the affairs of the equally notorious

Mr Boyes. Wimsey represented that, as a collector of first editions, he would be glad to secure copies of all Philip Boyes's works. Mr Cole regretted extremely that he could not help him, and, under the influence of an expensive cigar, became quite confidential.

'Without wishing to seem callous, my dear Lord Peter,' he said, throwing himself back in his chair, and creasing his three chins into six or seven as he did so, 'between you and me, Mr Boyes could not have done better for himself than to go and get murdered like this. Every copy was sold out a week after the result of the exhumation became known, two large editions of his last book were disposed of before the trial came on – at the original price of seven and sixpence, and the libraries clamoured so for the early volumes that we had to reprint the lot. Unfortunately we had not kept the type standing, and the printers had to work night and day, but we did it. We are rushing the three-and-sixpennies through the binders now, and the shilling edition is arranged for. Positively, I don't think you could get a first edition in London for love or money. We have nothing here but our own file copies, but we are putting out a special memorial edition, with portraits, on hand-made paper, limited and numbered, at a guinea. Not the same thing of course, but – '

Wimsey begged to put his name down for a set at a guinea a-piece, adding:

'Sad and all that, don't you know, that the author can't benefit by it, what?'

'Deeply distressing,' agreed Mr Cole, compressing his fat cheeks by two longitudinal folds from the nostril to the mouth. 'And sadder still that there can be no more work to come from him. A very talented young man, Lord Peter. We shall always feel a melancholy pride, Mr Grimsby and myself, in knowing that we recognised his quality, before there was any likelihood of financial remuneration. A *succes d'estime*, that was all, until this very grievous occurrence. But, when the work is good, it is not our habit to boggle about monetary returns.'

'Ah well!' said Wimsey, 'it sometimes pays to cast your bread upon the waters. Quite religious, isn't it – you know, the bit about "plenteously bringing out good works may of thee be plenteously rewarded". Twenty-fifth after Trinity.'

'Quite,' said Mr Cole, with a certain lack of enthusiasm,

60

possibly because he was imperfectly acquainted with the Book of Common Prayer, or possibly because he detected a hint of mockery in the other's tone. 'Well, I have very much enjoyed this chat. I am sorry I can do nothing for you about first editions.'

Wimsey begged him not to mention it, and with a cordial farewell ran hastily down the stairs.

His next visit was to the office of Mr Challoner, Harriet Vane's agent. Challoner was an abrupt, dark, militant-looking little man, with untidy hair and thick spectacles.

'Boom?' said he, when Wimsey had introduced himself and mentioned his interest in Miss Vane. 'Yes, of course there is a boom. Rather disgusting, really, but one can't help that. We have to do our best for our client, whatever the circumstances. Miss Vane's books have always sold reasonably well – round about the three or four thousand mark in this country – but of course this business has stimulated things enormously. The last book has gone to three new editions, and the new one has sold seven thousand before publication.'

'Financially, all to the good, eh?'

'Oh, yes – but frankly I don't know whether these artificial sales do very much good to an author's reputation in the long run. Up like a rocket, down like the stick, you know. When Miss Vane is released –'

'I am glad you say "when".'

'I am not allowing myself to contemplate any other possibility. But *when* that happens, public interest will be liable to die down very quickly. I am, of course, securing the most advantageous contracts I possibly can at the moment, to cover the next three or four books, but I can only really control the advances. The actual receipts will depend on the sales, and that is where I foresee a slump. I am, however, doing well with serial rights, which are important from the point of view of immediate returns.'

'On the whole, as a business man, you are not altogether glad that this has happened?'

'Taking the long view, I am not. Personally, I need not say that I am extremely grieved, and feel quite positive that there is some mistake.'

'That's my idea,' said Wimsey.

'From what I know of your lordship, I may say that your interest and assistance are the best stroke of luck Miss Vane could have had.'

'Oh, thanks – thanks very much. I say – this arsenic book – you couldn't let me have a squint at it, I suppose?'

'Certainly, if it would help you.' He touched a bell. 'Miss Warburton, bring me a set of galleys of *Death in the Pot*. Trufoot's are pushing publication on as fast as possible. The book was still unfinished when the arrest took place. With rare energy and courage, Miss Vane has put the finishing touches and corrected the proofs herself. Of course, everything had to go through the hands of the prison authorities. However, we were anxious to conceal nothing. She certainly knows all about arsenic, poor girl. These are complete, are they, Miss Warburton? Here you are. Is there anything else?'

'Only one thing. What do you think of Messrs Grimsby & Cole?'

'I never contemplate them,' said Mr Challoner. 'Not thinking of doing anything with them, are you, Lord Peter?'

'Well, I don't know that I am – seriously.'

'If you do, read your contract carefully. I won't say bring it to us – '

'If ever I do publish with Grimsby & Cole,' said Lord Peter, 'I promise to do it through you.'

Chapter VII

LORD PETER WIMSEY almost flounced into Holloway Prison the next morning. Harriet Vane greeted him with a kind of rueful smile.

'So you've reappeared?'

'Good Lord, yes! Surely you expected me to? I fancied I'd left that impression. I say – I've thought of a good plot for a detective story.'

'Really?'

'Top-hole. You know, the sort people bring out and say, "I've often thought of doing it myself, if I could only find time to sit down and write it." I gather that sitting down is all that is necessary for producing masterpieces. Just a moment, though, I must get through my business first. Let me see – ' He made belief to consult a note-book. 'Ah, yes. Do you happen to know whether Philip Boyes made a will?'

'I believe he did, when we were living together.'

'In whose favour?'

'Oh, in mine. Not that he had much to leave, poor man. It was chiefly that he wanted a literary executor.'

'Are you, in point of fact, his executrix now?'

'Good heavens! I never thought of that. I took it for granted he would have altered it when we parted. I think he must have, or I should have heard about it when he died, shouldn't I?'

She looked candidly at him, and Wimsey felt a little uncomfortable.

'You didn't *know* he had altered it, then? Before he died, I mean?'

'I never thought a word more about it, as a matter of fact. If I had thought – of course I should have assumed it. Why?'

'Nothing,' said Wimsey. 'Only I'm rather glad the will wasn't brought up at the thingummybob.'

'Meaning the trial? You needn't be so delicate about mentioning it. You mean, if I had thought I was still his heir, I might have murdered him for his money. But it didn't amount to a hill of beans, you know. I was making four times as much as he was.'

'Oh, yes. It was only this silly plot I'd got in my mind. But it is rather silly, now I come to think of it.'

'Tell me.'

'Well, you see – ' Wimsey choked a little, and then rattled his idea out with an exaggerated lightness.

'Well – it's about a girl (or a man would do, but we'll call it a girl) who writes novels – crime stories, in fact. And she has a – a friend who also writes. Neither of them best-sellers, you see, but just ordinary novelists.'

'Yes? That's a kind of thing that might happen.'

'And the friend makes a will, leaving his money – receipts from books and so on – to the girl.'

'I see.'

'And the girl – who has got rather fed up with him, you know – thinks of a grand scoop that will make both of them best-sellers.'

'Oh, yes?'

'Yes. She polishes him off by the same method she has used in her latest crime-thriller.'

'A daring stroke,' said Miss Vane, with grave approval.

'Yes. And, of course, his books immediately become best-sellers. And she grabs the pool.'

'That's really ingenious. An entirely new motive for murder – the thing I've been looking for for years. But – don't you think it would be a little dangerous? She might even be suspected of the murder.'

'Then *her* books would become best-sellers, too.'

'How true that is! But possibly she wouldn't live to enjoy the profits.'

'That, of course,' said Wimsey, 'is the snag.'

'Because, unless she were suspected and arrested and tried, the scoop would only half come off.'

'There you are,' said Wimsey. 'But, as an experienced mystery-monger, couldn't you think of a way round that?'

'I daresay. She might prove an ingenious alibi, for instance. Or, if she were very wicked, manage to push the blame on

64

somebody else. Or lead people to suppose that her friend had made away with himself.'

'Too vague,' said Wimsey. 'How would she do that?'

'I can't say, offhand. I'll give it careful thought and let you know. Or – here's an idea!'

'Yes?'

'She is a person with a monomania – no, no – not a homicidal one. That's dull, and not really fair to the reader. But there is somebody she wishes to benefit – somebody, say a father, mother, sister, lover, or cause, that badly needs money. She makes a will in his, her, or its favour, and lets herself be hanged for the crime, knowing that the beloved object will then come in for the money. How's that?'

'Great!' cried Wimsey, carried away. 'Only – wait a minute. They wouldn't give her the friend's money, would they? You're not allowed to profit by a crime.'

'Oh, hang! That's true. It would only be her own money, then. She could make that over by a deed of gift. Yes – look! If she did that immediately after the murder – a deed of gift of everything she possessed – that would include everything she came into under the friend's will. It would then all go direct to the beloved object, and I don't believe the law could stop it!'

She faced him with dancing eyes.

'See here,' said Wimsey. 'You're not safe. You're too clever by half. But, I say, it's a good plot, isn't it?'

'It's a winner! Shall we write it?'

'By Jove, let's!'

'Only, you know, I'm afraid we shan't get the chance.'

'You're not to say that. Of course we're going to write it. Damn it, what am I here for? Even if I could be reconciled to losing you, I couldn't lose the chance of writing my best-seller!'

'But what you've done so far is to provide me with a very convincing motive for murder. I don't know that that's going to help us a great lot.'

'What I've done,' said Wimsey, 'is to prove that that was not the motive, anyway.'

'Why?'

'You wouldn't have told me if it had been. You would have gently led me away from the subject. And besides –'

'Well?'

'Well, I've seen Mr Cole of Grimsby & Cole, and I know who is going to get the major part of Philip Boyes's profits. And I don't somehow fancy that he is the beloved object.'

'No?' said Miss Vane, 'and why not? Don't you know that I passionately dote on every chin on his face?'

'If it's chins you admire,' said Wimsey, 'I will try to grow some, though it will be rather hard work. Anyway, keep smiling – it suits you.'

* * *

'It's all very well, though,' he thought to himself, when the gates had closed behind him. 'Bright back-chat cheers the patient, but gets us no forrarder. How about this fellow Urquhart? He looked all right in court, but you never can tell. I think I'd better pop round and see him.'

He presented himself accordingly in Woburn Square, but was disappointed. Mr Urquhart had been called away to a sick relative. It was not Hannah Westlock who answered the door, but a stout elderly woman, whom Wimsey supposed to be the cook. He would have liked to question her, but felt that Mr Urquhart would hardly receive him well if he discovered that his servants had been pumped behind his back. He therefore contented himself with inquiring how long Mr Urquhart was likely to be away.

'I couldn't rightly say, sir. I understand it depends how the sick lady gets on. If she gets over it, he'll be back at once, for I know he is very busy just now. If she should pass away, he would be engaged some time with settling up the estate.'

'I see,' said Wimsey. 'It's a bit awkward, because I wanted to speak to him rather urgently. You couldn't give me his address, by any chance?'

'Well, sir, I don't rightly know if Mr Urquhart would wish it. If it's a matter of business, sir, they could give you information at his office in Bedford Row.'

'Thanks very much,' said Wimsey, noting down the number. 'I'll call there. Possibly they'd be able to do what I want without bothering him.'

'Yes, sir. Who should I say called?'

Wimsey handed over his card, writing at the top, '*In re* R. U. Vane', and added:

'But there is a chance he may be back quite soon?'

'Oh, yes, sir. Last time he wasn't away more than a couple of days, and a merciful providence I am sure that was, with poor Mr Boyes dying in that dreadful manner.'

'Yes, indeed,' said Wimsey, delighted to find the subject introducing itself of its own accord. 'That must have been a shocking upset for you all.'

'Well, there,' said the cook. 'I don't hardly like to think of it, even now. A gentleman dying in the house like that, and poisoned too, when one's had the cooking of his dinner – it do seem to bring it home to one, like.'

'It wasn't the dinner that was at fault, anyway,' said Wimsey, genially.

'Oh, dear, no, sir – we proved that most careful. Not that any accident could happen in my kitchen – I should like to see it! But people do say such things if they get half a chance. Still, there wasn't a thing ate but master and Hannah and I had some of it, and very thankful I was for that, I needn't tell you.'

'You must be, I am sure,' Wimsey was framing a further inquiry, when the violent ringing of the area bell interrupted them.

'There's that butcher,' said the cook. 'You'll excuse me, sir. The parlourmaid's in bed with the influenza, and I'm single-handed this morning. I'll tell Mr Urquhart you called.'

She shut the door, and Wimsey departed for Bedford Row, where he was received by an elderly clerk, who made no difficulty about supplying Mr Urquhart's address.

'Here it is, my lord. Care of Mr Wrayburn. Appleford, Windle, Westmorland. But I shouldn't think he would be very long away. In the meantime, could we do anything for you?'

'No, thanks. I rather wanted to see him personally, don't you know. As a matter of fact, it's about that very sad death of his cousin, Mr Philip Boyes.'

'Indeed, my lord? Shocking affair, that. Mr Urquhart was greatly upset, with it happening in his own house. A very fine young man was Mr Boyes. He and Mr Urquhart were great friends, and he took it greatly to heart. Were you present at the trial, my lord?'

'Yes. What did you think of the verdict?'

The clerk pursed up his lips.

'I don't mind saying I was surprised. It seemed to me a very clear case. But juries are very unreliable, especially nowadays, with women on them. We see a good deal of the fair sex in this profession,' said the clerk, with a sly smile 'and very few of them are remarkable for possessing the legal mind.'

'How true that is,' said Wimsey. 'If it wasn't for them, though, there'd be much less litigation, so it's all good for business.'

'Ha, ha! Very good, my lord. Well, we have to take things as they come, but in my opinion – I'm an old-fashioned man – the ladies were most adorable when they adorned and inspired and did not take any active part in affairs. Here's our young lady clerk – I don't say she wasn't a good worker – but a whim comes over her and away she goes to get married, leaving me in the lurch, just when Mr Urquhart is away. Now, with a young man, marriage steadies him, and makes him stick closer to his job, but with a young woman, it's the other way about. It's right she should get married, but it's inconvenient, and in a solicitor's office one can't get temporary assistance very well. Some of the work is confidential, of course, and, in any case, an atmosphere of permanence is desirable.'

Wimsey sympathised with the head-clerk's grievance, and bade him an affable good morning. There is a telephone box in Bedford Row, and he darted into it and immediately rang up Miss Climpson.

'Lord Peter Wimsey speaking – oh, hullo, Miss Climpson! How is everything? All bright and beautiful? Good! – Yes, now listen. There's a vacancy for a confidential female clerk at Mr Norman Urquhart's, the solicitor's, in Bedford Row. Have you got anybody? – Oh, good! – Yes, send them all along – I particularly want to get someone in there – Oh, no! no special inquiry – just to pick up any gossip about the Vane business – Yes, pick out the steadiest-looking, not too much face-powder, and see that their skirts are the regulation four inches below the knee – the head-clerk's in charge, and the last girl left to be married, so he's feeling anti-sex-appeal. Right oh! Get her in and I'll give her her instructions. Bless you, may your shadow never grow bulkier!'

Chapter VIII

'BUNTER!'

'My lord?'

Wimsey tapped with his fingers a letter he had just received.

'Do you feel at your brightest and most truly fascinating? Does a livelier iris, winter weather notwithstanding, shine upon the burnished Bunter? Have you got that sort of conquering feeling? The Don Juan touch, so to speak?'

Bunter, balancing the breakfast tray on his fingers, coughed deprecatingly.

'You have a good, upstanding, impressive figure, if I may say so,' pursued Wimsey, 'a bold and roving eye when off duty, a ready tongue, Bunter – and, I am persuaded, you have a way with you. What more should any cook or house-parlourmaid want?'

'I am always happy,' replied Bunter, 'to exert myself to the best of my capacity in your lordship's service.'

'I am aware of it,' admitted his lordship. 'Again and again I say to myself, "Wimsey, this cannot last. One of these days this worthy man will cast off the yoke of servitude and settle down in a pub or something," but nothing happens. Still, morning by morning, my coffee is brought, my bath is prepared, my razor laid out, my ties and socks sorted, and my bacon and eggs brought to me in a lordly dish. No matter. This time I demand a more perilous devotion – perilous for us both, my Bunter, for if you were to be carried away, a helpless martyr to matrimony, who then would bring my coffee, prepare my bath, lay out my razor, and perform all those other sacrificial rites? And yet –'

'Who is the party, my lord?'

'There are two of them, Bunter, two ladies lived in a bower,

Binnorie, O Binnorie! The parlourmaid you have seen. Her name is Hannah Westlock. A woman in her thirties, I fancy, and not ill-favoured. The other, the cook – I cannot lisp the tender syllables of her name, for I'd not know it, but doubtless it is Gertrude, Cecily, Magdalen, Margaret, Rosalys, or some other sweet symphonious sound – a fine woman, Bunter, on the mature side, perhaps, but none the worse for that.'

'Certainly not, my lord. If I may say so, the woman of ripe years and queenly figure is frequently more susceptible to delicate attentions than the giddy and thoughtless young beauty.'

'True. Let us suppose, Bunter, that you were to be the bearer of a courteous missive to one Mr Norman Urquhart of Woburn Square. Could you, in the short space of time at your disposal, insinuate yourself, snakelike, as it were, into the bosom of the household?'

'If you desire it, my lord, I will endeavour to insinuate myself to your lordship's satisfaction.'

'Noble fellow. In case of an action for breach, or any consequences of that description, the charges will, of course, be borne by the management.'

'I am obliged to your lordship. When would your lordship wish me to commence?'

'As soon as I have written a note to Mr Urquhart. I will ring.'

'Very good, my lord.'

Wimsey moved over to the writing desk. After a few moments he looked up, a little peevishly.

'Bunter, I have a sensation of being hovered over. I do not like it. It is unusual and it unnerves me. I implore you not to hover. Is the proposition distasteful, or do you want me to get a new hat? What is troubling your conscience?'

'I beg your lordship's pardon. It had occurred to my mind to ask your lordship, with every respect –'

'Oh, God, Bunter – don't break it gently. I can't bear it. Stab and end the creature – to the heft! What is it?'

'I wish to ask you, my lord, whether your lordship thought of making any changes in your establishment?'

Wimsey laid down his pen and stared at the man.

'Changes, Bunter? When I have just so eloquently expressed to you my undying attachment to the loved routine of coffee, bath, razor, sock, eggs and bacon, and the old, familiar faces? You're not giving me warning, are you?'

'No, indeed, my lord. I should be very sorry to leave your lordship's service. But I had thought it possible that, if your lordship was about to contract new ties – '

'I *knew* it was something in the haberdashery line! By all means, Bunter, if you think it necessary. Had you any particular pattern in mind?'

'Your lordship misunderstands me. I referred to domestic ties, my lord. Sometimes, when a gentleman reorganises his household on a matrimonial basis, the lady may prefer to have a voice in the selection of the gentleman's personal attendant, in which case – '

'Bunter!' said Wimsey, considerably startled, 'may I ask where you have contracted these ideas?'

'I ventured to draw an inference, my lord.'

'This comes of training people to be detectives. Have I been nourishing a sleuth-hound on my own hearth-stone? May I ask if you have gone so far as to give a name to the lady?'

'Yes, my lord.'

There was a pause.

'Well?' said Wimsey, in a rather subdued tone, 'what about it, Bunter?'

'A very agreeable lady, if I may say so, my lord.'

'It strikes you that way, does it? The circumstances are unusual, of course.'

'Yes, my lord. I might perhaps make so bold as to call them romantic.'

'You may make so bold as to call them damnable, Bunter.'

'Yes, my lord,' said Bunter, in a tone of sympathy.

'You won't desert the ship, Bunter?'

'Not on any account, my lord.'

'Then don't come frightening me again. My nerves are not what they were. Here is the note. Take it round and do your best.'

'Very good, my lord.'

'Oh, and Bunter.'

'My lord?'

'It seems that I am being obvious. I have no wish to be any-

71

thing of the kind. If you see me being obvious, will you drop me a hint?'

'Certainly, my lord.'

Bunter faded gently out, and Wimsey stepped anxiously to the mirror.

'I can't see anything,' he said to himself. 'No lily on my cheek with anguish moist and fever-dew. I suppose, though, it's hopeless to try and deceive Bunter. Never mind. Business must come first. I've stopped one, two, three, four earths. What next? How about this fellow Vaughan?'

* * *

When Wimsey had any researches to do in Bohemia, it was his custom to enlist the help of Miss Marjorie Phelps. She made figurines in porcelain for a living, and was therefore usually to be found either in her studio or in someone else's studio. A telephone call at 10 a.m. would probably catch her scrambling eggs over her own gas stove. It was true that there had been passages, about the time of the Bellona Club affair, between her and Lord Peter which made it a little embarrassing and unkind to bring her in on the subject of Harriet Vane, but, with so little time in which to pick and choose his tools, Wimsey was past worrying about gentlemanly scruples. He put the call through and was relieved to hear an answering 'Hullo!'

'Hullo, Marjorie! This is Peter Wimsey. How goes it?'

'Oh, fine, thanks. Glad to hear your melodious voice again. What can I do for the Lord High Investigator?'

'Do you know one Vaughan, who is mixed up in the Philip Boyes murder mystery?'

'Oh, Peter! Are you on to that? How gorgeous! Which side are you taking?'

'For the defence.'

'Hurray!'

'Why this pomp of jubilee?'

'Well, it's much more exciting and difficult, isn't it?'

'I'm afraid it is. Do you know Miss Vane, by the way?'

'Yes and no. I've seen her with the Boyes-Vaughan crowd.'

'Like her?'

'So-so.'

72

'Like him? Boyes, I mean?'

'Never stirred a heart-beat.'

'I said, did you like him?'

'One didn't. One either fell for him or not. He wasn't the merry bright-eyed pal of the period, you know.'

'Oh! What's Vaughan?'

'Hanger-on.'

'Oh?'

'House-dog. Nothing must interfere with the expansion of my friend the genius. That sort.'

'Oh!'

'Don't keep saying "Oh!" Do you want to meet the man Vaughan?'

'If it's not too much trouble.'

'Well, turn up tonight with a taxi and we'll go the rounds. We're certain to drop across him somewhere. Also the rival gang, if you want them – Harriet Vane's supporters.'

'Those girls who gave evidence?'

'Yes. You'll like Eiluned Price, I think. She scorns everything in trousers, but she's a good friend at a pinch.'

'I'll come, Marjorie. Will you dine with me?'

'Peter, I'd adore to, but I don't think I will. I've an awful lot to do.'

'Right-ho! I'll roll round about nine, then.'

Accordingly, at 9 o'clock, Wimsey found himself in a taxi with Marjorie Phelps, headed for a round of the studios.

'I've been doing some intensive telephoning,' said Marjorie, 'and I think we shall find him at the Kropotky's. They are pro-Boyes, Bolshevik, and musical, and their drinks are bad, but their Russian tea is safe. Does the taxi wait?'

'Yes; it sounds as if we might want to beat a retreat.'

'Well, it's nice to be rich. It's down the court here on the right, over the Petrovitchs' stable. Better let me grope first.'

They stumbled up a narrow and encumbered stair, at the top of which a fine confused noise of a piano, strings, and the clashing of kitchen utensils announced that some sort of entertainment was in progress.

Marjorie hammered loudly on a door. and, without waiting for an answer, flung it open. Wimsey, entering on her heels, was struck in the face, as by an open hand, by a thick muffling

73

wave of heat, sound, smoke, and the smell of frying.

It was a very small room, dimly lit by a single electric bulb, smothered in a lantern of painted glass, and it was packed to suffocation with people, whose silk legs, bare arms, and pallid faces loomed at him like glow-worms out of the obscurity. Coiling wreaths of tobacco smoke swam slowly to and fro in the midst. In one corner an anthracite stove, glowing red and mephitical, vied with a roaring gas-oven in another corner to raise the atmosphere to roasting pitch. On the stove stood a vast and steaming kettle; on a sidetable stood a vast and steaming samovar; over the gas, a dim figure stood turning sausages in a pan with a fork, while an assistant attended to something in the oven, which Wimsey, whose nose was selective, identified among the other fragrant elements in this compound atmosphere, and identified rightly, as kippers. At the piano, which stood just inside the door, a young man with bushy red hair was playing something of a Czechoslovakian flavour, to a violin obbligato by an extremely loose-jointed person of indeterminate sex in a Fair Isle jumper. Nobody looked round at their entrance. Marjorie picked her way over the scattered limbs on the floor and, selecting a lean young woman in red, bawled into her ear. The young woman nodded and beckoned to Wimsey. He negotiated a passage, and was introduced to the lean woman by the simple formula: 'Here's Peter – this is Nina Kropotky.'

'So pleased,' shouted Madame Kropotky through the clamour. 'Sit by me. Vanya will get you something to drink. It is beautiful, yes? That is Stanislas – such a genius – his new work on the Piccadilly Tube Station – great *n'est-ce pas*? Five days he was continually travelling upon the escalator to absorb the tone-values.'

'Colossal!' yelled Wimsey.

'So – you think? Ah! you can appreciate! You understand it is really for the big orchestra. On the piano it is nothing. It needs the brass, the effects, the tympani – b'rrrrrrr! – So! But one seizes the form, the outline. Ah! it finishes! Superb! magnificent!'

The enormous clatter ceased. The pianist mopped his face and glared haggardly round. The violinist put down its instrument and stood up, revealing itself, by its legs, to be female. The room exploded into conversation. Madame Kropotky leapt

74

over her seated guests and embraced the perspiring Stanislas on both cheeks. The frying-pan was lifted from the stove in a fusillade of spitting fat, a shriek went up for 'Vanya!' and presently a cadaverous face was pushed down to Wimsey's and a deep guttural voice barked at him: 'What will you drink?' while simultaneously a plate of kippers came hovering perilously over his shoulder.

'Thanks,' said Wimsey, 'I have just dined – just *dined,*' he roared despairingly, 'full up, *complet*!'

Marjorie came to the rescue with a shriller voice and more determined refusal.

'Take those dreadful things away, Vanya. They make me sick. Give us some tea, tea, tea!'

'Tea!' echoed the cadaverous man, 'they want tea! What do you think of Stanislas's tone-poem? Strong, modern, eh? The soul of rebellion in the crowd – the clash, the revolt at the heart of the machinery. It gives the bourgeois something to think of, oh, yes!'

'Bah!' said a voice in Wimsey's ear, as the cadaverous man turned away, 'it is nothing. Bourgeois music. Programme music. Pretty! – You should hear Vrilovitch's "Ecstasy on the letter Z". That is pure vibration with no antiquated pattern in it. Stanislas – he thinks much of himself, but it is old as the hills – you can sense the resolution at the back of all his discords. Mere harmony in camouflage. Nothing in it. But he takes them all in because he had red hair and reveals his bony structure.'

The speaker certainly did not err along these lines, for he was as bald and round as a billiard-ball. Wimsey replied soothingly:

'Well, what can you do with the wretched and antiquated instruments of our orchestra? A diatonic scale, bah! Thirteen miserable, bourgeois semi- ones, pooh! To express the infinite complexity of modern emotion, you need a scale of thirty-two notes to the octave.'

'But why cling to the octave?' said the fat man. 'Till you can cast away the octave and its sentimental associations, you walk in fetters of convention.'

'That's the spirit!' said Wimsey. 'I would dispense with all definite notes. After all, the cat does not need them for his midnight melodies, powerful and expressive as they are. The love-hunger of the stallion takes no account of octave or interval in

75

giving forth the cry of passion. It is only man, trammelled by a stultifying convention – oh, hullo, Marjorie, sorry – what is it?'

'Come and talk to Ryland Vaughan,' said Marjorie. 'I have told him you are a tremendous admirer of Philip Boyes's books. Have you read them?'

'Some of them. But I think I'm getting light-headed.'

'You'll feel worse in an hour or so. So you'd better come now.' She steered him to a remote spot near the gas-oven, where an extremely elongated man was sitting curled upon a floor cushion, eating caviare out of a jar with a pickle-fork. He greeted Wimsey with a sort of lugubrious enthusiasm.

'Hell of a place,' he said, 'hell of a business altogether. This stove's too hot. Have a drink. What the devil else can one do? I come here because Philip used to come here. Habit, you know. I hate it, but there's nowhere else to go.'

'You knew him very well, of course,' said Wimsey, seating himself in a waste-paper basket, and wishing he was wearing a bathing-suit.

'I was his only real friend,' said Ryland Vaughan, mournfully. 'All the rest only cared to pick his brains. Apes! parrots! all the bloody lot of them.'

'I've read his books and thought them very fine,' said Wimsey, with some sincerity. 'But he seemed to me an unhappy soul.'

'Nobody understood him,' said Vaughan. 'They called him difficult – who wouldn't be difficult with so much to fight against? They sucked the blood out of him, and his damned thieves of publishers took every blasted coin they could lay their hands on. And then that bitch of a woman poisoned him. My god, what a life!'

'Yes, but what made her do it – if she did do it?'

'Oh, she did it all right. Sheer, beastly spite and jealousy, that's all there was to it. Just because she couldn't write anything but tripe herself. Harriet Vane's got the bug all these damned women have got – fancy they can do things. They hate a man and they hate his work. You'd think it would have been enough for her to help and look after a genius like Phil, wouldn't you? Why, damn it, he used to ask her advice about his work – her advice! Good Lord!'

'Did he take it?'

'Take it? She wouldn't give it. Told him she never gave opinions on other authors' work. *Other* authors! The impudence of it! Of course she was out of things among us all, but why couldn't she realise the difference between her mind and his? Of course it was hopeless from the start for Philip to get entangled with that kind of woman. Genius must be served, not argued with. I warned him at the time, but he was infatuated. And then, to want to marry her – !'

'Why did he?' asked Wimsey.

'Remains of parsonical upbringing, I suppose. It was really pitiful. Besides, I think that fellow Urquhart did a lot of mischief. Sleek family lawyer – d'you know him?'

'No.'

'He got hold of him – put up to it by the family, I imagine. I saw the influence creeping over Phil long before the real trouble began. Perhaps it's a good thing he's dead. It would have been ghastly to watch him turn conventional and settle down.'

'When did this cousin start getting hold of him, then?'

'Oh – about two years ago – a little more, perhaps. Asked him to dinner and that sort of thing. The minute I saw him I knew he was out to ruin Philip, body and soul. What he wanted – what Phil wanted, I mean – was freedom and room to turn about in, but what with the woman and the cousin and the father in the background – oh, well! It's no use crying about it now. His work is left, and that's the best part of him. He's left me that to look after, at least. Harriet Vane didn't get her finger in that pie, after all.'

'I'm sure it's absolutely safe in your hands,' said Wimsey.

'But when one thinks what there might have been,' said Vaughan, turning his bloodshot eyes miserably on Lord Peter, 'it's enough to make one cut one's throat, isn't it?'

Wimsey expressed agreement.

'By the way,' he said, 'you were with him all that last day, till he went to his cousin's. You don't think he had anything on him in the way of – poison or anything? I don't want to seem unkind – but he was unhappy – it would be rotten to think that he –'

'No,' said Vaughan, 'no. That I'll swear he never did. He would have told me – he trusted me in those last days. I shared

77

all his thoughts. He was miserably hurt by that damned woman, but he wouldn't have gone without telling me or saying good-bye. And besides – he wouldn't have chosen that way. Why should he? I could have given him –'

He checked himself, and glanced at Wimsey, but, seeing nothing in his face beyond sympathetic attention, went on:

'I remember talking to him about drugs. Hyoscine – veronal – all that sort of thing. He said, "If ever I want to go out, Ryland you'll show me the way." And I would have – if he'd really wanted it. But arsenic! Philip, who loved beauty so much – do you think he would have chosen arsenic? the suburban poisoner's outfit? That's absolutely impossible.'

'It's not an agreeable sort of thing to take, certainly,' said Wimsey.

'Look here,' said Vaughan, hoarsely and impressively – he had been putting a constant succession of brandies on top of the caviare, and was beginning to lose reserve – 'look here! See this!' He pulled a small bottle from his breast pocket. 'That's waiting till I've finished editing Phil's books. It's a comfort to have it there to look at, you know. Peaceful. Go out through the ivory gate – that's classical – they brought me up on the classics. These people would laugh at a fellow, but you needn't tell them I said it – funny, the way it sticks – *"tende-bantque manus ripoe ulterioris amore, ulterioris' amore"* – what's that bit about the souls thronging thick as leaves in Vallombrosa – no, that's Milton – *amorioris ultore – ultoriore* – damn it – poor Phil!'

Here Mr Vaughan burst into tears and patted the little bottle.

Wimsey, whose head and ears were thumping as though he were sitting in an engine-room, got up softly and withdrew. Somebody had begun a Hungarian song, and the stove was white-hot. He made signals of distress to Marjorie, who was sitting in a corner with a group of men. One of them appeared to be reading his own poems with his mouth nearly in her ear, and another was sketching something on the back of an envelope, to the accompaniment of yelps of merriment from the rest. The noise they made disconcerted the singer, who stopped in the middle of a bar, and cried angrily:

'Ach! this noise; these interruptions! they are intolerable! I lose myself! Stop! I begin all over again, from the beginning.'

Marjorie sprang up, apologising.

'I'm a brute – I'm not keeping your menagerie in order, Nina. We're being perfect nuisances. Forgive me, Marya, I'm in a bad temper. I'd better pick up Peter and toddle away. Come and sing to me another day, darling, when I'm feeling better and there is more room for my feelings to expand. Goodnight, Nina – we've enjoyed it frightfully – and Boris, that poem's the best thing you've done, only I couldn't hear it properly. Peter, tell them what a rotten mood I'm in tonight and take me home.'

'That's right,' said Wimsey, 'nervy, you know – bad effect on the manners and so on.'

'Manners,' said a bearded gentleman suddenly and loudly, 'are for the bourgeois.'

'Quite right,' said Wimsey. 'Beastly bad form, and gives you repressions in the what-not. Come on Marjorie, or we shall all be getting polite.'

'I begin again,' said the singer, 'from the beginning.'

'Whew!' said Wimsey, on the staircase.

'Yes, I know. I think I'm a perfect martyr to put up with it. Anyway, you've seen Vaughan. Nice dopey specimen, isn't he?'

'Yes, but I don't think he murdered Philip Boyes, do you? I had to see him to make sure. Where do we go next?'

'We'll try Joey Trimbles's. That's the stronghold of the opposition show.'

Joey Trimbles occupied a studio over a mews. Here there was the same crowd, the same smoke, more kippers, still more drinks, and still more heat and conversation. In addition there was a blaze of electric light, a gramophone, five dogs, and a strong smell of oil-paints. Sylvia Marriott was expected. Wimsey found himself involved in a discussion of free love, D. H. Lawrence, the prurience of prudery, and the immoral significance of long skirts. In time, however, he was rescued by the arrival of a masculine-looking middle-aged woman with a sinister smile and a pack of cards, who proceeded to tell everybody's fortune. The company gathered around her, and at the same time a girl came in and announced that Sylvia had sprained her ankle and couldn't come. Everybody said warmly, 'Oh, how sickening, poor dear!' and forgot the subject immediately.

'We'll scoot off,' said Marjorie. 'Never mind about saying

goodbye. Nobody marks you. It's good luck about Sylvia because she'll be at home and can't escape us. I sometimes wish they'd all sprain their ankles. And yet, you know, nearly all those people are doing very good work. Even the Kropotky crowd. I used to enjoy this kind of thing myself once.'

'We're getting old, you and I,' said Wimsey. 'Sorry, that's rude. But do you know, I'm getting on for forty, Marjorie.'

'You wear well. But you are looking a bit fagged tonight, Peter, dear. What's the matter?'

'Nothing at all but middle-age.'

'You'll be settling down if you're not careful.'

'Oh, I've been settled for years.'

'With Bunter and the books. I envy you sometimes, Peter.'

Wimsey said nothing. Marjorie looked at him almost in alarm, and tucked her arm in his.

'Peter – do please be happy. I mean, you've always been the comfortable sort of person that nothing could touch. Don't alter, will you?'

That was the second time Wimsey had been asked not to alter himself; the first time, the request had exalted him; this time, it terrified him. As the taxi lurched along the rainy Embankment, he felt for the first time the dull and angry helplessness which is the first warning stroke of triumph of mutability. Like the poisoned Athulf in the *Fool's Tragedy*, he could have cried, 'Oh, I am changing, changing, fearfully changing.' Whether his present enterprise failed or succeeded, things would never be the same again. It was not that his heart would be broken by a disastrous love – he had outlived the luxurious agonies of youthful blood, and in this very freedom from illusion he recognised the loss of something. From now on, every hour of light-heartedness would be, not a prerogative, but an achievement – one more axe or case-bottle or fowling-piece rescued, Crusoe-fashion, from a sinking ship.

For the first time, too, he doubted his own power to carry through what he had undertaken. His personal feelings had been involved before this in his investigations, but they had never before clouded his mind. He was fumbling – grasping uncertainly here and there at fugitive and mocking possibilities. He asked questions at random, doubtful of his object, and the shortness of the time, which would once have stimulated, now frightened and confused him.

'I'm sorry, Marjorie,' he said, rousing himself, 'I'm afraid I'm being damned dull. Oxygen-starvation, probably. D'you mind if we have the window down a bit? That's better. Give me good food and a little air to breathe and I will caper, goat-like, to a dishonourable old age. People will point me out, as I creep, bald and yellow and supported by discreet corsetry, into the nightclubs of my great-grandchildren, and they'll say, "Look, darling! that's the wicked Lord Peter, celebrated for never having spoke a reasonable word for the last ninety-six years. He was the only aristocrat who escaped the guillotine in the revolution of 1960. We keep him as a pet for the children." And I shall wag my head and display my up-to-date dentures and say, "Ah, ha! They don't have the fun we used to have in my young days, the poor, well-regulated creatures!" '

'There won't be any nightclubs then for you to creep into, if they're as disciplined as all that.'

'Oh, yes – nature will have her revenge. They will slink away from the Government Communal Games to play solitaire in catacombs over a bowl of unsterilised skim-milk. Is this the place?'

'Yes; I hope there's someone to let us in at the bottom, if Sylvia's bust her leg. Yes – I hear footsteps. Oh, it's you, Eiluned; how's Sylvia?'

'Pretty all right, only swelled up – the ankle, that is. Coming up?'

'Is she visible?'

'Yes, perfectly respectable.'

'Good, because I'm bringing Lord Peter Wimsey up, too.'

'Oh,' said the girl. 'How do you do? You detect things, don't you? Have you come for the body or anything?'

'Lord Peter's looking into Harriet Vane's business for her.'

'Is he? That's good. Glad somebody's doing something about it.' She was a short, stout girl with a pugnacious nose and a twinkle. 'What do you say it was? I say he did it himself. He was the self-pitying sort, you know. Hullo, Syl – here's Marjorie, with a bloke who's going to get Harriet out of jug.'

'Produce him instantly!' was the reply from within. The door opened upon a small bedsitting-room, furnished with the severest simplicity, and inhabited by a pale, spectacled young woman in a Morris chair, her bandaged foot stretched out upon a packing-case.

'I can't get up, because, as Jenny Wren said, my back's bad and my legs queer. Who's the champion, Marjorie?'

Wimsey was introduced, and Eiluned Price immediately inquired, rather truculently:

'Can he drink coffee, Marjorie? Or does he require masculine refreshment?'

'He's perfectly godly, righteous, and sober, and drinks anything but cocoa and fizzy lemonade.'

'Oh! I only asked because some of your male belongings need stimulating, and we haven't got the wherewithal, and the pub's just closing.'

She stumped over to a cupboard, and Sylvia said:

'Don't mind Eiluned; she likes to treat 'em rough. Tell me, Lord Peter, have you found any clues or anything?'

'I don't know,' said Wimsey. 'I've put a few ferrets down a few holes. I hope something may come up the other end.'

'Have you seen the cousin yet – the Urquhart creature?'

'Got an appointment with him for tomorrow. Why?'

'Sylvia's theory is that he did it,' said Eiluned.

'That's interesting. Why?'

'Female intuition,' said Eiluned, bluntly. 'She doesn't like the way he does his hair.'

'I only said he was too sleek to be true,' protested Sylvia. 'And who else could it have been? I'm sure it wasn't Ryland Vaughan; he's an obnoxious ass, but he is genuinely heartbroken about it all.'

Eiluned sniffed scornfully, and departed to fill a kettle at a tap on the landing.

'And, whatever Eiluned thinks, I can't believe Phil Boyes did it himself.'

'Why not?' asked Wimsey.

'He talked such a lot,' said Sylvia. 'And he really had too high an opinion of himself. I don't think he would have wilfully deprived the world of the privilege of reading his books.'

'He would,' said Eiluned. 'He'd do it out of spite, to make the grown-ups sorry. No, thanks' – as Wimsey advanced to carry the kettle – 'I'm quite capable of carrying six pints of water.'

'Crushed again!' said Wimsey.

'Eiluned disapproves of conventional courtesies between the sexes,' said Marjorie.

'Very well,' replied Wimsey, amiably. 'I will adopt an attitude of passive decoration. Have you any idea, Miss Marriott, why this over-sleek solicitor should wish to make away with his cousin?'

'Not the faintest. I merely proceed on the old Sherlock Holmes basis that when you have eliminated the impossible, then whatever remains, however improbable, must be true.'

'Dupin said that before Sherlock. I grant the conclusion, but in this case I question the premises. No sugar, thank you.'

'I thought all mèn liked to make their coffee into syrup.'

'Yes, but then I am very unusual. Haven't you noticed it?'

'I haven't had much time to observe you, but I'll count the coffee as a point in your favour.'

'Thanks frightfully. I say – can you people tell me just what was Miss Vane's reaction to the murder?'

'Well – ' Sylvia considered a moment. 'When he died – she was upset, of course – '

'She was startled,' said Miss Price, 'but it's my opinion she was thankful to be rid of him. And no wonder. Selfish beast! He'd made use of her and nagged her to death for a year and insulted her at the end. And he was one of your greedy sort that wouldn't let go. She *was* glad, Sylvia – what's the good of denying it?'

'Yes, perhaps. It was a relief to know he was finished with. But she didn't know then that he'd been murdered.'

'No. The murder spoilt it a bit – if it was a murder, which I don't believe. Philip Boyes was always determined to be a victim, and it was very irritating of him to succeed in the end. I believe that's what he did it for.'

'People do do that kind of thing,' said Wimsey, thoughtfully. 'But it's difficult to prove. I mean, a jury is much more inclined to believe in some tangible sort of reason, like money. But I can't find any money in this case.'

Eiluned laughed.

'No, there never was much money, except what Harriet

made. The ridiculous public didn't appreciate Phil Boyes. He couldn't forgive her that, you know.'

'Didn't it come in useful?'

'Of course, but he resented it all the same. She ought to have been ministering to his work, not making money for them both with her own independent trash. But that's men all over.'

'You haven't much opinion of us, what?'

'I've known too many borrowers,' said Eiluned Price, 'and too many that wanted their hands held. All the same, the women are just as bad, or they wouldn't put up with it. Thank heaven, I've never borrowed and never lent – except to women, and they pay back.'

'People who work hard usually do pay back, I fancy,' said Wimsey, ' – except geniuses.'

'Women geniuses don't get coddled,' said Miss Price, grimly, 'so they learn not to expect it.'

'We're getting rather off the subject, aren't we?' said Marjorie.

'No,' replied Wimsey. 'I'm getting a certain amount of light on the central figures in the problem – what journalists like to call the protagonists.' His mouth gave a wry little twist. 'One gets a lot of illumination in that fierce light that beats upon a scaffold.'

'Don't say that,' pleaded Sylvia.

A telephone rang somewhere outside, and Eiluned Price went out to answer it.

'Eiluned's anti-man,' said Sylvia, 'but she's a very reliable person.'

Wimsey nodded.

'But she's wrong about Phil – she couldn't stick him, naturally, and she's apt to think – '

'It's for you, Lord Peter,' said Eiluned, returning. 'Fly at once – all is known. You're wanted by Scotland Yard.'

Wimsey hastened out.

'That you, Peter? I've been scouring London for you. We've found the pub.'

'Never!'

'Fact. And we're on the track of a packet of white powder.'

'Good God!'

'Can you run down first thing tomorrow? We may have it for you.'

'I will skip like a ram and hop like a high hill. We'll beat you yet, Mr Bleeding Chief Inspector Parker.'

'I hope you will,' said Parker, amiably, and rang off.

Wimsey pranced back into the room.

'Miss Price's price has gone to odds on,' he announced. 'It's suicide, fifty to one and no takers. I am going to grin like a dog and run about the city.'

'I'm sorry I can't join you,' said Sylvia Marriott, 'but I'm glad if I'm wrong.'

'I'm glad I'm right,' said Eiluned Price, stolidly.

'And you are right and I am right and everything is quite all right,' said Wimsey.

Marjorie Phelps looked at him and said nothing. She suddenly felt as though something inside her had been put through a wringer.

Chapter IX

By what ingratiating means Mr Bunter had contrived to turn
the delivery of a note into the acceptance of an invitation to
tea was best known to himself. At half-past four on the day
which ended so cheerfully for Lord Peter, he was seated in the
kitchen of Mr Urquhart's house, toasting crumpets. He had
been trained to a great pitch of dexterity in the preparation of
crumpets, and if he was somewhat lavish in the matter of
butter, that hurt nobody except Mr Urquhart. It was natural
that the conversation should turn to the subject of murder.
Nothing goes so well with a hot fire and buttered crumpets as a
wet day without and a good dose of comfortable horrors within.
The heavier the lashing of the rain and the ghastlier the details,
the better the flavour seems to be. On the present occasion, all
the ingredients of an enjoyable party were present in full force.

''Orrible white, he looked, when he came in,' said Mrs
Pettican the cook. 'I see him when they sent for me to bring
up the 'ot bottles. Three of them, they 'ad, one to his feet and
one to his back and the big rubber one to 'is stummick. White
and shiverin', he was, and that dreadful sick, you never would
believe. And he groaned pitiful.'

'Green, he looked to me, Cook,' said Hannah Westlock, 'or
you might perhaps call it a greenish-yellow. I thought it was
jaundice a-coming on – more like them attacks he had in the
spring.'

'He was a bad colour then,' agreed Mrs Pettican, 'but nothing like to what he was that last time. And the pains and
cramps in his legs was agonising. That struck Nurse Williams
very forcible – a nice young woman she was, and not stuck-up
like some as I could name. "Mrs Pettican," she said to me,
which I call it better manners than callin' you Cook as they

86

mostly do, as though they paid your wages for the right of callin' you out of your name – "Mrs Pettican," said she, "never did I see anythink to equal them cramps except in one other case that was the dead spit of this one," she said, "and you mark my words, Mrs Pettican, them cramps ain't there for nothin'." Ah! little did I understand her meanin' at the time.'

'That's a regular feature of these arsenical cases, or so his lordship tells me,' replied Bunter. 'A very distressing symptom. Had he ever had anything of the sort before?'

'Not what you could call cramps,' said Hannah, 'though I remember when he was ill in the spring he complained of getting the fidgets in the hands and feet. Something like pins-and-needles, by what I understand him to say. It was a worrit to him, because he was finishing one of his articles in a hurry, and what with that and his eyes being so bad, the writing was a trial to him, poor thing.'

'From what the gentleman for the prosecution said, talking it out with Sir James Lubbock,' said Mr Bunter, 'I gathered that those pins-and-needles, and bad eyes and so on, were a sign he'd been given arsenic regularly, if I may so phrase it.'

'A dreadful wicked woman she must 'a been,' said Mrs Pettican, ' – 'ev another crumpet, do, Mr Bunter – a-torturin' of the poor soul that long-winded way. Bashin' on the 'ed or the 'asty use of a carvin' knife when roused I can understand, but the 'orrors of slow poisonin' is the work of a fiend in 'uman form, in my opinion.'

'Fiend is the only word, Mrs Pettican,' agreed the visitor.

'And the wickedness of it,' said Hannah, 'quite apart from the causing of a painful death to a fellow-being. Why, it's only the mercy of Providence we weren't all brought under suspicion.'

'Yes, indeed,' said Mrs Pettican. 'Why, when master told us about them diggin' poor Mr Boyes up and findin' him full of that there nasty arsenic, it give me sech a turn, I felt as if the room was a-goin' round like the gallopin' 'orses at the roundabouts. "Oh, sir!" I ses, "what, in our 'ouse!" That's what I ses, and he ses, "Mrs Pettican," he ses, "I sincerely hope not."'

Mrs. Pettican, having imparted this Macbeth-like flavour to the story was pleased with it, and added:

'Yes, that's what I said to 'im. "In our 'ouse," I said, and I'm sure I never slep' a wink for three nights afterwards, what with the police and the fright and one thing and another.'

'But of course you had no difficulty in proving that it hadn't happened in this house?' suggested Bunter. 'Miss Westlock gave her evidence so beautiful at the trial, I'm sure she made it clear as clear could be to judge and jury. The judge congratulated you, Miss Westlock, and I'm sure he didn't say nearly enough – so plainly and well as you spoke up before the whole Court.'

'Well, I never was one to be shy,' confessed Hannah, 'and then, what with going through it all so careful with the master and then with the police, I knew what the questions would be and was prepared, as you might say.'

'I wonder you could speak so exactly to every little detail, all that time ago,' said Bunter, with admiration.

'Well, you see, Mr Bunter, the very morning after Mr Boyes was took ill, master comes down to us and he says, sitting in that chair ever so friendly, just as you might be yourself, "I'm afraid Mr Boyes is very ill," he says. "He thinks he must have ate something as disagreed with him," he says, "and perhaps as it might be the chicken. So I want you and Cook," he says, "to run through with me everything we had for dinner last night to see if we can think what it could have been." "Well, sir," I said, "I don't see that Mr Boyes could have ate anything unwholesome here, for Cook and me had just the same, put aside yourself, sir, and it was all as sweet as it could be," I said.'

'And I said the same,' said the Cook. 'Sech a plain, simple dinner as it was, too – no oysters nor mussels not anythink of that sort, as it's well known shell-fish is poison to some people's stummicks, but a good stren'thenin' drop o' soup, and a bit of nice fish, and a casseroled chicken with turnips and carrots done in the gravy, and a omelette, wot could be lighter and better? Not but there's people as can't relish eggs in any form, my own mother was just the same, give her so much as a cake what had bin made with a egg in it and she'd be that sick and come out all over spots like nettle-rash, you'd be surprised. But Mr Boyes was a great gentleman for eggs, and omelettes was his particular favourite.'

'Yes, he made the omelette himself that very night, didn't he?'

'He did,' said Hannah, 'and well I remember it, for Mr Urquhart asked particular after the eggs, was they new-laid, and I reminded him they was some he had brought in himself that afternoon from that shop on the corner of Lamb's Conduit Street, where they always have them fresh from the farm, and I reminded him that one of them was a little cracked and he'd said, "We'll use that in the omelette tonight, Hannah," and I brought out a clean bowl from the kitchen and put them straight in – the cracked one and three more besides, and never touched them again till I brought them to table. "And what's more, sir," I said, "there's the other eight still here out of the dozen, and you can see for yourself they're as good and fresh as they can be." Didn't I, Cook?'

'Yes, Hannah, And as for the chicken, that was a little beauty. It was that young and tender, I says to Hannah at the time as it seemed a shame to casserole it, for it would 'ave roasted beautiful. But Mr Urquhart is very partial to a casseroled chicken; he says as there's more flavour to 'em that way, and I dunno but what he's right.'

'If done with a good beef stock,' pronounced Mr Bunter, judicially, 'the vegetables well packed in layers, on a foundation of bacon, not too fat, and the whole well seasoned with salt, pepper, and paprika, there are few dishes to beat a casseroled chicken. For my own part, I would recommend a *soupcon* of garlic, but I am aware that such is not agreeable to all tastes.'

'I can't a-bear the smell or sight of the stuff,' said Mrs Pettican, frankly, 'but as for the rest I'm with you, always allowing that the giblets is added to the stock, and I would personally favour mushrooms when in season, but not them tinned or bottled sorts as looks pretty but has no more taste to 'em than boot-buttons, if so much. But the secret is in the cooking, as you knew well, Mr Bunter, the lid being kep' well sealed down to 'old the flavour and the cookin' bein' slow to make the juices perambulate through *and* through each other as you might say. I'm not denyin' as sech is very 'ighly enjoyable, and so Hannah and me found it, though fond of a good roast fowl also, when well-basted with a good rich stuffing to rejuice the dryness. But as to roasting it, Mr Urquhart wouldn't hear of it, and bein' as it's him that pays the bills, he has the right to give his orders.'

'Well,' said Bunter, 'it's certain if there had been anything unwholesome about the casserole, you and Miss Westlock could scarcely have escaped it.'

'No, indeed,' said Hannah, 'for I won't conceal that, being blessed with hearty appetites, we finished it every bit, except a little piece I gave to the cat. Mr Urquhart asked to see the remains of it next day, and seemed quite put out to find it was all gone and the dish washed up – as though any washing-up was ever left overnight in *this* kitchen.'

'I couldn't a-bear myself if I had to begin the day with dirty dishes,' said Mrs Pettican. 'There was a drop of the soup left – not much, jest a wee drain, and Mr Urquhart took that up to show to the doctor, and he tasted it and said it was very good, so Nurse Williams told us, though she didn't have none of it herself.'

'And as for the Burgundy,' said Hannah Westlock, 'which was the only thing Mr Boyes had to himself, like, Mr Urquhart told me to cork it up tight and keep it. And just as well we did, because, of course, the police asked to see it when the time came.'

'It was very far-seeing of Mr Urquhart to take such precautions,' said Bunter, 'when there wasn't any thought at the time but that the poor man died naturally.'

'That's what Nurse Williams said,' replied Hannah, 'but we put it down to him being a solicitor and knowing what ought to be done in a case of sudden death. Very particular he was, too – got me to put a bit of sticking-plaster over the mouth of the bottle and write my initials on it, so that it shouldn't be opened accidental. Nurse Williams always said he expected an inquest, but Dr Weare being there to speak to Mr Boyes having had these kind of bilious attacks all his life, of course there was no question raised about giving the certificate.'

'Of course not,' said Bunter, 'but it's very fortunate, as it turns out, that Mr Urquhart should have understood his duty so well. Many's the case his lordship has seen in which an innocent man has been brought near to the gallows for lack of a simple little precaution like that.'

'And when I think how near Mr Urquhart was to being

away from 'ome at the time,' said Mrs Pettican, 'the thought fair gives me palpitations. Called away, he was, to that tiresome old woman what's always a-dying and never dies. Why, he's there now – Mrs Wrayburn, up in Windle. Rich as Sneezes, she is, by all accounts, and no good to nobody, for she's quite childish, so they say. A wicked old woman she was, too, in 'er day, and 'er other relations wouldn't 'ave nothink to do with 'er, only Mr Urquhart, and I don't suppose 'e wouldn't, neither, only 'e's her solicitor and it's his duty so to do.'

'Duty does not always lie in pleasant places,' commented Mr Bunter, 'as you and I well know, Mrs Pettican.'

'Them that are rich,' said Hannah Westlock, 'find no difficulty about getting their duties performed for them. Which I make bold to say, Mrs Wrayburn would not have done if she had been poor, great-aunt or no great-aunt, knowing Mr Urquhart.'

'Ah!' said Bunter.

'I pass no comments,' said Miss Westlock, 'but you and me, Mr Bunter, know how the world goes.'

'I suppose Mr Urquhart stands to gain something when the old woman does peg out,' suggested Bunter.

'That's as may be; he's not a talker,' said Hannah, 'but it stands to reason he wouldn't be always giving up his time and tearing off to Westmorland for nothing. Though I couldn't care myself to put my hand to money that's wickedly come by. It would not bring a blessing with it, Mr Bunter.'

'It's easy talking, my girl, when you ain't likely to be put in the way of temptation,' said Mrs. Pettican. 'There's many great families in the kingdom what never would 'a bin 'eard of if somebody 'adn't bin a little easier in their ways than what we've bin brought up to. There's skelintons in a many cupboards if the truth was known.'

'Ah!' said Bunter, 'I believe you. I've seen diamond necklaces and fur coats that should have been labelled "Wages of Sin" if deeds done in the dark were to be proclaimed upon the house-tops, Mrs Pettican. And there are families that hold their heads high that wouldn't ever have existed but for some king or other taking his amusements on the wrong side of the blanket, as the old saying goes.'

'They say as some that was high up wasn't too high to take

notice of old Mrs Wrayburn in her young days,' said Hannah, darkly. 'Queen Victoria wouldn't never allow her to act before the Royal Family – she knew too much about her goings-on.'

'An actress, was she?'

'And a very beautiful one, they say, though I can't rightly recollect what her stage name was,' mused Mrs Pettican. 'It was a queer one, I know – 'Yde Park, or somethink of that. This Wrayburn as she married, 'e was nobody – jest to kiver up the scandal, that's what she married 'im for. Two children she 'ad – but 'ose I would not take it upon me to say – and they both died in the cholera, which no doubt it was a judgement.'

'That's not what Mr Boyes called it,' said Hannah, with a self-righteous sniff. 'The Devil took care of his own, that was his way of putting it.'

'Ah! he talked careless,' said Mrs Pettican, 'and no wonder, seeing the folks he lived with. But he'd a sobered down in time if he'd bin spared. A very pleasant way 'e 'ad with 'im when 'e liked. Come in here, he would, and chat upon one thing and another, very amusing-like.'

'You're too soft with the gentlemen, Mrs Pettican,' said Hannah. 'Anyone as has taking ways and poor health is ewe-lambs to you.'

'So Mr Boyes knew all about Mrs Wrayburn?'

'Oh, yes – it was all in the family, you see, and no doubt Mr Urquhart would 'a told him more than he'd say to us. Which train did Mr Urquhart say he was a-comin' by, Hannah?'

'He said dinner for half-past seven. That'll be the six-thirty, I should think.'

Mrs Pettican glanced at the clock and Bunter, taking this as a hint, rose and made his farewells.

'And I 'opes as you'll come again, Mr Bunter,' said the Cook, graciously. 'The master makes no objections to respectable gentlemen visitors at tea-time. Wednesday is my 'arf-day.'

'Mine is Friday,' added Hannah, 'and every other Sunday. If you should be Evangelical, Mr Bunter, the Rev. Crawford in Judd Street is a beautiful preacher. But maybe you'll be going out of town for Christmas.'

Mr Bunter replied that the season would undoubtedly be spent at Duke's Denver, and departed in a shining halo of vicarious splendour.

Chapter X

'HERE you are, Peter,' said Chief Inspector Parker, 'and here is the lady you are anxious to meet. Mrs Bulfinch, allow me to introduce Lord Peter Wimsey.'

'Pleased, I am sure,' said Mrs Bulfinch. She giggled, and dabbed her large, blonde face with powder.

'Mrs Bulfinch, before her union with Mr Bulfinch, was the life and soul of the saloon bar at the Nine Rings in Gray's Inn Road,' said Mr Parker, 'and well known to all for her charm and wit.'

'Go on,' said Mrs Bulfinch, 'you're a one, aren't you? Don't you pay no attention to him, your lordship. You know what these police fellows are.'

'Sad dogs,' said Wimsey, shaking his head. 'But I don't need his testimonials; I can trust my own eyes and ears, Mrs Bulfinch, and I can only say that, if I had had the happiness to make your acquaintance before it was too late, it would have been my lifetime's ambition to wipe Mr Bulfinch's eye.'

'You're every bit as bad as he is,' said Mrs Bulfinch, highly gratified, 'and what Bulfinch would say to you I *don't* know. Quite upset, he was, when the officer came round to ask me to pop along to the Yard. "I don't like it, Gracie," he says, "we've always bin respectable in this house and no trouble with disorderlies nor drinks after hours, and once you get among them fellows you don't know the things you may be asked." "Don't be so soft," I tells him; "the boys all know me and they haven't got nothing against me, and if it's just to tell them about the gentleman that left the packet behind him at the Rings, I haven't no objection to tell them, having nothing to reproach myself with. What'd they think," I said, "if I refused to go? Ten to one they'd think there was something funny about it."

"Well," he says, "I'm coming with you." "Oh, are you?" I says, "and how about the new barman you was going to engage this morning? For," I said, "serve in the jug and bottle I will not, never having been accustomed to it, so you can do as you like." So I came away and left him to it. Mind you, I like him for it. I ain't saying nothing against Bulfinch, but, police or no police, I reckon I know how to take care of myself.'

'Quite so,' said Parker, patiently. 'Mr Bulfinch need feel no alarm. All we want you to do is to tell us, to the best of your recollection, about that young man you spoke of and help us to find the white paper packet. You may be able to save an innocent person from being convicted, and I am sure your husband could not object to that.'

'Poor thing!' said Mrs Bulfinch, 'I'm sure when I read the account of the trial I said to Bulfinch – '

'Just a moment. If you wouldn't mind beginning at the beginning, Mrs Bulfinch, Lord Peter would understand better what you have to tell us.'

'Why, of course. Well, my lord, before I was married I was barmaid at the Nine Rings, as the Chief Inspector says. Miss Montague I was then – it's a better name than Bulfinch, and I was almost sorry to say goodbye to it, but there! a girl has to make a lot of sacrifices when she marries and one more or less is nothing to signify. I never worked there but in the saloon bar, for I wouldn't undertake the four-ale business, it not being a refined neighbourhood, though there's a lot of very nice legal gentlemen drops in of an evening on the saloon side. Well, as I was saying, I was working there up to my marriage, which was last August Bank Holiday, and I remember one evening a gentleman coming in – '

'Could you remember the date, do you think?'

'Not within a day or so I couldn't, for I wouldn't wish to swear to a fib, but it wasn't far off the longest day, for I remember making that same remark to the gentleman for something to say, you know.'

'That's near enough,' said Parker. 'Round about June 20th, or 21st, or something like that?'

'That's right, as near as I can speak to it. And as to the time of night, that I *can* tell you – knowing how keen you 'tecs always are on the hands of the clock.' Mrs Bulfinch giggled again and looked archly round for applause. 'There was a gentleman sitting there – I didn't know him, he was a stranger to the district – and he asked what was our closing hour and I told him 11 o'clock, and he said, "Thank God! I thought I was going to be turned out at 10.30," and I looked at the clock and said, "Oh, you're all right, anyhow, sir; we always keep that clock a quarter of an hour fast." The clock said twenty past, so I know it must have been five past ten really. So we got talking a bit about these prohibitionists and the way they had been trying it on again to get our licensing-hour altered to half-past ten, only we had a good friend on the Bench in Mr Judkins, and while we was discussing it, I remember so well, the door was pushed open hurried-like and a young gentleman comes in, almost falls in, I might say, and he calls, "Give me a double brandy, quick." Well, I didn't like to serve him all at once, he looked so white and queer I thought he'd had one or two over the eight already, and the boss was most particular about that sort of thing. Still, he spoke all right – quite clear and not repeating himself nor nothing, and his eyes, though they did look a bit funny, weren't fixed-like, if you understand me. We get to size folks up pretty well in our business, you know. He sort of held on to the bar, all scrunched up together and bent double, and he says, "Make it a stiff one, there's a good girl. I'm feeling awful bad." The gentleman I'd been talking to, he says to him, "Hold up," he says, "what's the matter?" and the gentleman says, "I'm going to be ill." And he puts his hands across his waistcoat like so!'

Mrs Bulfinch clasped her waist and rolled her big blue eyes dramatically.

'Well, then I see he wasn't drunk, so I mixed him a double Martell with just a splash of soda and he gulps it down, and says "That's better." And the other gentleman puts his arm round him and helps him to a seat. There was a good many other people in the bar, but they didn't notice much, being full of the racing news. Presently the gentleman asks me for a glass of water, and I fetched it to him, and he says, "Sorry if I frightened you, but I've just had a bad shock, and it must have gone to my inside. I'm subject to gastric trouble," he says, "and any worry or shock always affects my stomach. However," he says, "perhaps this will stop it." And he takes out a white paper

95

packet with some powder in it, and drops it into the glass of water and stirs it up with a fountain-pen and drinks it off.'

'Did it fizz or anything?' asked Wimsey.

'No; it was just a plain powder, and it took a bit of time to mix. He drank it off and said, "That settles it," or "That'll settle it," or something of that sort. And then he says, "Thanks very much. I'm better now and I'd better get home in case it takes me again." And he raised his hat – he was quite the gentleman – and off he goes.'

'How much powder do you think he put in?'

'Oh, a good dollop. He didn't measure it or anything, just shot it in out of the packet. Near a dessertspoonful it might have been.'

'And what happened to the packet?' prompted Parker.

'Ah, there you are.' Mrs Bulfinch took a glance at Wimsey's face and seemed pleased with the effect she was producing.

'We'd just got the last customer out – about five past eleven, that would be – and George was locking the door, when I see something white on the seat. Somebody's handkerchief I thought it was, but when I picked it up, I see it was the paper packet. So I said to George, "Hullo! the gentleman's left his medicine behind him." So George asked what gentleman, and I told him, and he said, "What is it?" and I looked, but the label had been torn off. It was just one of them chemist's packets, you know, with the ends turned up and a label stuck across, but there wasn't a bit of the label left.'

'You couldn't even see whether it had been printed in black or in red?'

'Well, now.' Mrs Bulfinch considered. 'Well, no, I couldn't say that. Now you mention it, I do seem to recollect that there was something red about the packet, somewhere, but I can't clearly call it to mind. I wouldn't swear. I know there wasn't any name or printing of any kind, because I looked to see what it was.'

'You didn't try tasting it, I suppose?'

'Not me. It might have been poison or something. I tell you, he was a funny-looking customer.' (Parker and Wimsey exchanged glances.)

'Was that what you thought at the time?' inquired Wimsey,

'or did it only occur to you later on – after you'd read about the case, you know?'

'I thought it at the time, of course,' retorted Mrs Bulfinch, snappishly. 'Aren't I telling you that's why I didn't taste it? I said so to George at the time, what's more. Besides, if it wasn't poison, it might be "snow" or something. "Best not touch it," that's what I said to George, and he said, "Chuck it in the fire." But I wouldn't have that. The gentleman might have come back for it. So I stuck it up on the shelf behind the bar, where they keep the spirits, and never thought of it again from that day to yesterday, when your policeman came round about it.'

'It's been looked for there,' said Parker, 'but they can't seem to find it anywhere.'

'Well, I don't know about that. I put it there and I left the Rings in August, so what's gone with it I can't say. Daresay they threw it away when they were cleaning. Wait a bit, though – I'm wrong when I say I never thought about it again. I did just wonder about it when I read the report of the trial in the *News of the World*, and I said to George, "I wouldn't be surprised if that was the gentleman who came into the Rings one night and seemed so poorly – just fancy!" I said – just like that. And George said, "Now don't get fancies, Gracie my girl; you don't want to get mixed up in a police case." George has always held his head high, you see.'

'It's a pity you didn't come forward with this story,' said Parker, severely.

'Well, how was I to know it was important? The taxi-driver had seen him a few minutes afterwards and he was ill then, so the powder couldn't have had anything to do with it, if it was him, which I couldn't swear to. And anyhow, I didn't see about it till the trial was all over and finished with.'

'There will be a new trial, though,' said Parker, 'and you may have to give evidence at that.'

'You know where to find me,' said Mrs Bulfinch, with spirit. 'I shan't run away.'

'We're very much obliged to you for coming now,' added Wimsey, pleasantly.

'Don't mention it,' said the lady. 'Is that all you want, Mr Chief Inspector?'

'That's all at present. If we find the packet, we may ask you to identify it. And, by the way, it's advisable not to discuss these matters with your friends, Mrs Bulfinch. Sometimes ladies get talking, and one thing leads to another, and in the end they remember incidents that never took place at all. You understand.'

'I never was one for talking,' said Mrs Bulfinch, offended. 'And it's my opinion, when it comes to putting two and two together to make five of 'em, the ladies aren't in it with the gentlemen.'

'I may pass this on to the solicitors for the defence, I suppose?' said Wimsey, when the witness had departed.

'Of course,' said Parker, 'that's why I asked you to come and hear it – for what it's worth. Meanwhile, we shall of course have a good hunt for the packet.'

'Yes,' said Wimsey, thoughtfully, 'yes – you will have to do that – naturally.'

*   *   *

Mr Crofts did not look best pleased when this story was handed on to him.

'I warned you, Lord Peter,' he said, 'what might come of showing our hand to the police. Now they've got hold of this incident, they will have every opportunity to turn it to their own advantage. Why didn't you leave it to us to make the investigation?'

'Damn it,' said Wimsey, angrily, 'it was left to you for about three months and you did absolutely damn all. The police dug it up in three days. Time's important in this case, you know.'

'Very likely, but don't you see that the police won't rest now till they've found this precious packet.'

'Well?'

'Well, and suppose it isn't arsenic at all? If you'd left it in our hands, we could have sprung the thing on them at the last moment, when it was too late to make inquiries, and then we should have knocked the bottom out of the prosecution. Give the jury Mrs Bulfinch's story as it stands and they'd have to admit there was some evidence that the deceased poisoned himself. But now, of course, the police will find or fake something and show that the powder was perfectly harmless.'

'And supposing they find it and it *is* arsenic?'

'In *that* case, of course,' said Mr Crofts, 'we shall get an acquittal. But do you believe in that possibility, my lord?'

'It's perfectly evident that *you* don't,' said Wimsey, hotly. 'In fact, you think your client's guilty. Well, I don't.'

Mr Crofts shrugged his shoulders.

'In our client's interests,' he said, 'we are bound to look at the unfavourable side of all evidence, so as to anticipate the points that are likely to be made by the prosecution. I repeat, my lord, that you have acted indiscreetly.'

'Look here,' said Wimsey, 'I'm not out for a verdict of "Not proven". As far as Miss Vane's honour and happiness are concerned, she might as well be found guilty as acquitted on a mere element of doubt. I want to see her absolutely cleared and the blame fixed in the right quarter. I don't want any shadow of doubt about it.'

'Highly desirable, my lord,' agreed the solicitor, 'but you will allow me to remind you that it is not merely a question of honour or happiness, but of saving Miss Vane's neck from the gallows.'

'And I say,' said Wimsey, 'that it would be better for her to be hanged outright than to live and have everybody think her a murderess who got off by a fluke.'

'Indeed?' said Mr Crofts. 'I fear that is not an attitude that the defence can very well adopt. May I ask if it is adopted by Miss Vane herself?'

'I shouldn't be surprised if it was,' said Wimsey. 'But she's innocent, and I'll make you damn well believe it before I've done.'

'Excellent, excellent,' said Mr Crofts, suavely; 'nobody will be more delighted than myself. But I repeat that, in my humble opinion, your lordship will be wiser not to betray too many confidences to Chief Inspector Parker.'

Wimsey was still simmering inwardly from his encounter when he entered Mr Urquhart's office in Bedford Row. The head clerk remembered him and greeted him with the deference due to an exalted and expected visitor. He begged his lordship to take a seat for a moment, and vanished into an inner office.

A woman typist, with a strong, ugly, rather masculine face, looked up from her machine as the door closed, and nodded abruptly to Lord Peter. Wimsey recognised her as one of the 'The Cattery', and put a commendatory mental note against Miss Climpson's name for quick and efficient organisation. No words passed, however, and in a few moments the head clerk returned and begged Lord Peter to step inside.

Norman Urquhart rose from his desk and held out a friendly hand of greeting. Wimsey had seen him at the trial, and noted his neat dress, thick, smooth, dark hair, and general appearance of brisk and businesslike respectability. Seeing him now more closely, he noticed that he was rather older than he had appeared at a distance. He put him down as being somewhere about the middle forties. His skin was pale and curiously clear, except for a number of little freckles, like sunspots, rather unexpected at that time of the year, and in a man whose appearance conveyed no other suggestion of an outdoor life. The eyes, dark and shrewd, looked a little tired, and were bistred about the orbits, as though anxiety were not unknown to them.

The solicitor welcomed his guest in a high, pleasant voice and asked what he could do for him.

Wimsey explained that he was interested in the Vane poisoning trial, and that he had the authority of Messrs Crofts & Cooper to come and bother Mr Urquhart with questions, adding, as usual, that he was afraid he was being a nuisance.

'Not at all, Lord Peter, not at all. I'm only too delighted to help you in any way, though really I'm afraid you have heard all I know. Naturally, I was very much taken aback by the result of the autopsy, and rather relieved, I must admit, to find that no suspicion was likely to be thrown on me, under the rather peculiar circumstances.'

'Frightfully tryin' for you,' agreed Wimsey. 'But you seem to have taken the most admirable precautions at the time.'

'Well, you know, I suppose we lawyers get into a habit of taking precautions. Not that I had any idea of poison at the time – or, needless to say, I should have insisted on an inquiry then and there. What was in my mind was more in the nature of some kind of food-poisoning; not botulism – the symptoms were all wrong for that – but some contamination from cooking utensils or from some bacillus in the food itself. I am glad it turned out not to be that, though the reality was infinitely worse in one way. I suppose, really, in all cases of sudden and unaccountable illness, an analysis of the secretions ought to be made as a routine part of the business, but Dr Weare appeared perfectly satisfied, and I trusted entirely to his judgement.'

'Obviously,' said Wimsey. 'One doesn't naturally jump to the idea that people are bein' murdered – though I daresay it happens more often than one is apt to suppose.'

'It probably does, and if I'd ever had the handling of a criminal case, the suspicion might have occurred to me, but my work is almost entirely conveyancing and that sort of business – and probate and divorce and so on.'

'Talkin' of probate,' said Wimsey, carelessly, 'had Mr Boyes any sort of financial expectations?'

'None at all that I know of. His father is by no means well off – the usual country parson with a small stipend and a huge vicarage and tumbledown church. In fact, the whole family belongs to the unfortunate professional middle-class – over-taxed and with very little financial stamina. I shouldn't think there were more than a few hundred pounds to come to Philip Boyes, even if he had outlived the lot of them.'

'I had an idea there was a rich aunt somewhere.'

'Oh, no – unless you're thinking of old Cremorna Garden. She's a great-aunt, on the mother's side. But she hasn't had anything to do with them for very many years.'

At this moment Lord Peter had one of those bursts of illumination which come suddenly when two unrelated facts make contact in the mind. In the excitement of hearing Parker's news about the white paper packet, he had paid insufficient attention to Bunter's account of the tea-party with Hannah Westlock and Mrs Pettican, but now he remembered something about an actress, 'with a name like 'Yde Park or something of that'. The readjustment made itself so smoothly and mechanically in his mind that his next question followed almost without a pause.

'Isn't that Mrs Wrayburn of Windle in Westmorland?'

'Yes,' said Mr Urquhart. 'I've just been up to see her, as a matter of fact. Of course, yes, you wrote to me there. She's been quite childish, poor old lady, for the last five years or so. A wretched life – dragging on like that, a misery to herself and everybody else. It always seems to me a cruel thing that one may not put these poor old people out of the way, as one would a favourable animal – but the law will not let us be so merciful.'

'Yes, we'd be hauled over the coals by the N.S.P.C.A. if we let a cat linger on in misery,' said Wimsey. 'Silly, isnt' it? But it's all of a piece with the people who write to the papers about keepin' dogs in draughty kennels and don't give a hoot – or a penny – to stop landlords allowin' a family of thirteen to sleep in an undrained cellar with no glass in the windows and no windows to put it in. It really makes me quite cross, sometimes, though I'm a peaceful sort of idiot as a rule. Poor old Cremorna Garden – she must be gettin' on now, though. Surely she can't last much longer.'

'As a matter of fact, we all thought she'd gone the other day. Her heart is giving out – she's over ninety, poor soul, and she gets these attacks from time to time. But there's amazing vitality in some of these ancient ladies.'

'I suppose you're about her only living relation now.'

'I suppose I am, except for an uncle of mine in Australia.' Mr Urquhart accepted the fact of the relationship without inquiring how Wimsey came to know about it. 'Not that my being there can do her any good. But I'm her man of business, too, so it's just as well I should be on the spot when anything happens.'

'Oh, quite, quite. And, being her man of business, of course you know how she has left her money.'

'Well, yes, of course. Though I don't quite see, if you'll forgive my saying so, what that has to do with the present problem.'

'Why, don't you see,' said Wimsey, 'it just occurred to me that Philip Boyes might have got himself into some kind of financial mess-up – it happens to the best of men – and have, well, taken the short way out of it. But, if he had any expectations from Mrs Wrayburn, and the old girl – I mean, the poor old lady – was so near shuffling off this mortal thingummy, why then, don't you know, he would have waited, or raised the wind on the strength of a post-obit or something or the other. You get my meaning, what?'

'Oh, I see – you are trying to make out a case for suicide. Well, I agree with you that it's the most hopeful defence for Miss Vane's friends to put up, and as far as that goes I can support you. Inasmuch, that is, as Mrs Wrayburn did not leave

Philip anything. Nor, so far as I know, had he the smallest reason to suppose she would do so.'

'You're positive of that?'

'Quite. As a matter of fact' – Mr Urquhart hesitated – 'well, I may as well tell you that he asked me about it one day, and I was obliged to tell him that he hadn't the least chance of getting anything from her.'

'Oh – he did actually ask?'

'Well, yes, he did.'

'That's rather a point, isn't it? How long ago would that be?'

'Oh – about eighteen months ago, I fancy. I couldn't be sure.'

'And as Mrs Wrayburn is now childish, I suppose he couldn't entertain any hope that she would ever alter the will?'

'Not the slightest.'

'No, I see. Well, I think we might make something of that. Great disappointment, of course – one would make out that he had counted a good deal upon it. Is it much, by the way?'

'Pretty fair – about seventy or eighty thousand.'

'Very sickening, to think of all that good stuff going west and not getting a look-in one's self. By the way, how about you? Don't you get anything? I beg your pardon, fearfully inquisitive and all that, but I mean to say, considering you've been looking after her for years and are her only available relation, so to speak, it would be a trifle thick, what?'

The solicitor frowned, and Wimsey apologised.

'I know, I know – I've been fearfully impudent. It's a failing of mine. And, anyhow, it'll all be in the papers when the old lady does pop off, so I don't know why I should be so anxious to pump you. Wash it out – I'm sorry.'

'There's no real reason why you shouldn't know,' said Mr Urquhart, slowly, 'though one's professional instinct is to avoid disclosing one's clients' affairs. As a matter of fact, I am the legatee myself.'

'Oh?' said Wimsey, in a disappointed voice. 'But in that case – that rather weakens the story, doesn't it? I mean to say, your cousin might very well have felt, in that case, that he could look to you for – that is – of course I don't know what your ideas might have been – '

Mr Urquhart shook his head.

'I see what you are driving at, and it is a very natural thought.

103

But actually, such a disposal of the money would have been directly contrary to the expressed wish of the testatrix. Even if I could legally have made it over, I should have been morally bound not to do so, and I had to make that clear to Philip. I might, of course, have assisted him with casual gifts of money from time to time, but, to tell the truth, I should hardly have cared to do so. In my opinion, the only hope of salvation for Philip would have been to make his way on his own work. He was a little inclined – though I don't like speaking ill of the dead – to – to rely too much on other people.'

'Ah, quite. No doubt that was Mrs Wrayburn's idea also?'

'Not exactly. No. It went rather deeper than that. She considered that she had been badly treated by her family. In short – well, as we have gone so far, I don't mind giving you her *ipsissima verba.*'

He rang a bell on his desk.

'I haven't got the will itself here, but I have the draft. Oh, Miss Murchison, would you kindly bring me the deed-box labelled "Wrayburn"? Mr Pond will show it to you. It isn't heavy.'

The lady from 'The Cattery' departed silently in quest of the box.

'This is all rather irregular, Lord Peter,' went on Mr Urquhart, 'but there are times when too much discretion is as bad as too little, and I should like you to see exactly why I was forced to take up this rather uncompromising attitude towards my cousin. Ah, thank you, Miss Murchison.'

He opened the deed-box with a key attached to a bunch which he took from his trousers pocket, and turned over a quantity of papers. Wimsey watched him with the expression of a rather foolish terrier who expects a tit-bit.

'Dear, dear,' ejaculated the solicitor, 'it doesn't seem to be – oh! of course, how forgetful of me. I'm so sorry; it's in my safe at home. I got it out for reference last June, when the previous alarm occurred about Mrs Wrayburn's illness, and in the confusion which followed on my cousin's death I quite forgot to bring it back. However, the gist of it was –'

'Never mind,' said Wimsey, 'there's no hurry. If I called at your house tomorrow, perhaps I could see it then.'

'By all means, if you think it important. I do apologise for

104

carelessness. In the meantime, is there anything else I can tell you about the matter?'

Wimsey asked a few questions, covering the ground already traversed by Bunter in his investigations, and took his departure. Miss Murchison was again at work in the outer office. She did not look up as he passed.

'Curious,' mused Wimsey, as he pattered along Bedford Row, 'everybody is so remarkably helpful about this case. They cheerfully answer questions which one has no right to ask and burst into explanations in the most unnecessary manner. None of them seems to have anything to conceal. It's quite astonishing. Perhaps the fellow really did commit suicide. I hope he did. I wish I could question *him*. I'd put him through it, blast him. I've got about fifteen different analyses of his character already – all different . . . It's very ungentlemanly to commit suicide without leaving a note to say you've done it – gets people into trouble. When I blow my brains out –'

He stopped.

'I hope I shan't want to,' he said. 'I hope I shan't need to want to. Mother wouldn't like it, and it's messy. But I'm beginning to dislike this job of getting people hanged. It's damnable for their friends . . . I won't think about hanging. It's unnerving.'

Chapter XI

WIMSEY presented himself at Mr Urquhart's house at 9 o'clock the next morning, and found that gentleman at breakfast.

'I thought I might catch you before you went down to the office,' said his lordship, apologetically. 'Thanks awfully, I've had my morning nosebag. No, really, thanks – I never drink before eleven. Bad for the inside.'

'Well, I've found the draft for you,' said Mr Urquhart pleasantly. 'You can cast your eye over it while I drink my coffee, if you'll excuse my going on. It exposes the family skeleton a little, but it's all ancient history now.'

He fetched a sheet of typescript from a side-table and handed it to Wimsey, who noticed, mechanically, that it had been typed on a Woodstock machine, with a chipped lower-case p, and an A slightly out of alignment.

'I'd better make quite clear the family connections of the Boyeses and the Urquharts,' he went on, returning to the breakfast table, 'so that you will understand the will. The common ancestor is old John Hubbard, a highly respectable banker at the beginning of the last century. He lived in Nottingham, and the bank, as usual in those days, was a private, family concern. He had three daughters, Jane, Mary, and Rosanna. He educated them well, and they ought to have been heiresses in a mild way, but the old boy made the usual mistakes, speculated unwisely, allowed his clients too much rope – the old story. The bank broke, and the daughters were left penniless. The eldest, Jane, married a man called Henry Brown. He was a schoolmaster, and very poor and quite repellently moral. They had one daughter, Julia, who eventually married a curate, the Rev. Arthur Boyes, and was the mother of Philip Boyes. The second daughter, Mary, did rather better financially, though socially

106

she married beneath her. She accepted the hand of one Josiah Urquhart, who was engaged in the lace-trade. This was a blow to the old people, but Josiah came originally of a fairly decent family, and was a most worthy person, so they made the best of it. Mary had a son, Charles Urquhart, who contrived to break away from the degrading associations of trade. He entered a solicitor's office, did well, and finally became a partner in the firm. He was my father, and I am his successor in the legal business.

'The third daughter, Rosanna, was made of different stuff. She was very beautiful, a remarkably fine singer, a graceful dancer, and altogether a particularly attractive and spoilt young person. To the horror of her parents, she ran away and went on the stage. They erased her name from the family Bible. She determined to justify their worst suspicions. She became the spoilt darling of fashionable London. Under her stage name of Cremorna Garden, she went from one disreputable triumph to another. And, mind you, she had brains, nothing of the Nell Gwynne business about her. She was the take-it-and-keep-it sort. She took everything – money, jewels, *appartements meublés*, horses, carriages, all the rest of it, and turned it into good consolidated funds. She was never prodigal of anything except her person, which she considered to be a sufficient return for all favours, and I daresay it was. I never saw her till she was an old woman, but, before she had the stroke which destroyed her brain and body, she still kept the remains of remarkable beauty. She was a shrewd old woman in her way, and grasping. She had those tight little hands, plump and narrow, that give nothing away – except for cash down. You know the sort.

'Well, the long and the short of it was that the eldest sister, Jane – the one who married the schoolmaster – would have nothing to do with the family black sheep. She and her husband wrapped themselves up in their virtue and shuddered when they saw the disgraceful name of Cremorna Garden billed outside the Olympic or the Adelphi. They returned her letters unopened and forbade her the house, and the climax was reached when Henry Brown tried to have her turned out of the church on the occasion of his wife's funeral.

'My grandparents were less strait-laced. They didn't call on

her and didn't invite her, but they occasionally took a box for
her performances and they sent her a card for their son's wedding, and were polite in a distant kind of way. In consequence,
she kept up a civil acquaintance with my father, and eventually
put her business into his hands. He took the view that property
was property, however acquired, and said that if a lawyer refused to handle dirty money he would have to show half his
clients the door.

'The old lady never forgot or forgave anything. The very
mention of the Brown-Boyes connection made her foam at the
mouth. Hence, when she came to make her will, she put in that
paragraph you have before you now. I pointed out to her that
Philip Boyes had had nothing to do with the persecution, as,
indeed, neither had Arthur Boyes, but the old sore rankled still,
and she wouldn't hear a word in his favour. So I drew up the
will as she wanted; if I didn't, somebody else would have done
so, you know.'

Wimsey nodded, and gave his attention to the will, which was
dated eight years previously. It appointed Norman Urquhart as
sole executor, and, after a few legacies to servants and to
theatrical charities, it ran as follows:

'All the rest of my property whatsoever and wheresoever
situated I give to my great-nephew Norman Urquhart of Bedford Row Solicitor for his lifetime and at his death to be
equally divided among his legitimate issue but if the said
Norman Urquhart should decease without legitimate issue
the said property to pass to [here followed the names of the
charities previously specified]. And I make this disposition of
my property in token of gratitude for the consideration
shown to me by my said great-nephew Norman Urquhart and
his father the late Charles Urquhart throughout their lives
and to ensure that no part of my property shall come into the
hands of my great-nephew Philip Boyes or his descendents.
And to this end and to mark my sense of the inhuman treatment meted out to me by the family of the said Philip Boyes
I enjoin upon the said Norman Urquhart as my dying wish
that he neither give lend nor convey to the said Philip Boyes
any part of the income derived from the said property enjoyed by him the said Norman Urquhart during his lifetime

108

nor employ the same to assist the said Philip Boyes in any manner whatsoever.'

'H'm!' said Wimsey, 'that's pretty clear, and pretty vindictive.'

'Yes, it is – but what are you to do with old ladies who won't listen to reason? She looked pretty sharply to see that I had got the wording fierce enough before she would put her name to it.'

'It must have depressed Philip Boyes all right,' said Wimsey. 'Thank you – I'm glad I've seen that; it makes the suicide theory a good deal more probable.'

In theory it might do so, but the theory did not square as well as Wimsey could have wished with what he had heard about the character of Philip Boyes. Personally, he was inclined to put more faith in the idea that the final interview with Harriet had been the deciding factor in the suicide. But this, too, was not quite satisfactory. He could not believe that Philip had felt that particular kind of affection for Harriet Vane. Perhaps, though, it was merely that he did not want to think well of the man. His emotions were, he feared, clouding his judgement a little.

He went back home and read the proofs of Harriet's novel. Undoubtedly she could write well, but undoubtedly she knew only too much about the administration of arsenic. Moreover, the book was about two artists who lived in Bloomsbury and led an ideal existence, full of love and laughter and poverty, till somebody unkindly poisoned the young man and left the young woman inconsolable and passionately resolved to avenge him. Wimsey ground his teeth and went down to Holloway Gaol, where he very nearly made a jealous exhibition of himself. Fortunately, his sense of humour came to the rescue when he had cross-examined his client to the verge of exhaustion and tears.

'I'm sorry,' he said; 'the fact is, I'm most damnably jealous of this fellow Boyes. I oughtn't to be, but I am.'

'That's just it,' said Harriet, 'and you always would be.'

'And if I was, I shouldn't be fit to live with. Is that it?'

'You would be very unhappy. Quite apart from all the other drawbacks.'

109

'But, look here,' said Wimsey, 'if you married me I shouldn't be jealous, because then I should know that you really liked me and all that.'

'You think you wouldn't be. But you would.'

'Should I? Oh, surely not. Why should I? It's just the same as if I married a widow. Are all second husbands jealous?'

'I don't know. But it's not quite the same. You'd never really trust me, and we should be wretched.'

'But, damn it all,' said Wimsey, 'if you would once say you cared a bit about me it would be all right. I should believe that. It's because you won't say it that I imagine all sorts of things.'

'You would go on imagining things in spite of yourself. You couldn't give me a square deal. No man ever does.'

'Never?'

'Well, hardly ever.'

'That would be rotten,' said Wimsey, seriously. 'Of course, if I turned out to be that sort of idiot, things would be pretty hopeless. I know what you mean. I knew a bloke once who got that jealous bug. If his wife wasn't always hanging round his neck, he said it showed he meant nothing to her, and if she did express her affection he called her a hypocrite. It got quite impossible, and she ran away with somebody she didn't care twopence for, and he went about saying that he had been right about her all along. But everybody else said it was his own silly fault. It's all very complicated. The advantage seems to be with the person who gets jealous first. Perhaps you could manage to be jealous of me. I wish you would, because it would prove that you took a bit of interest in me. Shall I give you some details of my hideous past?'

'Please don't.'

'Why not?'

'I don't want to know about all the other people.'

'Don't you, by Jove? I think that's rather hopeful. I mean, if you just felt like a mother to me, you would be anxious to be helpful and understanding. I loathe being helped and understood. And, after all, there was nothing in any of them – except Barbara, of course.'

'Who was Barbara?' asked Harriet, quickly.

'Oh, a girl. I owe her quite a lot, really,' replied Wimsey, musingly. 'When she married the other fellow, I took up sleuthing as a cure for wounded feelings, and it's really been great fun, take it all in all. Dear me, yes – I was very much bowled over that time. I even took a special course in logic for her sake.'

'Good gracious!'

'For the pleasure of repeating "Barbara celarent darii ferio baralipton". There was a kind of mysterious romantic lilt about the thing which was somehow expressive of passion. Many a moonlight night have I murmured it to the nightingales which haunt the garden of St John's – though, of course, I was a Balliol man myself, but the buildings are adjacent.'

'If anybody ever marries you, it will be for the pleasure of hearing you talk piffle,' said Harriet, severely.

'A humiliating reason, but better than no reason at all.'

'I used to piffle rather well myself,' said Harriet, with tears in her eyes, 'but it's got knocked out of me. You know – I was really meant to be a cheerful person – all this gloom and suspicion isn't the real me. But I've lost my nerve, somehow.'

'No wonder, poor kid. But you'll get over it. Just keep on smiling, and leave it to Uncle Peter.'

When Wimsey got home, he found a note awaiting him.

'DEAR LORD PETER, As you saw, I got the job. Miss Climpson sent six of us, all with different stories and testimonials, of course, and Mr Pond (the head clerk) engaged me, subject to Mr Urquhart's approval.

'I've only been here a couple of days, so there isn't very much I can tell you about my employer, personally, except that he has a sweet tooth and keeps secret stores of chocolate cream and Turkish delight in his desk, which he surreptitiously munches while he is dictating. He seems pleasant enough.

'But there's just one thing. I fancy it would be interesting to investigate his financial activities. I've done a good bit one way and another with stockbroking, you know, and yesterday in his absence I took a call for him which I wasn't meant to hear. It wouldn't have told the ordinary person anything, but it did me, because I knew something about the man at the other end. Find out if Mr U. had been doing anything with the Megatherium Trust before their big crash.

111

'Further reports when anything turns up.

'Yours sincerely,

'JOAN MURCHISON.'

'Megatherium Trust?' said Wimsey. 'That's a nice thing for a respectable solicitor to get mixed up with. I'll ask Freddy Arbuthnot. He's an ass about everything except stocks and shares, but he does understand them for some ungodly reason.'

He read the letter again, mechanically noting that it was typed on a Woodstock machine, with a chipped lower-case p, and a capital A that was out of alignment.

Suddenly he woke up and read it a third time, noticing, by no means mechanically, the chipped p and the irregular capital A.

Then he sat down, wrote a line on a sheet of paper, folded it, addressed it to Miss Murchison, and sent Bunter out to post it.

For the first time, in this annoying case, he felt the vague stirring of the waters as a living idea emerged slowly and darkly from the inmost deeps of his mind.

Chapter XII

WIMSEY was accustomed to say, when he was an old man and more talkative even than usual, that the recollection of that Christmas at Duke's Denver had haunted him in nightmares, every night regularly, for the following twenty years. But it is possible that he remembered it with advantages. There is no doubt that it tried his temper severely. It began inauspiciously at the tea-table, when Mrs 'Freak' Dimsworthy fluted out in her high, overriding voice: 'And is it true, Lord Peter, dear, that you are defending that frightful poisoning woman?' The question acted like the drawing of a champagne cork. The whole party's bottled-up curiosity about the Vane case creamed over in one windy gust of stinging froth.

'I've no doubt she did it, and I don't blame her,' said Captain Tommy Bates; 'perfectly foul blighter. Has his photograph on the dust-cover of his books, you know – that's the sort of squit he was. Wonderful, the rotters these highbrow females will fall for. The whole lot of 'em ought to be poisoned like rats. Look at the harm they do to the country.'

'But he was a very fine writer,' protested Mrs Featherstone, a lady in her thirties, whose violently compressed figure suggested that she was engaged in a perpetual struggle to compute her weight in terms of the first syllables of her name rather than the last. 'His books are positively Gallic in their audacity and restraint. Audacity is not rare – but that perfect concision of style is a gift which – '

'Oh, if you like dirt,' interrupted the Captain, rather rudely.

'I wouldn't call it that,' said Mrs Featherstone. 'He is frank, of course, and that is what people in this country will not forgive. It is part of our national hypocrisy. But the beauty of the writing puts it all on a higher plane.'

'Well, I wouldn't have the muck in the house,' said the Captain, firmly. 'I caught Hilda with it, and I said, "Now you send that book straight back to the library." I don't interfere, but one must draw the line somewhere.'

'How did you know what it was like?' asked Wimsey, innocently.

'Why James Douglas's article in the *Express* was good enough for me,' said Captain Bates. 'The paragraphs he quoted were filthy – positively filthy.'

'Well, it's a good thing we've all read them,' said Wimsey. 'Forewarned is forearmed.'

'We owe a great debt of gratitude to the Press,' said the Dowager Duchess; 'so kind of them to pick out all the plums for us and save us the trouble of reading the books, don't you think, and such a joy for the poor dear people who can't afford seven and sixpence, or even a library subscription. I suppose, though I'm sure that works out cheaply enough if one is a quick reader. Not that the cheap ones will take those books for I asked my maid, such a superior girl and so keen on improving her mind, which is more than I can say for most of my friends, but no doubt it is all due to free education for the people and I suspect her in my heart of voting Labour though I never ask because I don't think it's fair, and besides, if I did, I couldn't very well take any notice of it, could I?'

'Still, I don't suppose the young woman murdered him on that account,' said her daughter-in-law. 'From all accounts she was as bad as he was.'

'Oh, come,' said Wimsey, 'you can't think that, Helen. Damn it, she writes detective stories, and in detective stories virtue is always triumphant. They're the purest literature we have.'

'The Devil is always ready to quote Scripture when it pays him to do so,' said the younger Duchess, 'and they say the wretched woman's sales are going up by leaps and bounds.'

'It's my belief,' said Mr Harringay, 'that the whole thing is a publicity stunt gone wrong.' He was a large jovial man, extremely rich and connected with the City. 'You never know what these advertising fellows are up to.'

'Well, it looks like a case of hanging the goose that lays the golden eggs this time,' said Captain Bates, with a loud laugh. 'Unless Wimsey means to pull off one of his conjuring tricks.'

'I hope he does,' said Miss Titterton. 'I adore detective stories. I'd commute the sentence to penal servitude on condition that she turned out a new story every six months. It would be much more useful than picking oakum or sewing mail bags for the post office to mislay.'

'Aren't you being a bit previous?' suggested Wimsey, mildly. 'She's not convicted yet.'

'But she will be the next time. You can't fight facts, Peter.'

'Of course not,' said Captain Bates. 'The police know what they're about. They don't put people into the dock if there isn't something pretty shady about 'em.'

Now this was a fearful brick, for it was not so many years since the Duke of Denver had himself stood his trial on a mistaken charge of murder. There was a ghastly silence, broken by the Duchess, who said icily: 'Really, Captain Bates!'

'What? Eh? Oh, of course, I mean to say, I know mistakes do happen sometimes, but that's a very different thing. I mean to say, this woman, with no morals at all, that is, I mean – '

'Have a drink, Tommy,' said Lord Peter, kindly; 'you aren't quite up to your usual standard of tact today.'

'No, but do tell us, Lord Peter,' cried Mrs Dimsworthy, 'what the creature is *like*. Have you talked to her? I thought she had rather a nice voice, though she's as plain as a pancake.'

'Nice voice, Freakie? Oh, no,' said Mrs Featherstone. 'I should have called it rather sinister. It absolutely thrilled me. I got shudders all the way down my spine. A genuine *frisson*. And I think she would be quite attractive, with those queer, smudgy eyes, if she were properly dressed. A sort of *femme fatale*, you know. Does she try to hypnotise you, Peter?'

'I saw in the papers,' said Miss Titterton, 'that she had had hundreds of offers of marriage.'

'Out of one noose into the other,' said Harringay, with his noisy laugh.

'I don't think I should care to marry a murderess,' said Miss Titterton, 'especially one that's been trained on detective stories. One would be always wondering whether there was anything funny about the taste of the coffee.'

'Oh, these people are all mad,' said Mrs Dimsworthy. 'They have a morbid longing for notoriety. It's like the lunatics who make spurious confessions and give themselves up for crimes they haven't committed.'

'A murderess might make quite a good wife,' said Harringay. 'There was Madeleine Smith, you know – she used arsenic too, by the way – she married somebody and lived happily to a respectable old age.'

'But did her husband live to a respectable old age?' demanded Miss Titterton. 'That's more to the point, isn't it?'

'Once a poisoner, always a poisoner, *I* believe,' said Mrs Featherstone. 'It's a passion that grows upon you – like drink or drugs.'

'It's the intoxicating sensation of power,' said Mrs Dimsworthy. 'But Lord Peter, *do* tell us – '

'Peter!' said his mother, 'I do wish you'd go and see what's happened to Gerald. Tell him his tea is getting cold. I think he's in the stables talking to Freddy about thrush or cracked heels or something, so tiresome the way horses are always getting something the matter with them. You haven't trained Gerald properly, Helen, he used to be quite punctual as a boy. Peter was always the tiresome one, but he's becoming almost human in his old age. It's that wonderful man of his who keeps him in order, really a remarkable character and so intelligent, quite one of the old sort, you know, a perfect autocrat, and such manners too. He would be worth thousands to an American millionaire, most impressive, I wonder Peter isn't afraid he'll give warning one of these days, but I really believe he is positively attached to him, Bunter attached to Peter, I mean, though the other way on would be true too, I'm sure Peter pays more attention to his opinion than he does to mine.'

Wimsey had escaped, and was by now on his way to the stables. He met Gerald, Duke of Denver, returning, with Freddy Arbuthnot in tow. The former received the Dowager's message with a grin.

'Got to turn up, I suppose,' he said. 'I wish nobody had ever invented tea. Ruins your nerves and spoils your appetite for dinner.'

'Beastly sloppy stuff,' agreed the Hon. Freddy. 'I say, Peter, I've been wanting to get hold of you.'

'Same here,' said Wimsey, promptly. 'I'm feelin' rather exhausted with conversation. Let's wander through the billiard room and build our constitutions up before we face the barrage.'

'Today's great thought,' said Freddy, enthusiastically. He pattered happily after Wimsey into the billiard room, and flung himself down in a large chair. 'Great bore, Christmas, isn't it? All the people one hates most gathered together in the name of goodwill and all that.'

'Bring a couple of whiskies,' said Wimsey to the footman. 'And James, if anybody asks for Mr Arbuthnot or me, you rather think we have gone out. Well, Freddy, here's luck! Has anything transpired, as the journalists say?'

'I've been sleuthing like stink on the tracks of your man,' said Mr Arbuthnot. 'Really, don't you know, I shall soon be qualified to set up in your line of business. Our financial column, edited by Uncle Buthie – that sort of thing. Friend Urquhart has been very careful though. Bound to be – respectable family lawyer and all that. But I saw a man yesterday who knows a fellow who had it from a chappie that said Urquhart had been dipping himself a bit recklessly off the deep end.'

'Are you sure, Freddy?'

'Well, not to say sure. But this man, you see, owes me one, so to speak, for having warned him off the Megatherium before the band began to play, and he thinks, if he can get hold of the chappie that knows – not the fellow that told him, you understand, but the other one – that he might be able to get something out of him, don't you see, especially if I was able to put this other chappie in the way of something or the other, what?'

'And no doubt you have secrets to sell.'

'Oh, well, I daresay I could make it worth this other chappie's while, because I've got an idea, through this other fellow that my bloke knows, that the chappie is rather up against it, as you might say, through being caught short on some Airways stock, and if I was to put him in touch with Goldberg, don't you see, it might get him out of a hole and so on. And Goldberg will be all right, because, don't you see, he's a cousin of old Levy's, who was murdered, you know, and all these Jews stick together like leeches, and, as a matter of fact, I think it's very fine of them.'

'But what has old Levy got to do with it?' asked Wimsey,

his mind running over the incidents in that half-forgotten murder episode.

'Well, as a matter of fact,' said the Hon. Freddy, a little nervously, 'I've – er – done the trick as you might say. Rachel Levy is – er – in fact – going to become Mrs Freddy and all that sort of thing.'

'The devil she is,' said Wimsey, ringing the bell. 'Tremendous congratters and all that. It's been a long time working up, hasn't it?'

'Why, yes,' said Freddy. 'Yes, it has. You see, the trouble was that I was a Christian – at least, I was christened and all that, though I pointed out I wasn't at all a good one, except, of course, that one keeps up the family pew and turns out on Christmas Day and so on. Only it seems they didn't mind that so much as my bein' a Gentile. Well that, of course, is past prayin' for. And then there was the difficulty about the kids – if any. But I explained that I didn't mind what they counted them as – and I don't, you know, because, as I was saying, it would be all to the little beggars' advantage to be in with the Levy and Goldberg crowd, especially if the boys were to turn out anything in the financial way. And then I rather got round Lady Levy by sayin' I had served nearly seven years for Rachel – that was rather smart, don't you think?'

'Two more whiskies, James,' said Lord Peter. 'It was brilliant, Freddy. How did you come to think of it?'

'In church,' said Freddy, 'at Diana Rigby's wedding. The bride was fifty minutes late and I had to do something, and somebody had left a Bible in the pew, I saw that – I say, old Laban was a bit of a tough, wasn't he? – and I said to myself, "I'll work that off next time I call," and so I did, and the old lady was uncommonly touched by it.'

'And the long and the short of it is, you're fixed up,' said Wimsey. 'Well, cheerio, here's to it. Am I best man, Freddy, or do you bring it off at the Synagogue?'

'Well, yes – it is to be at the Synagogue – I had to agree to that,' said Freddy, 'but I believe some sort of bridegroom's friend comes into it. You'll stand by me, old bean, won't you? You keep your hat on, don't forget.'

'I'll bear it in mind,' said Wimsey, 'and Bunter will explain the procedure to me. He's bound to know. He knows everything. But look here, Freddy, you won't forget about this little inquiry, will you?'

'I won't, old chap – upon my word I won't. I'll let you know the very second I hear anything. But I really think you may count on there being something in it.'

Wimsey found some consolation in this. At any rate, he so far pulled himself together as to be the life and soul of the rather restrained revels at Duke's Denver. The Duchess Helen, indeed, observed rather acidly to the Duke that Peter was surely getting too old to play the buffoon, and that it would be better if he took things seriously and settled down.

'Oh, I dunno,' said the Duke, 'Peter's a weird fish – you never know what he's thinkin' about. He pulled me out of the soup once and I'm not going to interfere with him. You leave him alone, Helen.'

Lady Mary Wimsey, who had arrived late on Christmas Eve, took another view of the matter. She marched into her younger brother's bedroom at 2 o'clock on the morning of Boxing Day. There had been dinner and dancing and charades of the most exhausting kind. Wimsey was sitting thoughtfully over the fire in his dressing-gown.

'I say, old Peter,' said Lady Mary. 'you're being a bit fevered, aren't you? Anything up?'

'Too much plum-pudding,' said Wimsey, 'and too much country. I'm a martyr, that's what I am – burning in brandy to make a family holiday.'

'Yes, it's ghastly, isn't it? But how's life? I haven't seen you for an age. You've been away such a long time.'

'Yes – and you seem very much taken up with this house-decorating job you're running.'

'One must do something. I get rather sick of being aimless, you know.'

'Yes. I say, Mary, do you ever see anything of old Parker these days?'

Lady Mary stared into the fire.

'I've had dinner with him once or twice, when I was in town.'

'Have you? He's a very decent sort. Reliable, homespun – that sort of thing. Not amusing, exactly.'

'A little solid.'

119

'As you say – a little solid.' Wimsey lit a cigarette. 'I should hate anything upsettin' to happen to Parker. He'd take it hard. I mean to say, it wouldn't be fair to muck about with his feelin's and so on.'

Mary laughed.

'Worried, Peter?'

'N-no. But I'd rather like him to have fair play.'

'Well, Peter – I can't very well say yes or no till he asks me, can I?'

'Can't you?'

'Well, not to him. It would upset his ideas of decorum, don't you think?'

'I suppose it would. But it would probably upset them just as much if he did ask you. He would feel that the mere idea of hearing a butler announce "Chief Detective-Inspector and Lady Mary Parker" would have something shocking about it.'

'It's stalemate, then, isn't it?'

'You could stop dining with him.'

'I could do that, of course.'

'And the mere fact that you don't – I see. Would it be any good if I demanded to know his intentions in the true Victorian manner?'

'Why this sudden thirst for getting your family off your hands, old man? Peter – nobody's being horrible to you, are they?'

'No, no. I'm just feeling rather like a benevolent uncle, that's all. Old age creeping on. That passion for being useful which attacks the best of us when we're getting past our prime.'

'Like me with the house-decorating. I designed these pyjamas, by the way. Don't you think they're rather entertaining? But I expect Chief Inspector Parker prefers the old-fashioned nightgown, like Dr Spooner or whoever it was.'

'That would be a wrench,' said Wimsey.

'Never mind. I'll be brave and devoted. Here and now I cast off my pyjamas for ever!'

'No, no,' said Wimsey, 'not here and now. Respect a brother's feelings. Very well. I am to tell my friend Charles Parker that if he will abandon his natural modesty and propose, you will abandon your pyjamas and say yes.'

'It will be a great shock for Helen, Peter.'

'Blast Helen. I daresay it won't be the worst shock she'll get.'

'Peter, you're plotting something devilish. All right. If you want me to administer the first shock and let her down by degrees – I'll do it.'

'Right-ho!' said Wimsey, casually.

Lady Mary twisted one arm about his neck and bestowed on him one of her rare sisterly caresses.

'You're a decent old idiot,' she said, 'and you look played-out. Go to bed.'

'Go to blazes,' said Lord Peter amiably.

Chapter XIII

MISS MURCHISON felt a touch of excitement in her well-regulated heart as she rang the bell of Lord Peter's flat. It was not caused by the consideration of his title or his wealth or his bachelorhood, for Miss Murchison had been a business woman all her life, and was accustomed to visiting bachelors of all descriptions without giving a second thought to the matter. But his note had been rather exciting.

Miss Murchison was thirty-eight, and plain. She had worked in the same financier's office for twelve years. They had been good years on the whole, and it was not until the last two that she had even begun to realise that the brilliant financier who juggled with so many spectacular undertakings was juggling for his life under circumstances of increasing difficulty. As the pace grew faster, he added egg after egg to those which were already spinning in the air. There is a limit to the number of eggs which can be spun by human hands. One day an egg slipped and smashed – then another – then a whole omelette of eggs. The juggler fled from the stage and escaped abroad, his chief assistant blew out his brains, the audience booed, the curtain came down, and Miss Murchison, at thirty-seven, was out of a job.

She had put an advertisement in the papers and had answered many others. Most people appeared to want their secretaries young and cheap. It was discouraging.

Then her own advertisement had brought an answer from a Miss Climpson, who kept a typing bureau.

It was not what she wanted, but she went. And she found that it was not quite a typing bureau after all, but something more interesting.

Lord Peter Wimsey, mysteriously at the back of it all, had been abroad when Miss Murchison entered 'The Cattery', and she had never seen him till a few weeks ago. This would be the first time she had actually spoken to him. An odd-looking person, she thought, but people said he had brains. Anyhow –

The door was opened by Bunter, who seemed to expect her and showed her at once into a sitting-room lined with bookshelves. There were some fine prints on the walls, an Aubusson carpet, a grand piano, a vast Chesterfield, and a number of deep and cosy chairs, upholstered in brown leather. The curtains were drawn, a wood-fire blazed on the hearth, and before it stood a table, with a silver tea-service whose lovely lines were delightful to the eye.

As she entered, her employer uncoiled himself from the depths of an armchair, put down a black-letter folio which he had been studying, and greeted her in the cool, husky and rather languid tones which she had already heard in Mr Urquhart's office.

'Frightfully good of you to come round, Miss Murchison. Beastly day, isn't it? I'm sure you want your tea. Can you eat crumpets? Or would you prefer something more up-to-date?'

'Thanks,' said Miss Murchison, as Bunter hovered obsequiously at her elbow, 'I like crumpets very much.'

'Oh, good! Well, Bunter, we'll struggle with the teapot ourselves. Give Miss Murchison another cushion and then you can toddle off. Back at work, I suppose? How's our Mr Urquhart?'

'He's all right.' Miss Murchison had never been a chatty girl. 'There's one thing I wanted to tell you – '

'Plenty of time,' said Wimsey. 'Don't spoil your tea.' He waited on her with a kind of anxious courtesy which pleased her. She expressed admiration of the big bronze chrysanthemums heaped here and there about the room.

'Oh! I'm glad you like them. My friends say they give a feminine touch to the place, but Bunter sees to it, as a matter of fact. They make a splash of colour and all that, don't you think?'

'The books look masculine enough.'

'Oh, yes – they're my hobby, you know. Books – and crime, of course. But crime's not very decorative, is it? I don't care about collecting hangmen's ropes and murderers' overcoats. What are you to do with 'em? Is the tea all right? I ought to have asked you to pour out, but it always seems to me rather

123

unfair to invite a person and then make her do all the work. What do you do when you're not working, by the way? Do you keep a secret passion for anything?'

'I go to concerts,' said Miss Murchison. 'And when there isn't a concert I put something on the gramophone.'

'Musician?'

'No – never could afford to learn properly. I ought to have been, I daresay. But there was more money in being a secretary.'

'I suppose so.'

'Unless one is absolutely first-class, and I should never have been that. And third-class musicians are a nuisance.'

'They have a rotten time, too,' said Wimsey. 'I hate to see them in cinemas, poor beasts, playing the most ghastly tripe, sandwiched in with snacks of Mendelssohn and torn-off gobbets of the "Unfinished". Have a sandwich. Do you like Bach? Or only the moderns?'

He wriggled on to the piano stool.

'I'll leave it to you,' said Miss Murchison, rather surprised.

'I feel rather like the Italian Concerto this evening. It's better on the harpsichord, but I haven't got one here. I find Bach good for the brain. Steadying influence and all that.'

He played the Concerto through, and then, after few seconds' pause, went on to one of the "Forty-eight". He played well, and gave a curious impression of controlled power, which, in a man so slight and so fantastical in manner, was unexpected and even a little disquieting. When he had finished, he said, still sitting at the piano:

'Did you make the inquiry about the typewriter?'

'Yes; it was bought new three years ago.'

'Good. I gather, by the way, that you are probably right about Urquhart's connection with the Megatherium Trust. That was a very helpful observation of yours. Consider yourself highly commended.'

'Thank you.'

'Anything fresh?'

'No – except that the evening after you called at Mr Urquhart's office, he stayed on a long time after we had gone, typing something.'

Wimsey sketched an arpeggio with his right hand and demanded:

'How do you know how long he stayed and what he was doing if you had all gone?'

'You said you wanted to know of anything however small, that was in the least unusual. I thought it might be unusual for him to stay on by himself, so I walked up and down Princeton Street and round Red Lion Square till half-past seven. Then I saw him put the light out and go home. Next morning I noticed that some papers I had left just inside my typewriter cover had been disturbed. So I concluded that he had been typing.'

'Perhaps the charwoman disturbed them?'

'Not she. She never disturbs the dust, let alone the cover.'

Wimsey nodded.

'You have the makings of a first-class sleuth, Miss Murchison. Very well. In that case, our little job will have to be undertaken. Now, look here – you quite understand that I'm going to ask you to do something illegal?'

'Yes, I understand.'

'And you don't mind?'

'No. I imagine that if I'm taken up you will pay any necessary costs.'

'Certainly.'

'And if I go to prison?'

'I don't think it will come to that. There's a slight risk, I admit – that is if I'm wrong about what I think is happening – that you might be brought up for attempted theft or for being in possession of safe-breaking tools, but that is the most that could happen.'

'Oh, well, it's all in the game, I suppose.'

'You mean that?'

'Yes.'

'Splendid. Well – you know that deed-box you brought in to Mr Urquhart's room the day I was there?'

'Yes, the one marked Wrayburn.'

'Where is it kept? In the outer office, where you could get hold of it?'

'Oh, yes – on a shelf with a lot of others.'

'Good. Would it be possible for you to get left alone in the office any day for, say, half an hour?'

/ 'Well – at lunch-time I'm supposed to go out at half-past twelve and come back at half-past one. Mr Pond goes out then, but Mr Urquhart sometimes comes back. I couldn't be certain that he wouldn't pop out on me. And it would look funny if I wanted to stay on after four-thirty, I expect. Unless I pretended I had made a mistake and wanted to stay and put it right. I could do that. I might come extra early in the morning when the charwoman is there – or would it matter her seeing me?'

'It wouldn't matter very much,' said Wimsey, thoughtfully. 'She'd probably think you had legitimate business with the box. I'll leave it to you to choose the time.'

'But what am I to do? Steal the box?'

'Not quite. Do you know how to pick a lock?'

'Not in the least, I'm afraid.'

'I often wonder what we go to school for,' said Wimsey. 'We never seem to learn anything really useful. I can pick a pretty lock myself, but, as we haven't much time and as you'll need some rather intensive training, I think I'd better take you to an expert. Should you mind putting your coat on and coming round with me to see a friend?'

'Not at all. I should be delighted.'

'He lives in the Whitechapel Road, but he's a very pleasant fellow, if you can overlook his religious opinions. Personally, I find them rather refreshing. Bunter! Get us a taxi, will you?'

On the way to the East End, Wimsey insisted upon talking music – rather to Miss Murchison's disquietude; she began to think there was something a little sinister in this pointed refusal to discuss the object of their journey.

'By the way,' she ventured, interrupting something Wimsey was saying about fugal form, 'this person we are going to see – has he a name?'

'Now you mention it, I believe he has, but he's never called by it. It's Rumm.'

'Not very, perhaps, if he – er – gives lessons in lock-picking.'

'I mean his name's Rumm.'

'Oh; what is it then?'

'Dash it! I mean Rumm is his name.'

'Oh! I beg your pardon.'

'But he doesn't care to use it, now that he is a total abstainer.'

'Then what does one call him?'

'I call him Bill,' said Wimsey, as the taxi drew up at the entrance to a narrow court, 'but when he was at the head of his profession they called him "Blindfold Bill". He was a very great man in his time.'

Paying off the taxi-man (who had obviously taken them for welfare-workers till he saw the size of his tip, and now did not know what to make of them), Wimsey steered his companion down the dirty alley-way. At the far end was a small house, from whose lighted windows poured forth the loud strains of a chorus of voices, supported by a harmonium and other instruments.

'Oh, dear!' said Wimsey, 'we've struck a meeting. It can't be helped. Here goes.'

Pausing until the strains of 'Glory, glory, glory' had been succeeded by a sound as of fervent prayer, he hammered lustily at the door. Presently a small girl put her head out and, seeing Lord Peter, uttered a shrill cry of delight.

'Hullo, Esmeralda Hyacinth!' said Wimsey. 'Is Dad in?'

'Yes, sir, please, sir, they'll be so pleased, will you step in and oh, please?'

'Well?'

'Please, sir, will you sing "Nazareth"?'

'No, I will not sing "Nazareth" on any account, Esmeralda; I'm surprised at you.'

'Daddy says "Nazareth" isn't worldly, and you do sing it so beautiful,' said Esmeralda, her mouth drooping.

Wimsey hid his face in his hands.

'This comes of having done a foolish thing once,' he said. 'One never lives it down. I won't promise, Esmeralda, but we'll see. But I want to talk business with Dad when the meeting's over.'

The child nodded; at the same moment, the praying voice within the room ceased, amid ejaculations of 'Alleluia!' and Esmeralda, profiting by this momentary pause, pushed open the door and said loudly:

'Here's Mr Peter and a lady.'

The room was small, very hot, and very full of people. In one corner was the harmonium, with the musicians grouped about it. In the middle, standing by a round table covered with a red cloth, was a stout, square man, with a face like a bulldog. He

127

had a book in his hand, and appeared to be about to announce a hymn, but, seeing Wimsey and Miss Murchison, he came forward, stretching out a large and hearty hand.

'Welcome one and welcome all!' he said. 'Brethren, 'ere is a dear brother and sister in the Lord as is come out of the 'aunts of the rich and the riotous living of the West End to join with us in singing the Songs of Zion. Let us sing and give praise. Alleluia! We know that many shall come from the East *and* from the West and sit down at the Lord's feast, while many that thinks theirselves chosen shall be cast into outer darkness. Therefore let us not say, because this man wears a shiny eye-glass, that he is not a chosen vessel, or, because this woman wears a di'mond necklace and rides in 'er Rolls-Royce, she will not therefore wear a white robe and a gold crown in the New Jerusalem, nor because these people travels in the Blue Train to the Rivereera, therefore they shall not be seen a-castin' down their golden crowns by the River of the Water of Life. We 'ears that there talk sometimes in 'yde Park o' Sundays, but it's bad and foolish and leads to strife and envyings and not to charity. All we like sheep 'ave gone astray and well I may say so, 'avin' been a black and wicked sinner myself till this 'ere gentleman for such 'e truly is laid 'is 'and upon me as I was a-bustin' of 'is safe and was the instrument under God of turnin' me from the broad way that leadeth to destruction. Oh, brethren, what a 'appy day that was for me, alleluia! What a shower of blessings come to me by the grace of the Lord! Let us unite now in thanksgiving for 'Eaven's mercies in Number One 'Undred and Two. (Esmeralda, give our dear friends a 'ymn-book.)'

'I'm sorry,' said Wimsey to Miss Murchison. 'Can you bear it? I fancy this is the final outbreak.'

The harmonium, harp, sackbut, psaltery, dulcimer, and all kinds of music burst out with a blare which nearly burst the eardrum, the assembly lifted its combined voices, and Miss Murchison, to her amazement, found herself joining – at first self-consciously and then with a fine fervour – in that stirring chant –

> *'Sweeping through the gates,*
> *Sweeping through the gates of the New Jerusalem*
> *Washed in the Blood of the Lamb.'*

Wimsey, who appeared to find it all very good fun, carolled away happily, without the slightest embarrassment; whether because he was accustomed to the exercise, or merely because he was one of those imperturbably self-satisfied people who cannot conceive of themselves as being out of place in any surroundings, Miss Murchison was unable to determine.

To her relief, the religious exercise came to an end with the hymn, and the company took their leave, with many hand-shakings all round. The musicians emptied the condensed moisture from their wind-instruments politely into the fireplace and the lady who played the harmonium drew the cover over the keys and came forward to welcome the guests. She was introduced simply as Bella, and Miss Murchison concluded, rightly, that she was the wife of Mr Bill Rumm and the mother of Esmeralda.

'Well, now,' said Bill, 'it's dry work preachin' and singin' – you'll take a cup of tea or coffee, now, won't you?'

Wimsey explained that they had just had tea, but begged that the family might proceed with their own meal.

'It ain't 'ardly supper-time yet,' said Mrs Rumm. 'P'raps if you was to do your business with the lady and gentleman, Bill, they might feel inclined to take a bite with us later. It's trotters,' she added, hopefully.

'It's very kind of you,' said Miss Murchison, hesitatingly.

'Trotters want a lot of beating,' said Wimsey, 'and since our business will take a little time we'll accept with pleasure – if you're sure we're not putting you out.'

'Not at all,' said Mrs Rumm, heartily. 'Eight beautiful trotters they is, and with a bit of cheese they'll go round easy. Come along, 'Meraldy – your Dad's got business.'

'Mr Peter's going to sing,' said the child, fixing reproachful eyes on Wimsey.

'Now don't you worrit his lordship,' rebuked Mrs Rumm. 'I declare I'm ashamed of you.'

'I'll sing after supper, Esmeralda,' said Wimsey. 'Hop along now like a good girl or I'll make faces at you. Bill, I've brought you a new pupil.'

'Always 'appy to serve you, sir, knowing as it's the Lord's work. Glory be.'

'Thank you,' said Wimsey, modestly. 'It's a simple matter,

Bill, but as the young lady is inexperienced with locks and so on, I've brought her along to be coached. You see, Miss Murchison, before Bill here saw the light – '

'Praise God!' put in Bill.

'He was the most accomplished burglar and safe-breaker in the three kingdoms. He doesn't mind my telling you this, because he's taken his medicine and finished with it all and is now a very honest and excellent locksmith of the ordinary kind.'

'Thanks be to Him that giveth the victory!'

'But from time to time, when I need a little help in a righteous cause, Bill gives me the benefit of his great experience.'

'And oh! what 'appiness it is, miss, to turn them talents w'ich I so wickedly abused to the service of the Lord. His 'oly Name be blessed that bringeth good out of evil.'

'That's right,' said Wimsey, with a nod. 'Now, Bill, I've got my eye on a solicitor's deed-box, which may or may not contain something which will help me to get an innocent person out of trouble. This young lady can get access to the box, Bill, if you can show her the way inside it.'

'If?' grunted Bill, with sovereign contempt. ' 'Course I can! Deed-box, that's nuffin'. That ain't no field for a man's skill. Robbin' the kid's money-box, that's what it is with they trumpery little locks. There ain't a deed-box in this 'ere city wot I wouldn't open blindfold in boxing-gloves with a stick of boiled macaroni.'

'I know, Bill; but it isn't you that's got to do it. Can you teach the lady how to work it?'

'Sure I can. What kinder lock is it, lady?'

'I don't know,' said Miss Murchison. 'An ordinary lock, I think. I mean, it has the usual sort of key – not a Bramah, or anything of that kind. Mr – that is, the solicitor has one set of keys and Mr Pond has another – just plain keys with barrels and wards.'

'Ho!' said Bill, 'then 'arf an hour will teach you all you want, Miss.' He went to a cupboard and brought out half a dozen lock-plates and a bunch of curious, thin wire hooks, strung on a ring like keys.

'Are those pick-locks?' asked Miss Murchison, curiously.

'That's what they are, miss. Ingines of Satan!' He shook his head as he lovingly fingered the bright steel. 'Many's the time sech keys as these 'ave let pore sinners in by the back gate into 'ell.'

'This time,' said Wimsey, 'they'll let a poor innocent out of prison into the sunshine – if any, in this beastly climate.'

'Praise Him for His manifold mercies! Well, miss, the first thing is to understand the construction of a lock. Now jest you look 'ere.'

He picked up one of the locks and showed how, by holding up the spring, the catch could be thrust back.

'There ain't no need of all them fancy words, you see, miss. The barrel and the spring – that's all there is to it. Jest you try.'

Miss Murchison accordingly tried, and forced several locks with an ease that astonished her.

'Well now, miss, the difficulty is, you see, that when the lock's in place, you can't use your eyes. But you 'as your 'earin' and you 'as the feelin', in your fingers, giv' you by Providence (praise His Name!) for that purpose. Now what you 'as to do, miss, is to shet your eyes and see with your fingers, like, w'en you've got your spring 'ooked back sufficient ter let the catch go past.'

'I'm afraid I'm very clumsy,' said Miss Murchison, at the fifth or sixth attempt.

'Now don't you fret, miss. Jest take it easy and you'll find the right way of it come to you all of a sudden, like. Jest feel when it seems to go sweet and use your 'ands independent. Would you like to 'ave a little go at a combination while you're 'ere, sir? I've got a beauty 'ere. Giv' to me it was by Sam, you know 'oo I mean. Many's the time I've tried to show 'im the error of 'is ways. "No, Bill," 'e ses, "I ain't got no use for religion," 'e ses, pore lost sheep, "but I ain't got no quarrel with you, Bill," ses 'e, "and I'd like for ter give you this 'ere little sooverneer." '

'Bill, Bill,' said Wimsey, shaking a reproachful finger, 'I'm afraid this wasn't honestly come by.'

'Well, sir, if I knowed the owner I'd 'and it over to 'im with the greatest of pleasure. It's quite good, you see. Sam put the soup in at the 'inges and it blowed the 'ole front clean off, lock and all. It's small, but it's a real beauty – new pattern to me,

131

that is. But I mastered it,' said Bill, with unregenerate pride, 'in an hour or two.'

'It'd have to be a good bit of work to beat you, Bill.' Wimsey set the lock up before him, and began to manipulate the knob, his fingers moving with micrometer delicacy and his ear bent to catch the fall of the tumblers.

'Lord!' said Bill – this time with no religious intention – 'wot a cracksman you'd a-made, if you'd a-given your mind to it – which the Lord in His mercy forbid you should!'

'Too much work in that life for me, Bill,' said Wimsey. 'Dash it! I lost it that time.'

He turned the knob back and started over again.

By the time the trotters arrived, Miss Murchison had acquired considerable facility with the more usual types of lock and a greatly enhanced respect for burglary as a profession.

'And don't you let yourself be 'urried, miss,' was Bill's final injunction, 'else you'll leave scratches on the lock and do yourself no credit. Lovely bit of work, that, ain't it, Lord Peter, sir?'

'Beyond me, I'm afraid,' said Wimsey, with a laugh.

'Practice,' said Bill, 'that's all it is. If you'd a-started early enough you'd a-been a beautiful workman.' He sighed. 'There ain't many of 'em nowadays – glory be! – that can do a real artistic job. It fair goes to my 'eart to see a elegant bit o' stuff like that blowed all to bits with gelignite. Wot's gelignite? Any fool can 'andle it as doesn't mind makin' a blinkin' great row. Brutal, I calls it.'

'Now, don't you get 'ankerin' back after them things, Bill,' said Mrs Rumm, reprovingly. 'Come along, do, now and eat yer supper. Ef anybody's goin' ter do sech a wicked thing as breakin' safes, wot do it matter whether it's done artistic or inartistic?'

'Ain't that jest like a woman? – beggin' yer pardon, miss.'

'Well, you know it's true,' said Mrs Rumm.

'I know those trotters look very artistic,' said Wimsey, 'and that's quite enough for me.'

The trotters having been eaten, and 'Nazareth' duly sung, to the great admiration of the Rumm family, the evening closed pleasantly with the performance of a hymn, and Miss Murchison found herself walking up the Whitechapel Road, with a bunch of pin-locks in her pocket and some surprising items of knowledge in her mind.

'You make some very amusing acquaintances, Lord Peter.'

'Yes – rather a jape, isn't it? But Blindfold Bill is one of the best. I found him on my premises one night and struck up a sort of alliance with him. Took lessons from him and all that. He was a bit shy at first, but he got converted by another friend of mine – it's a long story – and the long and short of it was, he got hold of this locksmith business, and is doing very well at it. Do you feel quite competent about locks now?'

'I think so. What am I to look for when I get the box open?'

'Well,' said Wimsey, 'the point is this. Mr Urquhart showed me what purported to be the draft of a will made five years ago by Mrs Wrayburn. I've written down the gist of it on a bit of paper for you. Here it is. Now the snag about it is that that draft was typed on a machine which, as you tell me, was bought new from the makers only three years ago.'

'Do you mean that's what he was typing that evening he stayed late at the office?'

'It looks like it. Now, why? If he had the original draft, why not show me that? Actually, there was no need for him to show it to me at all, unless it was to mislead me about something. Then, though he said he had the thing at home, and must have known he had it there, he pretended to search for it in Mrs Wrayburn's box. Again, why? To make me think that it was already in existence when I called. The conclusion I drew is that, if there is a will, it's not along the lines of the one he showed me.'

'It looks rather like that, certainly.'

'What I want you to look for is the real will – either the original or the copy ought to be there. Don't take it away, but try to memorise the chief points in it, especially the names of the chief legatee or legatees and of the residuary legatee. Remember that the residuary legatee gets everything which isn't specifically left to somebody else, or anything which falls in by a legatee's dying before the testatrix. I specially want to know whether anything was left to Philip Boyes or if any mention of the Boyes family is made in the will. Failing a will, there might be some other interesting document, such as a secret trust, instructing the executor to dispose of the money in some special way. In short, I want particulars of any document which may seem to be of interest. Don't waste too much time making notes. Carry the provisions in your head if you can and note them down privately when you get away from the office. And be sure you don't leave those skeleton keys about for people to find.'

Miss Murchison promised to observe these instructions, and, a taxi coming up at that moment, Wimsey put her into it and sped her to her destination.

Chapter XIV

MR NORMAN URQUHART glanced at the clock, which stood at 4.15, and called through the open door:

'Are those affidavits nearly ready, Miss Murchison?'

'I am just on the last page, Mr Urquhart.'

'Bring them in as soon as you've finished. They ought to go round to Hansons's tonight.'

'Yes, Mr Urquhart.'

Miss Murchison galloped noisily over the keys, slamming the shift-lever over with unnecessary violence, and causing Mr Pond once more to regret the intrusion of female clerks. She completed her page, ornamented the foot of it with a rattling of fancy lines and dots, threw over the release, spun the roller, twitching the foolscap sheets from under it in vicious haste, flung the carbons into the basket, shuffled the copies into order, slapped them vigorously on all four edges to bring them into symmetry, and bounced with them into the inner office.

'I haven't had time to read them through,' she announced.

'Very well,' said Mr Urquhart.

Miss Murchison retired, shutting the door after her. She gathered her belongings together, took out a hand-mirror and unashamedly powdered her rather large nose, stuffed a handful of odds-and-ends into a bulging handbag, pushed some papers under her typewriter cover ready for the next day, jerked her hat from the peg and crammed it on her head, tucking wisps of hair underneath it with vigorous and impatient fingers.

Mr Urquhart's bell rang – twice.

'Oh, bother!' said Miss Murchison, with heightened colour. She snatched the hat off again, and answered the summons.

'Miss Murchison,' said Mr Urquhart, with an expression of considerable annoyance, 'do you know that you have left out

135

a whole paragraph on the first page of this?'

Miss Murchison flushed still more deeply.

'Oh, have I? I'm very sorry.'

Mr Urquhart held up a document resembling in bulk that famous one of which it was said that there was not truth enough in the world to fill so long an affidavit.

'It is very annoying,' he said. 'It is the longest and most important of the three, and is urgently required first thing tomorrow morning.'

'I can't think how I could have made such a silly mistake,' muttered Miss Murchison. 'I will stay on this evening and re-type it.'

'I'm afraid you will have to. It is unfortunate, as I shall not be able to look it through myself, but there is nothing else to be done. Please check it carefully this time, and see that Hansons's have it before 10 o'clock tomorrow.'

'Yes, Mr Urquhart. I will be extremely careful. I am very sorry indeed. I will make sure that it is quite correct and take it round myself.'

'Very well, that will do,' said Mr Urquhart. 'Don't let it happen again.'

Miss Murchison picked up the papers and came out, looking flustered. She dragged the cover off the typewriter with much sound and fury, jerked out the deskdrawers till they slammed against the drawer-stops, shook the top sheets, carbons, and flimsies together as a terrier shakes a rat, and attacked the machine tempestuously.

Mr Pond, who had just locked his desk, and was winding a silk scarf about his throat, looked at her in mild astonishment.

'Have you some more typing to do tonight, Miss Murchison?'

'Got to do the whole bally thing again,' said Miss Murchison. 'Left out a paragraph on page one – it would be page one, of course – and he wants the tripe round at Hansons's by 10 o'clock.'

Mr Pond groaned slightly and shook his head.

'Those machines make you careless,' he reproved her. 'In the old days, clerks thought twice about making foolish mistakes, when it meant copying the whole document out again by hand.'

'Glad I didn't live then,' said Miss Murchison, shortly. 'One might as well have been a galley-slave.'

'And we didn't knock off at half-past four, either,' said Mr Pond. 'We *worked* in those days.'

'You may have worked longer,' said Miss Murchison, 'but you didn't get through as much in the time.'

'We worked accurately and neatly,' said Mr Pond, with emphasis, as Miss Murchison irritably disentangled two keys which had jammed together under her hasty touch.

Mr Urquhart's door opened, and the retort on the typist's lips was silenced. He said goodnight and went out. Mr Pond followed him.

'I suppose you will have finished before the cleaner goes, Miss Murchison,' he said. 'If not please remember to extinguish the light and to hand the key to Mrs Hodges in the basement.'

'Yes, Mr Pond. Goodnight.'

'Goodnight.'

His steps pattered through the entrance, sounded again loudly as he passed the window, and died away in the direction of Brownlow Street. Miss Murchison continued typing till she calculated that he was safely on the tube at Chancery Lane. Then she rose, with a quick glance round her, and approached a high tier of shelves, stacked with black deed-boxes, each of which bore the name of a client in bold white letters.

WRAYBURN was there, all right, but had mysteriously shifted its place. This in itself was unaccountable. She clearly remembered having replaced it, just before Christmas, on top of the pile MORTIMER – SCROGGINS – LORD COOTE – DOLBY BROS and WINGFIELD; and here it was, on the day after Boxing Day, at the bottom of a pile, heaped over and kept down by BODGERS SIR J. PENKRIDGE – FLATSBY & COATEN – TRUBODY LTD and UNIVERSAL BONE TRUST. Somebody had been spring cleaning, apparently, over the holidays, and Miss Murchison thought it improbable that it was Mrs Hodges.

It was tiresome, because all the shelves were full, and it would be necessary to lift down all the boxes and stand them somewhere before she could get out WRAYBURN. And Mrs Hodges would be in soon, and though Mrs Hodges didn't really matter, it might look odd . . .

Miss Murchison pulled the chair from her desk (for the shelf was rather high) and, standing on it, lifted down UNIVERSAL

137

BONE TRUST. It was heavyish and the chair (which was of the revolving kind, and not the modern type with one spindly leg and a stiffly sprung back, which butts you in the lower spine and keeps you up to your job) wobbled unsteadily, as she carefully lowered the box and balanced it on the narrow top of the cupboard. She reached up again and took down TRUBODY LTD, and placed it on BONE TRUST. She reached up for the third time and seized FLATSBY & COATEN. As she stopped with it a step sounded in the doorway and an astonished voice said behind her:

'Are you looking for something, Miss Murchison?'

Miss Murchison started so violently that the treacherous chair swung through a quarter-turn, nearly shooting her into Mr Pond's arms. She came down awkwardly, still clasping the black deed-box.

'How you startled me, Mr Pond! I thought you had gone.'

'So I had,' said Mr Pond, 'but when I got to the Underground I found I had left a little parcel behind me. So tiresome – I had to come back for it. Have you seen it anywhere? A little round jar, done up in brown paper.'

Miss Murchison set FLATSBY & COATEN on the seat of the chair and gazed about her.

'It doesn't seem to be in my desk,' said Mr Pond. 'Dear, dear, I shall be so late. And I can't go without it, because it's wanted for dinner – in fact, it's a little jar of caviare. We have guests tonight. Now, where can I have put it?'

'Perhaps you put it down when you washed your hands,' suggested Miss Murchison, helpfully.

'Well, now, perhaps I did.' Mr Pond fussed out and she heard the door of the little lavabo in the passage open with a loud creak. It suddenly occurred to her that she had left her handbag open on her desk. Suppose the skeleton keys were visible. She darted towards the bag, just as Mr Pond returned in triumph.

'Much obliged to you for your suggestion, Miss Murchison. It was there all the time. Mrs Pond would have been so much upset. Well, goodnight again.' He turned towards the door. 'Oh, by the way, were you looking for something?'

'I was looking for a mouse,' replied Miss Murchison with a nervous giggle. 'I was just sitting working when I saw it run along the top of the cupboard and – er – up the wall behind those boxes.'

'Dirty little beasts,' said Mr Pond. 'The place is overrun with them. I have often said we ought to have a cat here. No hope of catching it now, though. You're not afraid of mice apparently?'

'No,' said Miss Murchison, holding her eyes, by a strenuous physical effort, on Mr Pond's face. If the skeleton keys were – as it seemed to her they must be – indecently exposing their spidery anatomy on her desk it would be madness to look in that direction. 'No. In your days I suppose all women were afraid of mice.'

'Yes, they were,' admitted Mr Pond, 'but then, of course, their garments were longer.'

'Rotten for them,' said Miss Murchison.

'They were very graceful in appearance,' said Mr Pond. 'Allow me to assist you in replacing those boxes.'

'You will miss your train,' said Miss Murchison.

'I have missed it already,' replied Mr Pond, glancing at his watch. 'I shall have to take the 5.30.' He politely picked up FLATSBY & COATEN and climbed perilously with it in his hands to the unsteady seat of the rotatory chair.

'It's extremely kind of you,' said Miss Murchison, watching him as he restored it to its place.

'Not at all. If you would kindly hand me up the others – '

Miss Murchison handed him TRUBODY LTD and UNIVERSAL BONE TRUST.

'There!' said Mr Pond, completing the pile and dusting his hands. 'Now let us hope the mouse has gone for good. I will speak to Mrs Hodges about procuring a suitable kitten.'

'That would be a very good idea,' said Miss Murchison. 'Goodnight, Mr Pond.'

'Goodnight, Miss Murchison.'

His footsteps pattered down the passage, sounded again more loudly beneath the window, and for the second time died away in the direction of Brownlow Street.

'Whew!' said Miss Murchison. She darted to her desk. Her fears had deceived her. The bag was shut and the keys invisible.

She pulled her chair back to its place and sat down, as a clash of brooms and pails outside announced the arrival of Mrs Hodges.

'Ho!' said Mrs Hodges, arrested on the threshold at sight of the lady clerk industriously typing away, 'beg your pardon, miss, but I didn't know as how anybody was here.'

'Sorry, Mrs Hodges. I've got a little bit of work to finish. But you carry on. Don't mind me.'

'Thet's all right, miss,' said Mrs Hodges. 'I can do Mr Partridge's office fust.'

'Well, if it's all the same to you,' said Miss Murchison. 'I've just got to type a few pages and – er – make a précis – notes, you know – of some documents for Mr Urquhart.'

Mrs Hodges nodded and vanished again. Presently a loud bumping noise overhead proclaimed her presence in Mr Partridge's office.

Miss Murchison waited no longer. She dragged her chair to the shelves again, took down swiftly, one after the other, BONE TRUST, TRUBODY LTD, FLATSBY & COATEN, SIR J. PENKRIDGE, and BODGERS. Her heart beat heavily as at last she seized WRAYBURN and carried it across to her desk.

She opened her bag and shook out its contents. The bunch of pick-locks clattered upon the desk, mixed up with a handkerchief, a powder compact, and a pocket comb. The thin and shining barrels seemed to burn her fingers.

As she picked the bunch over, looking for the most suitable implement, there came a loud rap at the window.

She wheeled round, terrified. There was nothing there. Thrusting the pick-locks into the pocket of her sports coat, she tip-toed across and looked out. In the lamplight she observed three small boys engaged in climbing the iron railings which guard the sacred areas of Bedford Row. The foremost child saw her and gesticulated, pointing downwards. Miss Murchison waved her hand and cried 'Be off with you!'

The child shouted something unintelligible and pointed again. Putting two and two together, Miss Murchison deduced from the rap at the window, the gesture, and the cry, that a valuable ball had fallen into the area. She shook her head with severity and returned to her task.

But the incident had reminded her that the window had no blinds and that, under the glare of the electric light, her movements were as visible to anybody in the street as though she stood on a lighted stage. There was no reason to suppose that Mr Urquhart or Mr Pond was about, but her uneasy conscience vexed her. Moreover, if a policeman should pass by, would he not be able to recognise pick-locks a hundred yards away? She peered out again. Was it her agitated fancy, or was that a sturdy form in dark blue emerging from Hand Court?

Miss Muchison fled in alarm and, snatching up the deed-box, carried it bodily into Mr Urquhart's private office.

Here, at least, she could not be overlooked. If anybody came in – even Mrs Hodges – her presence might cause surprise, but she would hear them coming and be warned in advance.

Her hands were cold and shaking, and she was not in the best condition to profit by Blindfold Bill's instructions. She drew a few deep breaths. She had been told not to hurry herself. Very well, then, she would not.

She chose a key with care and slipped it into the lock. For years, at it seemed to her, she scratched about aimlessly, till at length she felt the spring press against the hooked end. Pushing and lifting steadily with one hand, she introduced her second key. She felt the lever move – in another moment there was a sharp click and the lock was open.

There were not a great many papers in the box. The first document was a long list of securities, endorsed 'Securities deposited with Lloyd's Bank'. Then came the copies of some title-deeds, of which the originals were similarly deposited. Then came a folder filled with correspondence. Some of this consisted of letters from Mrs Wrayburn herself, the latest letter being dated five years previously. In addition there were letters from tenants, bankers, and stockholders, with copies of the replies written from the office and signed by Norman Urquhart.

Miss Murchison hastened impatiently through all this. There was no sign of a will or copy of a will – not even of the dubious draft that the solicitor had shown to Wimsey. Two papers only now remained at the bottom of the box. Miss Murchison picked up the first. It was a Power of Attorney, dated January 1925, giving Norman Urquhart full powers to act for Mrs Wrayburn. The second was thicker and tied neatly with red tape. Miss Murchison slipped this off and unfolded the document.

It was a Deed of Trust, making over the whole of Mrs Wrayburn's property to Norman Urquhart, in trust for herself, and providing that he should pay into her current account, from the estate, a certain fixed annual sum for personal expenses. The deed was dated July 1920, and attached to it was a letter, which Miss Murchison hastily read through.

'Appleford,
'Windle,
'15th May, 1920.

'MY DEAR NORMAN, Thank you very much, my dear boy, for your birthday letter and the pretty scarf. It is good of you to remember your old aunt so faithfully.

'It has occurred to me that, now that I am over eighty years old, it is time that I put my business into your hands entirely. You and your father have managed very well for me all these years, and you have, of course, always very properly consulted me before taking any step with regard to investments. But I am getting such a *very old woman now* that I am quite out of touch with the modern world, and I cannot pretend that my opinions are of any real value. I am a *tired* old woman, too, and though you always explain everything *most clearly*, I find the *writing of letters a gêne* and a burden to me at my advanced age.

'So I have determined to put my property in Trust with you for my lifetime, so that you may have full power to handle everything according to your own discretion, without having to consult me every time. And also, though I am strong and healthy yet, I am glad to say, and have my wits quite about me, still, that happy state of things might alter at any time. I might become paralysed or feeble in my head, or want to make some foolish use of my money, as silly old women have done before now.

'So will you draw up a deed of this kind and bring it to me and I will sign it. And at the same time I will give you instructions about my will.

'Thanking you again for your good wishes,
'Your affec. Great-Aunt,
'ROSANNA WRAYBURN.'

'Hurray!' said Miss Murchison. 'There *was* a will, then! And this trust – that's probably important, too.'

She read the letter again, skimmed through the clauses of the trust, taking particular notice that Norman Urquhart was named as sole trustee, and finally made a mental note of some of the larger and more important items in the list of securities. Then she replaced the documents in their original order, re-locked the box – which yielded to treatment like an angel – carried it out, replaced it, piled the other boxes above it, and was back at her machine, just as Mrs Hodges re-entered the office.

'Just finished, Mrs Hodges,' she called out cheerfully.

'I wondered ef yer would be,' said Mrs Hodges. 'I didn't hear the typewriter a-going.'

'I was making notes by hand,' said Miss Murchison. She crumpled together the spoiled front page of the affidavit and threw it into the waste-paper basket together with the retype which she had begun. From her desk drawer she produced a correctly typed first page, provided beforehand for the purpose, added it to the bundle of script, put the top copy and the required sets of flimsies into an envelope, sealed it, addressed it to Messrs Hanson & Hanson, put on her hat and coat, and went out, bidding a pleasant farewell to Mrs Hodges at the door.

A short walk brought her to Messrs Hansons' office, where she delivered the affidavit through the letter box. Then, with a brisk step and humming to herself, she made for the bus stop at the junction of Theobald's Road and Gray's Inn Road.

'I think I deserve a little supper in Soho,' said Miss Murchison.

She was humming again as she walked from Cambridge Circus into Frith Street. 'What *is* this beastly tune?' she asked herself abruptly. A little consideration reminded her that it was 'Sweeping through the gates, Sweeping through the gates . . . '

'Bless me!' said Miss Murchison. 'Going dotty, that's what I am.'

Chapter XV

LORD PETER congratulated Miss Murchison and gave her a rather special lunch at Rules, where there is a particularly fine old cognac for those that appreciate such things. Indeed, Miss Murchison was a little late in returning to Mr Urquhart's office, and in her haste omitted to hand back the skeleton keys. But when the wine is good and the company agreeable one cannot always think of everything.

Wimsey himself, by a great act of self-control, had returned to his own flat to think, instead of bolting away to Holloway Gaol. Although it was a work of charity and necessity to keep up the spirits of the prisoner (it was in this way that he excused his almost daily visits), he could not disguise from himself that it would be even more useful and charitable to get her innocence proved. So far, he had not made much real progress.

The suicide theory had been looking very hopeful when Norman Urquhart had produced the draft of the will; but his belief in that draft had now been thoroughly undermined. There was still a faint hope of retrieving the packet of white powder from the Nine Rings, but as the days passed remorselessly on, that hope diminished almost to vanishing point. It irked him to be taking no action in the matter – he wanted to rush to the Gray's Inn Road, to cross-question, bully, bribe, ransack every person and place in and about the Rings, but he knew that the police could do this better than he could.

Why had Norman Urquhart tried to mislead him about the will? He could so easily have refused all information. There must be some mystery about it. But if Urquhart were not, in fact, the legatee, he was playing rather a dangerous game. If the old lady died, and the will was proved, the facts would probably be published – and she might die any day.

How easy it would be, he thought, regretfully, to hasten Mrs Wrayburn's death a trifle. She was ninety-three and very frail. An overdose of something – a shake – a slight shock, even – It did not do to think after that fashion. He wondered idly who lived with the old woman and looked after her . . .

It was the 30th of December, and he still had no plan. The stately volumes on his shelves, rank after rank of saint, historian, poet, philosopher, mocked his impotence. All that wisdom and all that beauty, and they could not show him how to save the woman he imperiously wanted, from a sordid death by hanging. And he had thought himself rather clever at that kind of thing. The enormous and complicated imbecility of things was all round him like a trap. He ground his teeth and raged helplessly, striding about the suave, wealthy, futile room. The great Venetian mirror over the fireplace showed him his own head and shoulders. He saw a fair, foolish face, with straw-coloured hair sleeked back; a monocle clinging incongruously under a ludicrously-twitching brow; a chin shaved to perfection, hairless, epicene; a rather high collar, faultlessly starched, a tie elegantly knotted and matching in colour the handkerchief which peeped coyly from the breast-pocket of an expensive Savile-Row-tailored suit. He snatched up a heavy bronze from the mantelpiece – a beautiful thing; even as he snatched it, his fingers caressed the patina – and the impulse seized him to smash the mirror and smash the face – to break out into great animal howls and gestures.

Silly! One could not do that. The inherited inhibitions of twenty civilised centuries tied one hand and foot in bonds of ridicule. What if he did smash the mirror? Nothing would happen. Bunter would come in, unmoved and unsurprised, would sweep up the débris in a dust-pan, would prescribe a hot bath and massage. And next day a new mirror would be ordered, because people would come in and ask questions, and civilly regret the accidental damage to the old one. And Harriet Vane would still be hanged, just the same.

Wimsey pulled himself together, called for his hat and coat, and went away in a taxi to call on Miss Climpson.

'I have a job,' he said to her, more abruptly than was his wont, 'which I should like you to undertake yourself. I can't trust anybody else.'

145

'How *kind* of you to put it like that,' said Miss Climpson.

'The trouble is, I can't in the least tell you how to set about it. It all depends on what you find when you get there. I want you to go to Windle in Westmorland and get hold of an imbecile and paralysed old lady called Mrs Wrayburn, who lives at a house called Applefold. I don't know who looks after her, or how you are to get into the house. But you've got to do it, and you've got to find out where her will is kept, and, if possible, see it.'

'Dear me!' said Miss Climpson.

'And what's worse,' said Wimsey, 'you've only got about a week to do it in.'

'That's a very short time,' said Miss Climpson.

'You see,' said Wimsey, 'unless we can give some very good reason for delay, they're bound to take the Vane case almost first thing next sessions. If I could persuade the lawyers for the defence that there is the least chance of securing fresh evidence, they could apply for a postponement. But at present I have nothing that could be called evidence – only the vaguest possible hunch.'

'I see,' said Miss Climpson. 'Well, none of us can do more than our best, and it is very necessary to have faith. That moves mountains, we are told.'

'Then for Heaven's sake lay in a good stock of it,' said Wimsey, gloomily, 'because, as far as I can see, this job is like shifting the Himalayas and the Alps, with a spot of frosty Caucasus and a touch of the Rockies thrown in.'

'You may count on me to do my poor best,' replied Miss Climpson, 'and I will ask the dear vicar to say a Mass of special intention for one engaged in a difficult undertaking. When would you like me to start?'

'At once,' said Wimsey. 'I think you had better go just as your ordinary self, and put up at the local hotel – no – a boarding-house; there will be more opportunities for gossip. I don't know much about Windle, except that there is a boot-factory there and rather a good view, but it's not a large place, and I should think everybody would know about Mrs Wrayburn. She is very rich, and was notorious in her time. The person you'll have to cotton on to is the female – there must be one of some sort – who nurses and waits on Mrs Wrayburn and is, generally speaking, about her path and about her bed and all that. When you find out her special weakness, drive a wedge into it like one o'clock. Oh! by the way – it's quite possible the will isn't there at all, but in the hands of a solicitor-fellow called Norman Urquhart who hangs out in Bedford Row. If so, all you can do is to get the pump to work and find out anything – anything at all – to his disadvantage. He's Mrs Wrayburn's great-nephew, and he goes to see her sometimes.'

Miss Climpson made a note of these instructions.

'And now I'll tootle off and leave you to it,' said Wimsey. 'Draw on the firm for any money you want. And if you need any special outfit, send me a wire.'

* * *

On leaving Miss Climpson, Lord Peter Wimsey again found himself a prey to *Weltschmerz* and self-pity. But it now took the form of a gentle, pervading melancholy. Convinced of his own futility, he determined to do what little good lay in his power before retiring to a monastery or to the frozen wastes of the Antarctic. He taxi'd purposefully round to Scotland Yard, and asked for Chief Inspector Parker.

Parker was in his office, reading a report which had just come in. He greeted Wimsey with an expression which seemed more embarrassed than delighted.

'Have you come about that packet of powder?'

'Not this time,' said Wimsey. 'I don't suppose you'll ever hear anything more of that. No. It's – rather a more – er – delicate matter. It's about my sister.'

Parker started and pushed the report to one side.

'About Lady Mary?'

'Eer – yes. I understand she's been going about with you – er – dining – and all that sort of thing, what?'

'Lady Mary has honoured me – on one or two occasions – with her company,' said Parker. 'I did not think – I did not know – that is, I understood –'

'Ah! but *did* you understand, that's the point?' said Wimsey, solemnly. 'You see, Mary's a very nice-minded sort of girl, though I say it and –'

'I assure you,' said Parker, 'that there is no need to tell me

147

that. Do you suppose that I should misinterpret her kindness? It is the custom nowadays for women of the highest character to dine unchaperoned with their friends, and Lady Mary has – '

'I'm not suggesting a chaperon,' said Wimsey. 'Mary wouldn't stick it for one thing, and I think it's all bosh, anyhow. Still, bein' her brother, and all that – it's Gerald's job really, of course, but Mary and he don't altogether hit it off, you know, and she wouldn't be likely to burble any secrets into his ear, especially as it would all be handed on to Helen – what was I going to say? Oh, yes – as Mary's brother, you know, I suppose it's my so to speak duty to push round and drop the helpful word here and there.'

Parker jabbed the blotting-paper thoughtfully.

'Don't do that,' said Wimsey, 'it's bad for your pen. Take a pencil.'

'I suppose,' said Parker, 'I ought not to have presumed – '

'What did you presume, old thing?' said Wimsey, his head cocked, sparrow-fashion.

'Nothing to which anybody could object,' said Parker, hotly. 'What are you thinking of Wimsey? I quite see that it is unsuitable, from your points of view, that Lady Mary Wimsey should dine in public restaurants with a policeman, but if you imagine I have ever said a word to her that could not be said with the greatest propriety – '

' – in the presence of her mother, you wrong the purest and sweetest woman that ever lived, and insult your friend,' interrupted Peter, snatching the words from his mouth and rattling them to a glib conclusion. 'What a perfect Victorian you are, Charles. I should like to keep you in a glass case. Of course you haven't said a word. What I want to know is, why?'

Parker stared at him.

'For the last five years or so,' said Wimsey, 'you have been looking like a demented sheep at my sister, and starting like a rabbit whenever her name is mentioned. What do you mean by it? It is not ornamental. It is not exhilarating. You unnerve the poor girl. You give me a poor idea of your guts, if you will pardon the expression. A man doesn't like to see a man go all wobbly about his sister – at least, not with such a prolonged wobble. It's unsightly. It's irritating. Why not slap the manly thorax and say, "Peter, my dear old mangel-wurzel, I have decided to dig myself into the old family trench and be a brother to you"? What's stopping you? Is it Gerald? He's an ass, I know, but he's not a bad old stick, really. Is it Helen? She's a bit of a wart, but you needn't see much of her. Is it me? Because, if so, I'm thinking of becoming a hermit – there was a Peter the Hermit, wasn't there? – so I shouldn't be in your way. Cough up the difficulty, old thing, and we will have it removed in a plain van. Now, then!'

'Do you – are you asking me – ?'

'I'm asking you your intentions, damn it!' said Wimsey, 'and if that's not Victorian enough, I don't know what is. I quite understand your having given Mary time to recover from that unfortunate affair with Cathcart and the Goyles fellow, but, dash it all, my dear man, one can overdo the delicacy business. You can't expect a girl to stand on and off for ever, can you? Are you waiting for leap-year, or what?'

'Look here, Peter, don't be a damned fool. How can I ask your sister to marry me?'

'*How* you do it is your affair. You might say: "What about a spot of matrimony, old dear?" That's up-to-date, and plain and unmistakable. Or you could go down on one knee and say, "Will you honour me with your hand and heart?" which is pretty and old-fashioned and has the merit of originality in these times. Or you could write, or wire, or telephone. But I leave that to your own individual fancy.'

'You're not serious.'

'Oh, God! Shall I ever live down this disastrous reputation for tomfoolery? You're making Mary damned unhappy, Charles, and I wish you'd marry her and have done with it.'

'Making her unhappy?' said Parker, almost in a shout. 'Me – her – unhappy?'

Wimsey tapped his forehead significantly.

'Wood – solid wood! But the last blow seems to have penetrated. Yes, you – her – unhappy – do you get it now?'

'Peter – if you really thought that –'

'Now don't go off the deep end,' said Wimsey; 'it's wasted on me. Keep it for Mary. I've done my brotherly duty and there's an end of it. Calm yourself. Return to your reports –'

'Oh, Lord, yes,' said Parker. 'Before we go any further, I've got a report for you.'

'You have? Why didn't you say so at first?'

'You wouldn't let me.'

'Well, what is it?'

'We've found the packet.'

'What?'

'We've found the packet.'

'Actually found it?'

'Yes. One of the barmen –'

'Never mind the barmen. You're sure it's the right packet?'

'Oh, yes; we've identified it.'

'Get on. Have you analysed it?'

'Yes, we've analysed it.'

'Well, what is it?'

Parker looked at him with the eyes of one who breaks bad news, and said, reluctantly:

'Bicarbonate of soda.'

Chapter XVI

MR CROFTS, excusably enough, said, 'I told you so'; Sir Impey Biggs observed curtly, 'Very unfortunate.'

To chronicle Lord Peter Wimsey's daily life during the ensuing week would be neither kind nor edifying. An enforced inactivity will produce irritable symptoms in the best of men. Nor did the imbecile happiness of Chief Inspector Parker and Lady Mary Wimsey tend to soothe him, accompanied as it was by tedious demonstrations of affection for himself. Like the man in Max Beerbohm's story, Wimsey 'hated to be touching'. He was only moderately cheered by hearing from the industrious Freddy Arbuthnot that Mr Norman Urquhart was found to be more or less deeply involved in the disasters of the Megatherium Trust.

Miss Kitty Climpson, on the other hand, was living in what she herself liked to call a 'whirl of activity'. A letter, written the second day after her arrival in Windle, furnishes us with a wealth of particulars.

> 'Hillside View,
> 'Windle,
> 'Westmorland.
> 1*st Jan.,* 1930.

'MY DEAR LORD PETER, I feel sure you will be anxious to hear, at the *earliest possible* moment, *how* things are *going,* and though I have only been here *one* day, I really think I have *not* done so *badly* all things considered!

'My train got in quite late on Monday night, after a *most dreary* journey, with a *lugubrious* wait at *Preston,* though thanks to your kindness in insisting that I should travel *First Class,* I was not really at all tired! Nobody can realise what a *great* difference these extra comforts make, especially when one is *getting on* in years, and after the *uncomfortable* travelling which I had to endure in my days of poverty, I feel that I am living in almost *sinful* luxury! The carriage was *well* heated – indeed, *too much* so and I should have liked the window down, but that there was a *very* fat business man, *muffled* up to the eyes in *coats* and *woolly waistcoats* who *strongly* objected to fresh air! Men are such HOTHOUSE PLANTS nowadays, are they not, quite unlike my dear father, who would never permit a *fire* in the house *before* November the 1st, or *after* March 31st, even though the thermometer was at *freezing-point*!

'I had *no* difficulty in getting a comfortable room at the Station Hotel, *late* as it was. In the old days, an *unmarried* woman arriving *alone* at *midnight* with a *suitcase* would hardly have been considered *respectable* – what a wonderful difference one finds today! I am *grateful* to have lived to see such changes, because whatever old-fashioned people may say about the greater *decorum* and *modesty* of women in Queen Victoria's time, those who can remember the old conditions know how *difficult* and *humiliating* they were!

'Yesterday morning, of course, my *first* object was to find a *suitable boarding-house,* in accordance with your instructions, and I was *fortunate* enough to hit upon this house at the *second* attempt. It is very well run and *refined,* and there were three *elderly ladies* who are *permanent* boarders here, and are *well up* in all the GOSSIP of the town, so that nothing could be more *advantageous* for our purpose!

'As soon as I had engaged my room, I went out for a little *voyage of discovery*. I found a very helpful *policeman* in the High Street, and asked him where to find Mrs Wrayburn's house. He knew it quite well, and told me to take the *omnibus* and it would be a penny ride to the Fisherman's Arms and then about five minutes walk. So I followed his directions, and the bus took me right out into the country to a *cross-roads* with the Fisherman's Arms at the corner. The conductor was most polite and helpful and showed me the way, so I had *no difficulty* in finding the house.

'It is a *beautiful old place,* standing in its own grounds – quite a *big* house, built in the *eighteenth century,* with an *Italian* porch and a lovely green lawn with a cedar-tree and formal flower-beds, and in summer must be really a *garden of Eden*. I looked at it from the road for a little time – I did not think this would be at all *peculiar* behaviour, if anybody saw me, because *anybody* might be interested in such a fine old place. Most of the *blinds* were down, as though the greater part of the house were *uninhabited*, and I could not see any *gardener* or anybody about – I suppose there is not very much to be done in the garden this time of the year. One of the *chimneys* was smoking, however, so there were *some* signs of life about the place.

'I took a little *walk* down the road and then turned back and passed the house again, and this time I saw a servant just passing round the corner of the house, but of course she was *too far off* for me to speak to. So I took the omnibus back again and had lunch at Hillside View, so as to make acquaintance with my fellow-boarders.

'Naturally I did not want to seem *too eager* all at once, so I said nothing about Mrs Wrayburn's house *at first*, but just talked generally about Windle. I had some difficulty in parrying the *questions* of the good ladies, who *wondered* very much *why* a stranger had come to Windle at this time of the year, but without telling many actual *untruths* I think I left them with the *impression* that I had come into a little fortune (!) and was visiting the Lake District to find a suitable spot in which to settle next *summer*! I talked about *sketching* – as girls we were *all* brought up to dabble a little in watercolours, so that I was able to display quite sufficient *technical knowledge* to satisfy them!

'That gave me quite a *good* opportunity to ask about the *house*! Such a *beautiful* old place, I said, and did anybody live there? (Of *course* I did not blurt this out *all at once* – I waited till they had told me of the many *quaint spots* in the district that would interest an artist!) Mrs Pegler, a very stout, PUSSY old lady with a LONG TONGUE (!) was able to tell me *all* about it. My dear Lord Peter, what I do *not* know now about the *abandoned wickedness* of Mrs Wrayburn's early life is really NOT WORTH KNOWING!! But what was *more to the point* is that she told me the *name* of Mrs Wrayburn's *nurse-companion*. She is a MISS BOOTH, a retired nurse, about *sixty* years old, and she lives *all alone* in the house with Mrs Wrayburn, except for the *servants,* and a *housekeeper.* When I heard that Mrs Wrayburn was so *old,* and *paralysed* and *frail,* I said was it not very *dangerous* that Miss Booth should be the only attendant, but Mrs Pegler said the housekeeper was a *most trustworthy* woman who had been with Mrs Wrayburn for many years, and was *quite* capable of looking after her any time when Miss Booth was out. So it appears that Miss Booth does go out sometimes! Nobody in this house seems to *know* her *personally,* but they say she is often to be seen in the town in *nurse's uniform.* I managed to extract quite a good description of her, so if I should happen to meet her, I daresay I shall be *smart* enough to *recognise* her!

'That is really *all* I have been able to discover in *one* day. I hope you will not be *too* disappointed, but I was obliged to listen to a terrible amount of *local history* of one kind and another, and of course, I could not FORCE the conversation round to Mrs Wrayburn in any suspicious way.

'I will let you know as *soon* as I get the *least bit* more information.

'Most sincerely yours,
'KATHERINE ALEXANDRA CLIMPSON.'

Miss Climpson finished her letter in the privacy of her bedroom, and secured it carefully in her capacious handbag before going downstairs. A long experience of boarding-house life warned her that to display openly an envelope addressed even to a minor member of the nobility would be to court a quite unnecessary curiosity. True, it would establish her status, but at that moment Miss Climpson hardly wished to move in the limelight. She crept quietly out at the hall door, and turned her step towards the centre of the town.

On the previous day, she had marked down one principal tea-shop, two rising and competitive tea-shops, one slightly *passé* and declining tea-shop, a Lyons, and four obscure and, on the whole, negligible tea-shops which combined the service of refreshments with a trade in sweets. It was now half-past ten. In the next hour and a half she could, with a little exertion, pass in review all that part of the Windle population which indulged in morning coffee.

154

She posted her letter and then debated with herself where to begin. On the whole, she inclined to leave the Lyons for another day. It was an ordinary plain Lyons, without orchestra or soda-fountain. She thought that its clientèle would be chiefly housewives and clerks. Of the other four, the most likely was, perhaps, the Central. It was fairly large, well-lighted and cheerful, and strains of music issued from its doors. Nurses usually like the large, well-lighted, and melodious. But the Central had one drawback. Anyone coming from the direction of Mrs Wrayburn's house would have to pass all the others to get to it. This fact unfitted it for an observation post. From this point of view, the advantage lay with Ye Cosye Corner, which commanded the bus-stop. Accordingly, Miss Climpson decided to start her campaign from that spot. She selected a table in the window, ordered a cup of coffee and a plate of digestive biscuits, and entered upon her vigil.

After half an hour, during which no woman in nurse's costume had been sighted, she ordered another cup of coffee and some pastries. A number of people – mostly women – dropped in, but none of them could by any possibility be identified with Miss Booth. At half-past eleven, Miss Climpson felt that to stay any longer would be conspicuous and might annoy the management. She paid her bill and departed.

The Central had rather more people in it than Ye Cosye Corner, and was in some ways an improvement, having comfortable wicker chairs instead of fumed oak settles, and brisk waitresses instead of languid semi-gentlewomen in art-linen. Miss Climpson ordered another cup of coffee and a roll and butter. There was no window-table vacant, but she found one close to the orchestra from which she could survey the whole room. A fluttering dark-blue veil at the door made her heart beat, but it proved to belong to a lusty young person with two youngsters and a perambulator, and hope withdrew once more. By twelve o'clock, Miss Climpson decided that she had drawn blank at the Central.

Her last visit was to the Oriental – an establishment singularly ill-adapted for espionage. It consisted of three very small rooms of irregular shape, dimly lit by forty-watt bulbs in Japanese shades, and further shrouded by bead curtains and draperies. Miss Climpson, in her inquisitive way, wandered into all its nooks and corners, disturbing several courting couples, before returning to a table near the door and sitting down to consume her fourth cup of coffee. Half-past twelve came, but no Miss Booth. 'She can't come now,' thought Miss Climpson; 'she will have to get back and give her patient lunch.'

She returned to Hillside View with but little appetite for the joint of roast mutton.

At half-past three she sallied out again, to indulge in an orgy of teas. This time she included the Lyons and the fourth tea-shop, beginning at the far end of the town and working her way back to the bus-stop. It was while she was struggling with her fifth meal, in the window of Ye Cosye Corner, that a hurrying figure on the pavement caught her eye. The winter evening had closed in, and the street lights were not very brilliant, but she distinctly saw a stoutish, middle-aged nurse in a black veil and grey cloak pass along on the nearer pavement. By craning her neck, she could see her make a brisk spurt, scramble on the bus at the corner, and disappear in the direction of the Fisherman's Arms.

'How vexatious!' said Miss Climpson, as the vehicle disappeared. 'I must have just missed her somewhere. Or perhaps she was having tea in a private house. Well, I'm afraid this is a blank day. And I do feel so *full* of tea!'

It was fortunate that Miss Climpson had been blest by Heaven with a sound digestion, for the next morning saw a repetition of the performance. It was possible, of course, that Miss Booth only went out two or three times a week, or that she only went out in the afternoon, but Miss Climpson was taking no chances. She had at least achieved the certainty that the bus-stop was the place to watch. This time she took up her post at Ye Cosye Corner at 11 o'clock and waited till twelve. Nothing happened and she went home.

In the afternoon she was there again at three. By this time the waitress had got to know her, and betrayed a certain amused and tolerant interest in her comings and goings. Miss Climpson explained that she liked so much to watch the people pass, and spoke a few words in praise of the café and its service. She admired a quaint old inn on the opposite side of the street, and said she thought of making a sketch of it.

'Oh, yes,' said the girl, 'there's a many artists comes here for that.'

This gave Miss Climpson a bright idea, and the next morning she brought a pencil and sketchbook with her.

By the extraordinary perversity of things in general, she had no sooner ordered her coffee, opened the sketchbook, and started to outline the gables of the inn, than a bus drew up, and out of it stepped the stout nurse in the black and grey uniform. She did not enter Ye Cosye Corner, but marched on at a brisk pace down the opposite of the street, her veil flapping like a flag.

Miss Climpson uttered a sharp exclamation of annoyance, which drew the waitress's attention.

'How provoking!' said Miss Climpson. 'I have left my rubber behind. I must just run out and buy one.'

She dropped the sketchbook on the table and made for the door.

'I'll cover your coffee up for you, miss,' said the girl, helpfully. 'Mr Bulteel's, down near the Bear, is the best stationer's.'

'Thank you, thank you,' said Miss Climpson, and darted out.

The black veil was still flapping in the distance. Miss Climpson pursued breathlessly, keeping to the near side of the road. The veil dived into a chemist's shop. Miss Climpson crossed the road a little behind it and stared into a window full of baby-linen. The veil came out, fluttered undecidedly on the pavement, turned, passed Miss Climpson, and went into a boot-shop.

'If it's shoe-laces, it'll be quick,' thought Miss Climpson, 'but if it's trying-on it may be all morning.' She walked slowly past the door. By good luck a customer was just coming out, and, peering past him, Miss Climpson just caught a glimpse of the black veil vanishing into the back premises. She pushed the door boldly open. There was a counter for sundries in the front of the shop, and the doorway through which the nurse had vanished was labelled 'Ladies' Department'.

While buying a pair of brown silk laces, Miss Climpson debated with herself. Should she follow and seize this opportunity? Trying on shoes is usually a lengthy business. The subject is marooned for long periods in a chair, while the assistant climbs ladders and collects piles of cardboard boxes. It is also comparatively easy to enter into conversation with a person

157

who is trying on shoes. But there is a snag in it. To give colour to your presence in the fitting department, you must yourself try on shoes. What happens? The assistant first disables you by snatching off your right-hand shoe, and then disappears. And supposing, meanwhile, your quarry completes her purchase and walks out? Are you to follow, hopping madly on one foot? Are you to arouse suspicion by hurriedly replacing your own footgear and rushing out with laces flying and an unconvincing murmur about a forgotten engagement? Still worse, suppose you are in an amphibious condition, wearing one shoe of your own and one of the establishment's? What impression will you make by suddenly bolting with goods to which you are not entitled? Will not the pursuer very quickly become the pursued?

Having weighed this problem in her mind, Miss Climpson paid for her shoe-laces and retired. She had already bilked a tea-shop, and one misdemeanour in a morning was about as much as she could hope to get away with.

The male detective, particularly when dressed as a workman, an errand-boy, or a telegraph-messenger, is favourably placed for 'shadowing'. He can loaf without attracting attention. The female detective must not loaf. On the other hand, she can stare into shop-windows for ever. Miss Climpson selected a hat-shop. She examined all the hats in both windows attentively, coming back to gaze in a purposeful manner at an extremely elegant model with an eye-veil and a pair of excrescences like rabbits' ears. Just at the moment when any observer might have thought that she had at last made up her mind to go in and ask the price, the nurse came out of the boot-shop. Miss Climpson shook her head regretfully at the rabbit's ears, darted back to the other window, looked, hovered, hesitated – and tore herself away.

The nurse was now about thirty yards ahead, moving well, with the air of a horse that sights his stable. She crossed the street again, looked into a window piled with coloured wools, thought better of it, passed on, and turned in at the door of the Oriental Café.

Miss Climpson was in the position of one who, after prolonged pursuit, has clapped a tumbler over a moth. For the moment the creature is safe and the pursuer takes breath. The problem now is to extract the moth without damage.

It is easy, of course, to follow a person into a café and sit down at her table, if there is room there. But she may not welcome you. She may feel it perverse in you to thrust yourself upon her when other tables are standing empty. It is better to offer some excuse, such as restoring a dropped handkerchief or drawing attention to an open handbag. If the person will not provide you with an excuse, the next best thing is to manufacture one.

The stationer's shop was only a few doors off. Miss Climpson went in and purchased an indiarubber, three picture post-cards, a BB pencil, and a calendar, and waited while they were made up into a parcel. Then she slowly made her way across the street and turned into the Oriental.

In the first room she found two women and a small boy occupying one recess, an aged gentleman drinking milk in another, and a couple of girls consuming coffee and cakes in a third.

'Excuse me,' said Miss Climpson to the two women, 'but does this parcel belong to you? I picked it up just outside the door.'

The elder woman, who had evidently been shopping, hastily passed in review a quantity of miscellaneous packages, pinching each one by way of refreshing her memory as to the contents.

'I don't think it's mine, but really I can't say for certain. Let me see. That's eggs and that's bacon and – what's this, Gertie? Is that the mouse-trap? No, wait a minute, that's cough-mixture, that is – and that's Aunt Edith's cork soles, and that's Nugget – no, bloater paste, this here's the Nugget – why, bless my soul, I believe I *have* been and gone and dropped the mouse-trap – but that don't look like it to me.'

'No, Mother,' said the young woman, 'don't you remember, they were sending round the mouse-trap with the bath.'

'Of course, so they were. Well, that accounts for that. The mouse-trap and the two frying-pans, they was all to go with the bath, and that's all except the soap, which you've got, Gertie. No, thank you very much, all the same, but it isn't ours; somebody else must have dropped it.'

The old gentleman repudiated it firmly but politely, and the two girls merely giggled at it. Miss Climpson passed on. Two young women with their attendant young men duly thanked her in the second room, but said the parcel was not theirs.

Miss Climpson passed on into the third room. In one corner was a rather talkative party of people with an Airedale, and at the back, in the most obscure and retired of all the Oriental nooks and corners, sat the nurse, reading a book.

The talkative party had nothing to say to the parcel, and Miss Climpson, with her heart beating fast, bore down upon the nurse.

'Excuse me;' she said, smiling graciously, 'but I think this little parcel must be yours. I picked it up just in the doorway and I've asked all the other people in the café.'

The nurse looked up. She was a grey-haired, elderly woman, with those curious large blue eyes which disconcert the beholder by their intense gaze, and are usually an index of some emotional instability. She smiled at Miss Climpson and said pleasantly:

'No, no, it isn't mine. So kind of you. But I have all my parcels here.'

She vaguely indicated the cushioned seat which ran round three sides of the alcove, and Miss Climpson, accepting the gesture as an invitation, promptly sat down.

'How very odd,' said Miss Climpson. 'I made sure someone must have dropped it coming in here. I wonder what I had better do with it.' She pinched it gently. 'I shouldn't think it was valuable, but one never knows. I suppose I ought to take it to the police-station.'

'You could hand it to the cashier,' suggested the nurse, 'in case the owner came back here to claim it.'

'Well now, so I could,' cried Miss Climpson. 'How clever of you to think of it. Of course, yes, that would be the best way. You must think me very foolish, but the idea never occurred to me. I'm not a very practical person, I'm afraid, but I do so admire the people who are. I should never do to take up *your* profession, should I? Any little emergency leaves me *quite* bewildered.'

The nurse smiled again.

'It is largely a question of training,' she said. 'And of *self*-training, too, of course. All these little weaknesses can be cured by placing the mind under a Higher Control – don't you believe that?'

Her eyes rested hypnotically upon Miss Climpson's.

'I suppose that is true.'

'It is such a mistake,' pursued the nurse, closing her book and laying it down on the table, 'to imagine that anything in the mental sphere is large or small. Our least thoughts and actions are equally directed by the higher centres of spiritual power, if we can bring ourselves to believe it.'

A waitress arrived to take Miss Climpson's order.

'Oh, dear! I seem to have intruded myself upon your table . . . !'

'Oh, don't get up,' said the nurse.

'Are you sure? Really? Because I don't want to interrupt you – '

'Not at all. I live a very solitary life, and I am always glad to find a friend to talk to.'

'How nice of you. I'll have scones and butter, please, and a pot of tea. This is such a nice little café, don't you think? – so quiet and peaceful. If only those people wouldn't make such a noise with that dog of theirs. I don't like those great, big animals, and I think they're quite dangerous, don't you?'

The reply was lost on Miss Climpson, for she had suddenly seen the title of the book on the table, and the Devil, or a Ministering Angel (she was not quite sure which), was, so to speak, handing her a full-blown temptation on a silver salver. The book was published by the Spiritualist Press and was called *Can the Dead Speak?*

In a single moment of illumination, Miss Climpson saw her plan complete and perfect in every detail. It involved a course of deception from which her conscience shrank appalled, but it was certain. She wrestled with the demon. Even in a righteous cause, could anything so wicked be justified?

She breathed what she thought was a prayer for guidance, but the only answer was a small whisper in her ear, 'Oh, jolly good work, Miss Climpson!' and the voice was the voice of Peter Wimsey.

'Pardon me,' said Miss Climpson, 'but I see you are a student of spiritualism. How interesting that is!'

If there was one subject in the world about which Miss Climpson might claim to know something, it was spiritualism. It is a flower which flourishes bravely in a boarding-house

161

atmosphere. Time and again, Miss Climpson had listened while the apparatus of planes and controls, correspondences and veridical communications, astral bodies, auras, and ectoplastic materialisations was displayed before her protesting intelligence. That to the Church it was a forbidden subject she knew well enough, but she had been paid companion to so many old ladies and had been forced so many times to bow down in the House of Rimmon.

And then there had been the quaint little man from the Physical Research Society. He had stayed a fortnight in the same private hotel with her at Bournemouth. He was skilled in the investigation of haunted houses and the detection of poltergeists. He had rather liked Miss Climpson, and she had passed several interesting evenings hearing about the tricks of mediums. Under his guidance she had learnt to turn tables and produce explosive cracking noises; she knew how to examine a pair of sealed slates for the marks of the wedges which let the chalk go in on a long black wire to write spirit-messages. She had seen the ingenious rubber gloves which leave the impression of spirit hands in a bucket of paraffin-wax, and which, when deflated, can be drawn delicately from the hardened wax through a hole narrower than a child's wrist. She even knew theoretically, though she had never tried it, how to hold her hands to be tied behind her back so as to force that first deceptive knot which makes all subsequent knots useless, and how to flit about the room banging tambourines in the twilight in spite of having been tied up in a black cabinet with both fists filled with flour. Miss Climpson had wondered greatly at the folly and wickedness of mankind.

The nurse went on talking, and Miss Climpson answered mechanically.

'She's only a beginner,' said Miss Climpson to herself. 'She's reading a textbook . . . And she is quite uncritical . . . Surely she knows that that woman was exposed long ago . . . People like her shouldn't be allowed out alone – they're living incitements to fraud . . . I don't know this Mrs Craig she is talking about, but I should say she was as twisty as a corkscrew . . . I must avoid Mrs Craig; she probably knows too much . . . If the poor deluded creature will swallow that, she'll swallow anything.'

'It does seem *most* wonderful, doesn't it?' said Miss Climpson, aloud. 'But isn't it a wee bit *dangerous*? I've been told I'm sensitive myself, but I have never *dared* to try. Is it *wise* to open one's mind to these supernatural influences?'

'It's not dangerous if you know the right way,' said the nurse. 'One must learn to build up a shell of pure thoughts about the soul, so that no evil influences can enter it. I have had the most marvellous talks with the dear ones who have passed over . . . '

Miss Climpson refilled the teapot and sent the waitress for a plate of sugary cakes.

' . . . unfortunately I am not mediumistic myself – not yet, that is. I can't get anything when I'm alone. Mrs Craig says that it will come by practice and concentration. Last night I was trying with the ouija board, but it would only write spirals.'

'Your conscious mind is too active, I expect,' said Miss Climpson.

'Yes, I daresay that it is. Mrs Craig says that I am wonderfully sympathetic. We get the most wonderful results when we sit together. Unfortunately she is abroad just now.'

Miss Climpson's heart gave a great leap, so that she nearly spilled her tea.

'You yourself are a medium, then?' went on the nurse.

'I have been told so,' said Miss Climpson, guardedly.

'I wonder,' said the nurse, 'whether if we sat together –'

She looked hungrily at Miss Climpson.

'I don't really like –'

'Oh, do! You are such a sympathetic person. I'm sure we should get good results. And the spirits are so pathetically anxious to communicate. Of course, I wouldn't like to try unless I was sure of the person. There are so many fraudulent mediums about' – ('So you know that much!' thought Miss Climpson) – 'but with somebody like yourself one is absolutely safe. You would find it makes such a difference in your life. I used to be so unhappy over all the pain and misery in the world – we see so much of it, you know – till I realised the certainty of survival and how all our trials are merely sent to fit us for life on a higher plane.'

'Well,' said Miss Climpson, slowly, 'I'm willing just to try. But I can't say I really *believe* in it, you know.'

'You would – you would.'

'Of course, I've seen one or two strange things happen – things that couldn't be tricks, because I knew the people – and which I couldn't explain – '

'Come up and see me this evening, now do!' said the nurse, persuasively. 'We'll just have one quiet sitting and then we shall see whether you really are a medium. I've no doubt you are.'

'Very well,' said Miss Climpson. 'What is your name, by the way?'

'Caroline Booth – Miss Caroline Booth. I'm nurse to an old, paralysed lady in the big house along the Kendal Road.'

'Thank goodness for that, anyway,' thought Miss Climpson. Aloud she said:

'And my name is Climpson; I think I've got a card somewhere. No – I've left it behind. But I'm staying at Hillside View. How do I get to you?'

Miss Booth mentioned the address and the time of the bus and added an invitation to supper, which was accepted. Miss Climpson went home and wrote a hurried note:

'MY DEAR LORD PETER, I am sure you have been *wondering* what has *happened* to me. But *at last* I have NEWS! I have STORMED THE CITADEL!!! I am going to the *house* TONIGHT and you may expect GREAT THINGS!!!

'In *haste*,

'Yours very sincerely,

'KATHARINE A. CLIMPSON.'

Miss Climpson went out into the town again after lunch. First, being an honest woman, she retrieved her sketchbook from Ye Cosye Corner and paid her bill, explaining that she had run across a friend that morning and been detained. She then visited a number of shops. Eventually she selected a small metal soap-box which suited her requirements. Its sides were slightly convex, and when closed and pinched slightly, it sprang back with a hearty cracking noise. This, with a little contrivance and some powerful sticking-plaster, she fixed to a strong elastic garter. When clasped about Miss Climpson's bony knee and squeezed sharply against the other knee, the box emitted a series of cracks so satisfying as to convince the most sceptical. Miss Climpson, seated before the looking-glass, indulged in an hour's practice before tea, till the crack could be produced with the minimum of physical jerk.

Another purchase was a length of stiff black-bound wire, such as is used for making hat-brims. Used double, neatly bent to a double angle and strapped to the wrist, this contrivance was sufficient to rock a light table. The weight of a heavy table would be too much for it, she feared, but she had had no time to order blacksmith's work. She could try, anyway. She hunted out a black velvet rest-gown with long, wide sleeves, and satisfied herself that the wires could be sufficiently hidden.

At six o'clock, she put on this garment, fastened the soap-box to her leg – turning the box outward, lest untimely cracks should startle her fellow-travellers, muffled herself in a heavy rain-cloak of Inverness cut, took hat and umbrella, and started on her way to steal Mrs Wrayburn's will.

Chapter XVII

SUPPER was over. It had been served in a beautiful old panelled room with an Adam ceiling and fireplace, and the food had been good. Miss Climpson felt braced and ready.

'We'll sit in my own room, shall we?' said Miss Booth. 'It's the only really comfortable place. Most of this house is shut up, of course. If you'll excuse me, dear, I will just run up and give Mrs Wrayburn her supper and make her comfortable, poor thing, and then we can begin. I shan't be more than half an hour or so.'

'She's quite helpless, I suppose?'

'Yes, quite.'

'Can she speak?'

'Not to say speak. She mumbles sometimes, but one can't make anything of it. It's sad, isn't it, and her so rich. It will be a happy day for her when she passes over.'

'Poor soul!' said Miss Climpson.

Her hostess led her into a small, gaily-furnished sitting-room and left her there among the cretonne covers and the ornaments. Miss Climpson ran her eyes rapidly over the books, which were mostly novels, with the exception of some standard works on spiritualism, and then turned her attention to the mantelpiece. It was crowded with photographs, as the mantel-pieces of nurses usually are. Conspicuous among hospital groups and portraits inscribed 'From your grateful patient' was a cabinet photograph of a gentleman in the dress and moustache of the nineties, standing beside a bicycle, apparently upon a stone balcony in mid-air, with a distant view over a rocky gorge. The frame was silver, heavy, and ornate.

'Too young for a father,' said Miss Climpson, as she turned it over and pushed back the catch of the frame; 'either sweetheart or favourite brother. H'm! "My dearest Lucy, from her ever-loving Harry." Not a brother, I fancy. Photographer's address, Coventry. Cycle trade, possibly. Now what happened to Harry? Not matrimony, obviously. Death, or infidelity. First-class frame and central position; bunch of hot-house narcissi in a vase – I think Harry has passed over. What next? Family group? Yes. Names conveniently beneath. Dearest Lucy in a fringe, Papa and Mamma, Tom and Gertrude. Tom and Gertrude are older, but they may be still alive. Papa is a parson. Largish house – country rectory, perhaps. Photographer's address, Maidstone. Wait a minute. Here's Papa in another group, with a dozen small boys. Schoolmaster, or takes private pupils. Two boys have straw hats with zig-zag ribbons – school, probably, then. What's that silver cup? Thos Booth and three other names – Pembroke College Fours, 1883. Not an expensive college. Wonder whether Papa objected to Harry on account of the cycle-manufacturing connection? That book over there looks like a school prize. It is. Maidstone Ladies' College – for distinction in English Literature. Just so. Is she coming back? – No, false alarm. Young man in khaki, "Your loving nephew, G. Booth" – ah! Tom's son, I take it. Did he survive, I wonder? Yes – she is coming, this time.'

When the door opened, Miss Climpson was sitting by the fire, deeply engaged in *Raymond*.

'So sorry to keep you waiting,' said Miss Booth, 'but the poor old dear is rather restless this evening. She'll do now for a couple of hours, but I shall have to go up again later. Shall we begin at once? I'm *so* eager to try.'

Miss Climpson readily agreed.

'We usually use this table,' said Miss Booth, bringing forward a small, round table of bamboo, with a shelf between its legs. Miss Climpson thought she had never seen a piece of furniture more excellently adapted for the faking of phenomena, and heartily approved of Mrs Craig's choice.

'Do we sit in the light?' she inquired.

'Not in full light,' said Miss Booth. 'Mrs Craig explained to me that the blue rays of daylight or electricity are too hard for the spirits. They shatter the vibrations, you see. So we usually put out the light and sit in the firelight, which is quite bright enough for taking notes. Will you write down, or shall I?'

167

'Oh, I think you had better do it as you're more accustomed to it,' said Miss Climpson.

'Very well.' Miss Booth fetched a pencil and a pad of paper and switched off the light.

'Now we just sit down and place our thumbs and fingertips lightly on the table, near the edge. It's better to make a circle, of course, but one can't do that with two people. And just at first, I think it's better not to talk – till a *rapport* is established, you know. Which side will you sit?'

'Oh, this will do for me,' said Miss Climpson.

'You don't mind the fire on your back?'

Miss Climpson most certainly did not.

'Well, that's a good arrangement, because it helps to screen the rays from the table.'

'That's what I thought,' said Miss Climpson, truthfully.

They placed thumbs and fingertips on the table and waited.

Ten minutes passed.

'Did you feel any movement?' whispered Miss Booth.

'No.'

'It sometimes takes a little time.'

Silence.

'Ah! I thought I felt something then.'

'I've got a feeling like pins and needles in my fingers.'

'So have I. We shall get something soon.'

A pause.

'Would you like to rest a little?'

'My wrists ache rather.'

'They do till you get used to it. It's the power coming through them.'

Miss Climpson lifted her fingers and rubbed each wrist gently. The thin black hooks came quietly down to the edge of her black velvet sleeve.

'I feel sure there is power all about us. I can feel a cold thrill on my spine.'

'Let's go on,' said Miss Climpson. 'I'm quite rested now.'

Silence.

'I feel,' whispered Miss Climpson, 'as though something was gripping the back of my neck.'

'Don't move.'

'And my arms have gone dead from the elbow.'

'Hush! so have mine.'

Miss Climpson might have added that she had a pain in her deltoids, if she had known the name for them. This is not an uncommon result of sitting with the thumbs and fingers on a table without support for the wrist.

'I'm tingling from head to foot,' said Miss Booth.

At this moment the table gave a violent lurch. Miss Climpson had overestimated the force necessary to move bamboo furniture.

'Ah!'

After a slight pause for recuperation, the table began to move again, but more gently, till it was rocking with a regular see-saw motion. Miss Climpson found that by gently elevating one rather large foot, she could take practically all the weight off her wrist-hooks. This was fortunate, as she was doubtful whether their constitution would stand the strain.

'Shall we speak to it?' asked Miss Climpson.

'Wait a moment,' said Miss Booth. 'It wants to go sideways.'

Miss Climpson was surprised by this statement, which seemed to argue a high degree of imagination, but she obligingly imparted a slight gyratory movement to the table.

'Shall we stand up?' suggested Miss Booth.

This was disconcerting, for it is not easy to work a vibrating table while stooping and standing on one leg. Miss Climpson decided to fall into a trance. She dropped her head on her chest and uttered a slight moan. At the same time she pulled back her hands, releasing the hooks, and the table continued to revolve jerkily, spinning beneath their fingers.

A coal fell from the fire with a crash, sending up a bright jet of flame. Miss Climpson started, and the table ceased spinning and came down with a little thud.

'Oh, dear!' exclaimed Miss Booth. 'The light has dispersed the vibrations. Are you all right, dear?'

'Yes, yes,' said Miss Climpson vaguely. 'Did anything happen?'

'The power was tremendous,' said Miss Booth. 'I've never felt it so strong.'

'I think I must have fallen asleep,' said Miss Climpson.

'You were entranced,' said Miss Booth. 'The control was taking possession. Are you very tired, or can you go on?'

169

'I feel quite all right,' said Miss Climpson, 'only a little drowsy.'

'You're a wonderfully strong medium,' said Miss Booth.

Miss Climpson, surreptitiously flexing her ankle, was inclined to agree.

'We'll put a screen before the fire this time,' said Miss Booth. 'That's better. Now!'

The hands were replaced on the table, which began to rock again almost immediately.

'We won't lose any more time,' said Miss Booth. She cleared her throat slightly, and addressed the table.

'Is there a spirit here?'

Crack!

The table ceased moving.

'Will you give me one knock for "Yes" and two for "No"?'

Crack!

The advantage of this method of interrogation is that it obliges the inquirer to put the leading questions.

'Are you the spirit of one who has passed over?'

'Yes.'

'Are you Fedora?'

'No.'

'Are you one of the spirits who have visited me before?'

'No.'

'Are you friendly to us?'

'Yes.'

'Are you pleased to see us?'

'Yes. Yes. Yes.'

'Are you happy?'

'Yes.'

'Are you here to ask anything for yourself?'

'No.'

'Are you anxious to help us personally?'

'No.'

'Are you speaking on behalf of another spirit?'

'Yes.'

'Does he want to speak to my friend?'

'No.'

'To me then?'

'Yes. Yes. Yes. Yes.' (The table rocked violently.)

'Is it the spirit of a woman?'

'No.'

'A man?'

'Yes.'

A little gasp.

'Is it the spirit I have been trying to communicate with?'

'Yes.'

A pause and a tilting of the table.

'Will you speak to us by means of the alphabet? One knock for A, two for B, and so on?'

('Belated caution,' thought Miss Climpson.)

Crack!

'What is your name?'

Eight taps and a long indrawn breath.

One tap –

'H-A –'

A long succession of taps.

'Was that an R? You go too fast.'

Crack!

'H-A-R – is that right?'

'Yes.'

'Is it Harry?'

'Yes, yes, yes.'

'Oh, Harry! At last! How are you? Are you happy?'

'Yes – no – lonely.'

'It wasn't my fault, Harry.'

'Yes. Weak.'

'Ah, but I had my duty to think of. Remember who came between us.'

'Yes. F-A-T-H-E-'

'No, no, Harry! It was mo –'

' – A-D!' concluded the table, triumphantly.

'How can you speak so unkindly?'

'Love comes first.'

'I know that now. But I was only a girl. Won't you forgive me now?'

'All forgiven. Mother forgiven too.'

'I'm so glad. What do you do where you are, Harry?'

'Wait. Help. Atone.'

171

'Have you got any special message for me?'

'Go to Coventry!' (Here the table became agitated.)

This message seemed to overwhelm the seeker.

'Oh, it really is you, Harry! You haven't forgotten the dear old joke. Tell me – '

The table showed great signs of excitement at this point and poured out a volley of unintelligible letters.

'What do you want?'

'G-G-G – '

'It must be somebody else interrupting,' said Miss Booth. 'Who is that, please?'

'G-E-O-R-G-E' (very rapidly).

'George! I don't know any George, except Tom's boy. Has anything happened to him, I wonder.'

'Ha! ha! ha! not George Booth, George Washington.'

'George Washington?'

'Ha! ha!' (The table became convulsively agitated, so much so that the medium seemed hardly able to hold it. Miss Booth, who had been noting down the conversation, now put her hands back on the table, which stopped capering and began to rock.)

'Who is here now?'

'Pongo.'

'Who is Pongo?'

'Your control.'

'Who was that talking just now?'

'Bad spirit. Gone now.'

'Is Harry still there?'

'Gone.'

'Does anybody else want to speak?'

'Helen.'

'Helen who?'

'Don't you remember? Maidstone.'

'Maidstone? Oh, do you mean Ellen Pate?'

'Yes, Pate.'

'Fancy that! Good evening, Ellen. How nice to hear from you.'

'Remember row.'

'Do you mean the big row in the dormitory?'

'Kate bad girl.'

172

'No, I don't remember Kate, except Kate Hurley. You don't mean her, do you?'

'Naughty Kate. Lights out.'

'Oh, I *know* what she's trying to say. The cakes after lights were out.'

'That's right.'

'You still spell badly, Ellen.'

'Miss – Miss –'

'Mississippi? Haven't you learnt it yet?'

'Funny.'

'Are there many of our class where you are?'

'Alice and Mabel. Send love.'

'How sweet of them. Give them my love too.'

'Yes. All love. Flowers. Sunshine.'

'What do you –'

'P,' said the table, impatiently.

'Is that Pongo again?'

'Yes. Tired.'

'Do you want us to stop?'

'Yes. Another time.'

'Very well, goodnight.'

'Goodnight.'

The medium leaned back in her chair with an air of exhaustion which was perfectly justified. It is very tiring to rap out letters of the alphabet, and she was afraid the soap-box was slipping.

Miss Booth turned on the light.

'That was wonderful!' said Miss Booth.

'Did you get the answers you wanted?'

'Yes, indeed. Didn't you hear them?'

'I didn't follow it all,' said Miss Climpson.

'It is a little difficult, counting, till you're used to it. You must be dreadfully tired. We'll stop now and make some tea. Next time perhaps we could use the ouija. It doesn't take nearly so long to get the answers with that.'

Miss Climpson considered this. Certainly it would be less wearisome, but she was not sure of being able to manipulate it.

Miss Booth put the kettle on the fire and glanced at the clock.

'Dear me! it's nearly eleven. How the time has flown! I must

173

run up and see to my old dear. Would you like to read through the questions and answers? I don't suppose I shall be many minutes.'

Satisfactory so far, thought Miss Climpson. Confidence was well established. In a few days' time, she would be able to work her plan. But she had nearly tripped up over George. And it was stupid to have said 'Helen'. Nellie would have done for either – there was a Nellie in every school forty-five years ago. But, after all, it didn't much matter what you said – the other person was sure to help you out of it. How desperately her legs and arms were aching. Wearily she wondered if she had missed the last bus.

'I'm afraid you have,' said Miss Booth, when the question was put to her on her return. 'But we'll ring up a taxi. At my expense, of course, dear. I insist, as you were so good in coming all this way, entirely to please me. Don't you think the communications are too marvellous? Harry would never come before – poor Harry! I'm afraid I was very unkind to him. He married, but you see he has never forgotten me. He lived at Coventry, and we used to have a joke about it – that's what he meant by saying that. I wonder which Alice and Mabel that was. There was an Alice Gibbons and an Alice Roach – both such nice girls; I think Mabel must be Mabel Herridge. She married and went out to India years and years ago. I can't remember her married name, and I've never heard from her since, but she must have passed to the other side. Pongo is a new control. We must ask him who he is. Mrs Craig's control is Fedora – she was a slave-girl at the Court of Poppaea.'

'Really!' said Miss Climpson.

'She told us her story one night. So romantic. She was thrown to the lions because she was a Christian and refused to have anything to do with Nero.'

'How very interesting.'

'Yes, isn't it? But she doesn't speak very good English, and it's sometimes rather hard to understand her. And she sometimes lets the tiresome ones in. Pongo was very quick at getting rid of George Washington. You will come again, won't you? Tomorrow night?'

'Certainly, if you like.'

'Yes, please, do. And next time you must ask for a message for yourself.'

'I will indeed,' said Miss Climpson. 'It has all been *such* a revelation – quite *wonderful*. I never *dreamed* that I had such a gift.'

And that was true, also.

Chapter XVIII

IT was, of course, useless for Miss Climpson to try to conceal from the boarding-house ladies where she had been and what she had been doing. Her return at midnight in a taxi had already aroused the liveliest curiosity, and she told the truth to avoid being accused of worse dissipations.

'My dear Miss Climpson,' said Mrs Pegler, 'you will not, I trust, think me interfering, but I must caution you against having anything to do with Mrs Craig or her friends. I have no doubt Miss Booth is an excellent woman, but I do not like the company she keeps. Nor do I approve of spiritualism. It is a prying into matters which we are not intended to know about, and may lead to very undesirable results. If you were a married woman, I could explain myself more clearly, but you may take it from me that these indulgences may have serious effects upon the character in more ways than one.'

'Oh, Mrs Pegler,' said Miss Etheredge, 'I don't think you should say that. One of the most beautiful characters I know – a woman whom it is a privilege to call one's friend – is a spiritualist, and she is a real saint in her life and influence.'

'Very likely, Miss Etheredge,' replied Mrs Pegler, drawing her stout figure to its most impressive uprightness, 'but that is not the point. I do not say that a spiritualist *may* not live a good life, but I *do* say that the majority of them are most unsatisfactory people, and far from truthful.'

'I have happened to meet with a number of so-called mediums in the course of my life,' agreed Miss Tweall, acidly, 'and all of them, without *any* exception, were people I would not have trusted any further than I could see them – if as far.'

'That is very true of a great many of them,' said Miss Climpson, 'and I am sure *nobody* could have better opportunities of

176

judging than *myself*. But I think and hope that some of them are at least *sincere* if *mistaken* in their claims. What do *you* think, Mrs Liffey?' she added, turning to the proprietress of the establishment.

'We-ll,' said Miss Liffey – obliged, in her official capacity, to agree as far as possible with all parties – 'I must say, from what I have read, and that is not a great deal, for I have little time for reading, I think there is a certain amount of evidence to show that, in certain cases and under strictly safeguarded conditions, there is possibly some foundation of truth beneath the spiritualists' claims. Not that I should care to have anything to do with it personally; as Mrs Pegler says, I do not as a rule care very much for the sort of people who go in for it, though doubtless there are many exceptions. I think perhaps that the subject should be left to properly qualified investigators.'

'There I agree with you,' said Mrs Pegler. 'No words can express the disgust I feel at the intrusion of women like this Mrs Craig into realms that should be sacred to us all. Imagine, Miss Climpson, that that woman – whom I do not know and have no intention of knowing – actually had the impertinence once to write to me and say that she had received a message at one of her *séances*, as she calls them, purporting to come from my dear husband. I cannot tell you what I felt. To have the General's name actually brought up, in public, in connection with such wicked nonsense! And of course it was the purest invention, for the General was the *last* man to have anything to do with goings-on. "Pernicious poppycock," he used to call it in his bluff military way. And when it came to telling me, his widow, that he had come to Mrs Craig's house and played the accordion and asked for special prayers to deliver him from a place of punishment, I could only look on it as a calculated insult. The General was a regular church-goer and entirely opposed to prayers for the dead or anything popish; and as to being in any undesirable place, he was the best of men, even if he was a little abrupt at times. As for accordions, I hope, wherever he is, he has something better to do with his time.'

'A most shameful business,' said Miss Tweall.

'Who is this Mrs Craig?' asked Miss Climpson.

'Nobody knows,' said Mrs Pegler, ominously.

'She is said to be a doctor's widow,' said Mrs Liffey.

'It's my opinion,' said Miss Tweall, 'that she is no better than she should be.'

'A woman of her age,' said Mrs Pegler, 'with henna'd hair and earrings a foot long –'

'And going about in those extraordinary clothes,' said Miss Tweall.

'And having such very odd people to stay with her,' said Mrs Pegler. 'You remember that black man, Mrs Liffey, who wore a green turban and used to say his prayers in the front garden, till the police interfered.'

'What I should like to know,' said Miss Tweall, 'is where she gets her money from.'

'If you ask me, my dear, the woman's on the make. Heaven knows what she persuades people to do in these spiritualistic meetings.'

'But what brought her to Windle?' asked Miss Climpson. 'I should have thought London, or some big town, would have been a better place for her if she is the kind of person you describe.'

'I shouldn't be surprised if she was in hiding,' said Miss Tweall, darkly. 'There is such a thing as making a place too hot to hold you.'

'Without altogether subscribing to your wholesale condemnation,' said Miss Climpson, 'I must agree that physical research can be *very dangerous indeed* in the *wrong hands*, and, from what Miss Booth tells me, I do doubt very *much* whether Mrs Craig is a suitable guide for the inexperienced. Indeed, I quite felt it my *duty* to put Miss Booth on her guard, and that is what I am endeavouring to do. But, as you know, one has to do that kind of thing *very* tactfully – otherwise one may merely, so to speak, put the person's back up. The first step is to gain her *confidence*, and then, little by little, one may be able to induce a more wholesome frame of mind.'

'That's *so* true,' said Miss Etheredge, eagerly, her pale blue eyes lighting with something that was almost animation. 'I very nearly fell under the influence of a dreadful, fraudulent person myself, till my dear friend showed me a better way.'

'Maybe,' said Mrs Pegler, 'but in my opinion the whole thing is best left alone.'

Undeterred by this excellent advice, Miss Climpson kept her

appointment. After a spirited exhibition of table-rocking, Pongo consented to communicate by means of the ouija board, though at first he was rather awkward with it. He attributed this, however, to the fact that he had never learned to write while on earth. Asked who he was, he explained that he was an Italian acrobat of the Renaissance period, and that his full name was Pongocelli. He had lived a sadly irregular life, but had redeemed himself by heroically refusing to abandon a sick child during the time of the Great Plague in Florence. He had caught the plague and died of it, and was now working out the period of probation for his sins by serving as guide and interpreter to other spirits. It was a touching story, and Miss Climpson was rather proud of it.

George Washington was rather intrusive, and the *séance* also suffered from a number of mysterious interruptions from what Pongo described as a 'jealous influence'. Nevertheless, 'Harry' reappeared and delivered some consolatory messages, and there were further communications from Mabel Herridge, who gave a vivid description of her life in India. On the whole, and taking the difficulties into account, a successful evening.

On Sunday there was no *séance*, owing to the revolt of the medium's conscience. Miss Climpson felt that she could not really bring herself to do it. She went to church instead, and listened to the Christmas message with a distracted mind.

On Monday, however, the two inquirers again took their seats about the bamboo table, and the following is the report of the *séance*, as noted down by Miss Booth:

7.30 p.m.

On this occasion proceedings were begun at once with the ouija board; after a few minutes, a loud succession of raps announced the presence of a control.

Question: Good evening. Who is that?
Answer: Pongo here. Good evening. Heaven bless you.
Q. We are very glad to have you with us, Pongo.
A. Good – very good. Here we are again!
Q. Is that you, Harry?
A. Yes, only to give my love. Such a crowd.

Q. The more the better. We are glad to meet all our friends. What can we do for you?

A. Attend. Obey the spirits.

Q. We will do all we can, if you will tell us what to do.

A. Boil your heads!

Q. Go away, George, we don't want you.

A. Get off the line, silly.

Q. Pongo, can't you send him away?
(Here the pencil drew the sketch of an ugly face.)

Q. Is that your portrait?

A. That's me. G. W. Ha, ha!
(The pencil zigzagged violently and drove the board right over the edge of the table. When it was replaced it started to write in the hand we associate with Pongo.)

A. I have sent him away. Very noisy tonight. F. jealous and sends him to disturb us. Never mind. Pongo more powerful.

Q. Who do you say is jealous?

A. Never mind. Bad person. *Maladetta.*

Q. Is Harry still there?

A. No. Other business. There is a spirit here who wishes your help.

Q. Who is it?

A. Very hard. Wait.
(The pencil made a series of wide loops.)

Q. What letter is that?

A. Silly! don't be impatient. There is difficulty. I will try again.
(The pencil scribbled for a few minutes and then wrote a large C.)

Q. We have got the letter C. Is that right?

A. C-C-C –

Q. We have got C.

A. C-R-E –
(Here there was another violent interruption.)

A. (in Pongo's writing): She is trying, but there is much opposition. Think helpful thoughts.

Q. Would you like us to sing a hymn?

A. (Pongo again, very angry): Stupid! Be quiet! (Here the writing changed again.) M-O –

Q. Is that part of the same word?

A. R-N-A.

Q. Do you mean Cremorna?

A. (in the new writing): Cremorna, Cremorna. Through! Glad, glad, glad!

At this point, Miss Booth turned to Miss Climpson and said in a puzzled voice:

'This is very strange. Cremorna was Mrs Wrayburn's stage name. I do hope – surely she can't have passed away suddenly. She was perfectly comfortable when I left her. Had I better go and see?'

'Perhaps it's another Cremorna?' suggested Miss Climpson.

'But it's such an unusual name.'

'Why not ask who it is?'

Q. Cremorna – what is your second name?

A. (the pencil writing very fast): Rosegarden – easier now.

Q. I don't understand you.

A. Rose – Rose – Rose – silly!

Q. Oh! (My dear, she's mixing up the two names.) Do you mean Cremorna Garden?

A. Yes.

Q. Rosanna Wrayburn?

A. Yes.

Q. Have you passed over?

A. Not yet. In exile.

Q. Are you still in the body?

A. Neither in the body nor out of the body. Waiting. (*Pongo interposing*) When what you call the mind is departed, the spirit waits in exile for the Great Change. Why can't you understand? Make haste. Great difficulties.

Q. We are so sorry. Are you in trouble about something?

A. Great trouble.

Q. I hope it isn't anything in Dr Brown's treatment, or mine –

A. (*Pongo*) Do not be so foolish. (*Cremorna*) My will.

Q. Do you want to alter your will?

A. No.

Miss Climpson. That is fortunate, because I don't think it would be legal. What do you want us to do about it, dear Mrs Wrayburn?

181

A. Send it to Norman.

Q. To Norman Urquhart?

A. Yes. He knows.

Q. He knows what is to be done with it?

A. He wants it.

Q. Very well. Can you tell us where to find it?

A. I have forgotten. Search.

Q. Is it in the house?

A. I tell you I have forgotten. Deep waters. No safety. Failing, failing . . .

(Here the writing became very faint and irregular.)

Q. Try to remember.

A. In the B – B – B – (a confusion and the pencil staggering wildly) No good. (Suddenly, in a different hand and very vigorously) Get off the line, get off the line, get off the line.

Q. Who was that?

A. (*Pongo*) She has gone. The bad influence back. Ha, Ha! Get off! Finished now. (The pencil ran right out of the medium's control, and, on being replaced on the table, refused to answer any further questions.)

'How dreadfully vexatious!' exclaimed Miss Booth.

'I suppose you have no idea where the will is?'

'Not the least. "In the B – " she said. Now, what could that be?'

'In the Bank, perhaps,' suggested Miss Climpson.

'It might be. If so, of course, Mr Urquhart would be the only person who could get it out.'

'Then why hasn't he? She said he wanted it.'

'Of course. Then it must be somewhere in the house. What could B stand for?'

'Box, Bag, Bureau – ?'

'Bed? It might be almost anything.'

'What a pity she couldn't finish the message. Shall we try again! Or shall we look in all the likely places?'

'Let's look first, and then, if we can't find it, we can try again.'

'That's a good idea. There are some keys in one of the bureau drawers that belong to her boxes and things.'

'Why not try them?' said Miss Climpson, boldly.

'We will. You'll come and help, won't you?'

'If you think it advisable. I'm a stranger, you know.'

'The message came to you as much as to me. I'd rather you came with me. You might be able to suggest places.'

Miss Climpson made no further ado, and then went upstairs. It was a queer business – practically robbing a helpless woman in the interests of someone she had never seen. Queer. But the motive must be a good one, if it was Lord Peter's.

At the top of the beautiful staircase with its ample curve was a long, wide corridor, the walls hung thickly from floor to ceiling with portraits, sketches, framed autograph letters, programmes, and all the reminiscent bric-à-brac of the green-room.

'All her life is here and in these two rooms,' said the nurse. 'If this collection was to be sold, it would fetch a lot of money. I suppose it will be, some day.'

'Whom does the money go to, do you know?'

'Well, I've always thought it would be to Mr Norman Urquhart – he's a relation of hers; about the only one, I believe. But I've never been told anything about it.'

She pushed open a tall door, graceful with curved panels and classical architrave, and turned on the light.

It was a stately great room, with three tall windows and a ceiling gracefully moulded with garlands of flowers and flambeaux. The purity of its lines was, however, defaced and insulted by a hideous rose-trellised wallpaper, and heavy plush curtains of a hot crimson with thick gold fringes and ropes, like the drop-curtain of a Victorian play-house. Every foot of space was crammed thick with furniture – buhl cabinets incongruously jostling mahogany chiffoniers; whatnot tables strewn with ornaments cuddling the bases of heavy German marbles and bronzes; lacquer screens, Sheraton bureaux, Chinese vases, alabaster lamps, chairs, ottomans of every shape, colour, and period, clustered thick as plants wrestling for existence in a tropical jungle. It was the room of a woman without taste or moderation, who refused nothing and surrendered nothing, to whom the fact of possession had become the one steadfast reality in a world of loss and change.

'It may be in here or in the bedroom,' said Miss Booth. 'I'll get her keys.'

183

She opened a door on the right. Miss Climpson, endlessly inquisitive, tiptoed in after her.

The bedroom was even more of a nightmare than the sitting-room. A small electric reading-lamp burned dimly by the bed, huge and gilded, with hangings of rose brocade cascading in long folds from a tester supported by fat golden cupids. Outside the narrow circle of light loomed monstrous wardrobes, more cabinets, tall chests of drawers. The dressing-table, frilled and flounced, held a wide, threefold mirror, and a monstrous cheval-glass in the centre of the room darkly reflected the towering and shadowy outlines of the furniture.

Miss Booth opened the middle door of the largest wardrobe. It swung back with a creak, letting out a great gush of frangipani. Nothing, evidently, had been altered in this room since silence and paralysis had struck the owner down.

Miss Climpson stepped softly up to the bed. Instinct made her move cautiously as a cat, though it was evident that nothing would ever startle or surprise its occupant.

An old, old face, so tiny in the vast expanse of sheet and pillow that it might have been a doll, stared up at her with unblinking, unseeing eyes. It was covered with fine surface-wrinkles, like a hand sodden with soapy water, but all the great lines carved by experience had been smoothed out with the relaxing of the helpless muscles. It was both puffed and crumpled. It reminded Miss Climpson of a child's pink balloon, from which nearly all the air has leaked away. The escaping breath puffed through the lax lips in little blowing, snorting sounds and added to the resemblance. From under the frilled night-cap straggled a few lank wisps of whitened hair.

'Funny, isn't it,' said Miss Booth, 'to think that with her lying like that, her spirit can communicate with us.'

Miss Climpson was overcome by a sense of sacrilege. It was only by a great effort that she prevented herself from confessing the truth. She had pulled the garter with the soap-box above her knee for safety, and the elastic was cutting painfully into the muscles of her leg – a kind of reminder of her iniquities.

But Miss Booth had already turned away, and was pulling open the drawers of one of the bureaux.

Two hours passed, and they were still searching. The letter B opened up a particularly wide field of search. Miss Climpson had chosen it on that account, and her foresight was rewarded. By a little ingenuity, that useful letter could be twisted to fit practically any hiding-place in the house. The things that were neither bureaux, beds, bags, boxes, baskets, nor bibelot-tables could usually be described as big, black, brown, or buhl, at a pinch, as being bedroom or boudoir furniture, and since every shelf, drawer, and pigeon-hole in every object was crammed full of newspaper-cuttings, letters, and assorted souvenirs, the searchers soon found their heads, legs, and backs aching with effort.

'I'd no idea,' said Miss Booth, 'that there could be so many possible places.'

Miss Climpson, sitting on the floor, with her black hair uncoiling itself and her decent black petticoats rucked up nearly to the soap-box, agreed wearily.

'It's dreadfully exhausting, isn't it?' said Miss Booth. 'Wouldn't you like to stop? I can go on searching tomorrow by myself. It's a shame to tire you out in this way.'

Miss Climpson turned this over in her mind. If the will were found in her absence and sent to Norman Urquhart, would Miss Murchison be able to get hold of it before it was again hidden away or destroyed? She wondered.

Hidden away, not destroyed. The mere fact that the will had been sent to him by Miss Booth would prevent the solicitor from making away with it, for there would be a witness to its existence. But he might successfully conceal it for a considerable time – and time was of the essence of the adventure.

'Oh, I'm not a scrap tired,' she said brightly, sitting up on her heels and restoring her coiffure to something more like its usual neatness. She had a black note-book in her hand, taken from a drawer in one of the Japanese cabinets, and was turning its pages mechanically. A line of figures caught her eye: 12, 18, 4, 0, 9, 3, 15, and she wondered vaguely what they referred to.

'We've looked through everything here,' said Miss Booth. 'I don't believe we've missed anything – unless, of course, there is a secret drawer somewhere.'

'Could it be in a book, do you think?'

'A book! Why, of course it might. How silly of us not to think of that! In detective stories, wills are always hidden in books.'

'More often than in real life,' thought Miss Climpson, but she got up and dusted herself and said cheerfully:

'So they are. Are there many books in the house?'

'Thousands,' said Miss Booth. 'Downstairs in the library.'

'I shouldn't have expected Mrs Wrayburn to be a great reader, somehow.'

'Oh, I don't think she was. The books were bought with the house, so Mr Urquhart told me. They're nearly all old ones, you know – big things bound in leather. Dreadfully dull. I've never found a thing to read there. But they're just the sort of books to hide wills in.'

They emerged into the corridor.

'By the way,' said Miss Climpson, 'won't the servants think it funny of us to be wandering about the place so late?'

'They all sleep in the other wing. Beside, they know that I sometimes have visitors. Mrs Craig has often been here as late as this when we have had interesting sittings. There's a spare bedroom where I can put people up when I want to.'

Miss Climpson made no more objections, and they went downstairs and along the hall into the library. It was big, and books filled the walls and bays in serried ranks – a heart-breaking sight.

'Of course,' said Miss Booth, 'if the communication hadn't insisted on something beginning with B –'

'Well?'

'Well – I should have expected any papers to be in the safe down here.'

Miss Climpson groaned in spirit. The obvious place, naturally! If only her misplaced ingenuity – well! one must make the best of it.

'Why not look?' she suggested. 'The letter B may have been referring to something quite different. Or it may have been an interruption from George Washington. It would be quite like him to use words beginning with a B, don't you think?'

'But if it was in the safe, Mr Urquhart would know about it.'

Miss Climpson began to feel that she had let her invention play about too freely.

'It wouldn't do any harm to make sure,' she suggested.

'But I don't know the combination,' said Miss Booth. 'Mr Urquhart does, of course. We could write and ask him.'

An inspiration came to Miss Climpson.

'I believe I know it,' she exclaimed. 'There was a row of seven figures in that black note-book I was looking at just now, and it passed through my mind that they must be a memorandum of something.'

'Black Book!' cried Miss Booth. 'Why, there you are! How could we have been so silly! Of course Mrs Wrayburn was trying to tell us where to find the combination!'

Miss Climpson again blessed the all-round utility of the letter B.

'I'll run up and fetch it,' she cried.

When she came down again, Miss Booth was standing before a section of the bookshelves, which had swung out from the wall, disclosing the green door of a built-in safe. With trembling hands, Miss Climpson touched the milled knob and turned it.

The first attempt was unsuccessful, owing to the fact that the note did not make it clear which way the knob should be turned first, but at the second attempt the pointer swung over on the seventh figure with a satisfying click.

Miss Booth seized the handle, and the heavy door moved and stood open.

A bundle of papers lay inside. On the top, staring them in the face, was a long, sealed envelope. Miss Climpson pounced upon it.

'Will of Rosanna Wrayburn
5 June 1920.'

'Well, isn't that marvellous?' cried Miss Booth. On the whole, Miss Climpson agreed with her.

Chapter XIX

MISS CLIMPSON stayed the night in the spare bedroom.

'The best thing,' she said, 'will be for you to write a little letter to Mr Urquhart, explaining about the *séance,* and saying that you thought it best and safest to send the will on to him.'

'He will be very much surprised,' said Miss Booth. 'I wonder what he will say. Lawyers don't believe in spirit communications as a rule. And he'll think it rather funny that we should have managed to open the safe.'

'Well, but the spirit led us directly to the combination, didn't it? He could hardly expect you to ignore a message like that, could he? The proof of your good faith is that you are sending the will straight to him. And it would be as well, don't you think, if you asked him to come up and check the other contents of the safe and have the combination altered?'

'Wouldn't it be better if I kept the will and asked him to come for it?'

'But perhaps he requires it urgently.'

'Then why hasn't he been to fetch it?'

Miss Climpson noted with some irritation that, where spiritualistic messages were not concerned, Miss Booth showed signs of developing an independent judgement.

'Perhaps he doesn't know yet that he wants it. Perhaps the spirits foresaw an urgent need that will only arise tomorrow.'

'Oh, yes, that's quite likely. If only people would avail themselves more fully of the marvellous guidance given to them, so much might be foreseen and provided for! Well, I think you are right. We will find a big envelope to fit it, and I will write a letter and we will send it by the first post tomorrow.'

'It had better be registered,' said Miss Climpson. 'If you will entrust it to me, I will take it down to the post office first thing.'

'Will you? That will be a great relief to my mind. Well now, I'm sure you're as tired as I am, so I'll put on a kettle for the hot-water bottles and we'll turn in. Will you make yourself comfy in my sitting-room? I've only got to put the sheets on your bed. What? No, indeed, I can do it in a moment; *please* don't bother. I'm so used to making beds.'

'Then I'll see to the kettles,' said Miss Climpson. 'I simply *must* make myself useful.'

'Very well. It won't take long. The water is quite hot in the kitchen boiler.'

Left alone in the kitchen, with a kettle bumping and singing on its way to boiling-point, Miss Climpson wasted no time. She tiptoed quickly out again and stood with ear cocked at the foot of the stairs, listening to the nurse's footsteps as they pattered into the distance. Then she slipped into the little sitting-room, took up the will in its sealed envelope, and a long thin paper-knife which she had already marked down as a useful weapon, and hastened back to the kitchen.

It is astonishing how long a kettle which seems to be on the verge of boiling will take before the looked-for jet of steady steam emerges from its spout. Delusive little puffs and deceptive pauses in the song tantalise the watcher interminably. It seemed to Miss Climpson that there would have been time to make twenty beds before the kettle boiled that evening. But even a watched pot cannot absorb heat for ever. After what appeared to be an hour, but was actually about seven minutes, Miss Climpson, guilty and furtive, was holding the flap of the envelope before the scalding steam.

'I mustn't hurry,' said Miss Climpson, 'oh, blessed saints, I mustn't hurry, or I shall tear it.'

She slipped the paper-knife under the flap; it lifted; it opened cleanly, just as Miss Booth's step resounded in the passage.

Miss Climpson adroitly dropped the paper-knife behind the stove and thrust the envelope, with the flap doubled back to prevent it from re-sticking itself, behind a dish-cover on the wall.

'The water's ready!' she cried blithely. 'Where are the bottles?'

It is a tribute to her nerve that she filled them with a steady hand. Miss Booth thanked her, and departed upstairs, a bottle in each hand.

Miss Climpson pulled the will from its hiding-place, drew it from its envelope, and glanced swiftly through it.

It was not a long document, and, in spite of the legal phraseology, its purport was easily gathered. Within three minutes she had replaced it, moistened the gum and stuck the flap down again. She put it in her petticoat-pocket – for her garments were of a useful and old-fashioned kind – and went to hunt in the pantry. When Miss Booth returned, she was making tea peacefully.

'I thought it would refresh us after our labours,' she remarked.

'A very good idea,' said Miss Booth; 'in fact, I was just going to suggest it.'

Miss Climpson carried the tea-pot to the sitting-room, leaving Miss Booth to follow with the cups, milk and sugar on a tray. With the tea-pot on the hob and the will once more lying innocently on the table, she smiled and breathed deeply. Her mission was accomplished.

* * *

Letter from Miss Climpson to
Lord Peter Wimsey

Tuesday, Jan. 7, 1930

'MY DEAR LORD PETER, As my *telegram* this morning will have informed you, I have SUCCEEDED!! Though what excuse I can find in my *conscience* for the *methods* I have used, I *don't* KNOW! but I believe the Church takes into account the necessity of *deception* in certain *professions*, such as that of a *police-detective* or a SPY in time of WAR-FARE, and I *trust that* my *subterfuges* may be allowed to come under that *category*. However, you will not want to hear about my *religious scruples*! So I will hasten to let you know *what* I have DISCOVERED! !

'In my last letter I explained the *plan* I had in mind, so you will know what to do about the *Will itself*, which was duly *despatched* by *Registered Post* this morning under cover to *Mr Norman Urquhart*. How surprised he will be to get it! ! ! Miss Booth wrote an excellent *covering letter*, which I *saw* before it went, which explains the circumstances and *mentions* NO NAMES! ! I have wired Miss Murchison to *expect* the package, and I hope that when it comes she will contrive to be *present* at the opening, so as to constitute *yet another* WITNESS to its existence. In any case, I should not think he would *venture* to *tamper* with it. Perhaps Miss Murchison may be able to INVESTIGATE it in detail, which I had not *time* to do (it was all *most* adventurous! and I am looking forward to *telling* you ALL ABOUT IT when I come back), but in case she is *not* able to do so, I will give you the *rough outline*.

'The property consists of *real estate* (the house and grounds) and a *personalty* (am I not *good* at legal terms? ?) which I am not able to calculate *exactly*. But the gist of it all is this:

'The *real estate* is left to *Philip Boyes*, absolutely.

'*Fifty thousand pounds* is left to *Philip Boyes* also, in *cash*,

'The remainder (is not this called the residue?) is left to NORMAN URQUHART, who is appointed sole executor.

'There are a few *small legacies* to State Charities, of which I did not manage to memorise any *particulars*.

'There is a special paragraph, explaining that the greater part of the property is left to *Philip Boyes* in token that the testatrix FORGIVES the ill-treatment meted out to her by *his family*, for which he was *not responsible*.

'The date of the Will is 5 June 1920, and the *witnesses* are *Eva Gubbins*, housekeeper, and *John Briggs*, gardener.

'I hope, dear Lord Peter, that this information will be enough for your purpose. I had hoped that even *after* Miss Booth had enclosed the Will in a *covering envelope* I might be able to take it out and *peruse* it at leisure, but unfortunately she *sealed* it for greater security with Mrs Wrayburn's *private seal*, which I had not sufficient *dexterity* to *remove and replace*, though I understand it is possible to *do so* with a *hot knife*.

'You will *understand* that I cannot leave Windle *just yet* – it would look so odd to do so immediately after this occurrence. Besides, I am hoping, in a further series of "sittings", to *warn* Miss Booth against Mrs Craig and her "control"

Fedora, as I am *quite sure* that this person is *quite* as great a charlatan as I AM ! ! ! – and without my *altruistic* motives ! ! So you will not be surprised if I am away from Town for, say, *another week*! I am a little worried about the *extra expense* of this, but if you do not think it *justified* for the sake of safety, *let me know* – and I will alter my arrangements accordingly

'Wishing you *all success,* dear Lord Peter,

Most sincerely yours
'KATHARINE A. CLIMPSON.

'P.S. – I managed to do the "job" *very nearly* within the stipulated week, you see. I am *so sorry* it was not *quite* finished yesterday, but I was so *terrified* of *spoiling the* WHOLE THING by *rushing it*! !'

* * *

'Bunter,' said Lord Peter, looking up from this letter, 'I *knew* there was something fishy about that will.'

'Yes, my lord.'

'There is something about wills which brings out the worst side of human nature. People who under ordinary circumstances are perfectly upright and amiable, go as curly as corkscrews and foam at the mouth whenever they hear the words "I devise and bequeath". That reminds me, a spot of champagne in a silver tankard is no bad thing to celebrate on. Get up a bottle of the Pommery and tell Chief Inspector Parker I should be glad of a word with him. And bring me those notes of Mr Arbuthnot's. And oh, Bunter!'

'My lord?'

'Get Mr Crofts on the phone and give him my compliments, and say I have found the criminal and the motive and hope presently to produce proof of the way the crime was done, if he will see that the case is put off for a week or so.'

'Very good, my lord.'

'All the same, Bunter, I really don't know how it *was* done.'

'That will undoubtedly suggest itself before long, my lord.'

'Oh, yes,' said Wimsey, airily. 'Of course. Of course. I'm not worrying about a trifle like that.'

Chapter XX

'T'CH! t'ch!' said Mr Pond, clicking his tongue against his denture.

Miss Murchison looked up from her typewriter.

'Is anything the matter, Mr Pond?'

'No, nothing,' said the head clerk, testily. 'A foolish letter from a foolish member of your sex, Miss Murchison.'

'That's nothing new.'

Mr Pond frowned, conceiving the tone of his subordinate's voice to be impertinent. He picked up the letter and its enclosure and took them into the inner office.

Miss Murchison nipped swiftly across to his desk and glanced at the registered envelope which lay upon it, open. The postmark was 'Windle'.

'That's luck,' said Miss Murchison, to herself. 'Mr Pond is a better witness than I should be. I'm glad he opened it.'

She regained her place. In a few minutes Mr Pond emerged, smiling slightly.

Five minutes later, Miss Murchison who had been frowning over her shorthand note-book, rose up and came over to him.

'Can you read shorthand, Mr Pond?'

'No,' said the head clerk. 'In my day it was not considered necessary.'

'I can't make out this outline,' said Miss Murchison. 'It looks like "give consent to", but it may be only "give consideration to" – there's a difference, isn't there?'

'There certainly is,' said Mr Pond, dryly.

'P'raps I'd better not risk it,' said Miss Murchison. 'It's got to go off this morning. I'd better ask him.'

Mr Pond snorted – not for the first time – over the carelessness of the female typist.

Miss Murchison walked briskly across the room and opened the inner door without knocking – an informality which left Mr Pond groaning again.

Mr Urquhart was standing up with his back to the door, doing something or other at the mantelpiece. He turned round sharply, with an exclamation of annoyance.

'I have told you before, Miss Murchison, that I like you to knock before entering.'

'I am very sorry; I forgot.'

'Don't let it happen again. What is it?'

He did not return to his desk, but stood leaning against the mantelshelf. His sleek head, outlined against the drab-painted panelling, was a little thrown back, as though – Miss Murchison thought – he were protecting or defying somebody.

'I could not quite make out my shorthand note of your letter to Tewke & Peabody,' said Miss Murchison, 'and I thought it better to come and ask you.'

'I wish,' said Mr Urquhart, fixing a stern eye upon her, 'that you would take your notes clearly at the time. If I am going too fast for you, you should tell me so. It would save trouble in the end – wouldn't it?'

Miss Murchison was reminded of a little set of rules which Lord Peter Wimsey – half in jest and half in earnest – had once prepared for the guidance of 'The Cattery'. Of Rule Seven in particular, which ran: 'Always distrust the man who looks you straight in the eyes. He wants to prevent you from seeing something. Look for it.'

She shifted her eyes under her employer's gaze.

'I'm very sorry, Mr Urquhart. I won't let it occur again,' she muttered. There was a curious dark line at the edge of the panelling just behind the solicitor's head, as though the panel did not quite fit its frame. She had never noticed it before.

'Well, now, what is the trouble?'

Miss Murchison asked her question, got her answer, and retired. As she went, she cast a glance over the desk. The will was not there.

She went back and finished her letters. When she took them in to be signed, she seized the opportunity to look at the panelling again. There was no dark line to be seen.

Miss Murchison left the office promptly at half-past four. She

194

had a feeling that it would be unwise to linger about the premises. She walked briskly away through Hand Court, turned to the right along Holborn, dived to the right again through Featherstone Buildings, made a detour through Red Lion Street, and debouched into Red Lion Square. Within five minutes she was at her old walk round the square, and up Princeton Street. Presently, from a safe distance, she saw Mr Pond come out, thin, stiff, and stooping, and walk down Bedford Row towards Chancery Lane Station. Before very long Mr Urquhart followed. He stood a moment on the threshold, glancing to left and right, then came straight across the street towards her. For a moment she thought he had seen her, and she dived hurriedly behind a van that was standing at the kerb. Under its shelter, she withdrew to the corner of the street, where there is a butcher's shop, and scanned a windowful of New Zealand lamb and chilled beef. Mr Urquhart came nearer. His steps grew louder – then paused. Miss Murchison glued her eyes on a round of meat marked 4½ lb., 3s. 4d. A voice said: 'Good evening, Miss Murchison. Choosing your supper chop?'

'Oh! good evening, Mr Urquhart. Yes – I was just wishing that Providence had seen fit to provide more joints suitable for single people.'

'Yes – one gets tired of beef and mutton.'

'And pork is apt to be indigestible.'

'Just so. Well, you should cease to be single, Miss Murchison.'

Miss Murchison giggled.

'But this is so sudden, Mr Urquhart.'

Mr Urquhart flushed under his curious freckled skin.

'Goodnight,' he said abruptly, and with extreme coldness.

Miss Murchison laughed to herself as he strode off.

'Thought that would settle him. It's a great mistake to be familiar with your subordinates. They take advantage of you.'

She watched him out of sight on the far side of the square, then returned along Princeton Street, crossed Bedford Row, and re-entered the office building. The charwoman was just coming downstairs.

'Well, Mrs Hodges, it's me again! Do you mind letting me in? I've lost a pattern of silk. I think I must have left it in my desk, or dropped it on the floor. Have you come across it?'

'No, miss, I ain't done your office yet.'

'Then I'll have a hunt round for it. I want to get up to Bourne's before half-past six. It's such a nuisance.'

'Yes, miss, and such a crowd always with the buses and things. Here you are, miss.'

She opened the door, and Miss Murchison darted in.

'Shall I 'elp you look for it, miss?'

'No, thank you, Mrs Hodges, please don't bother. I don't expect it's far off.'

Mrs Hodges took up a pail and went to fill it at a tap in the backyard. As soon as her heavy steps had ascended again to the first floor, Miss Murchison made for the inner office.

'I must and will see what's behind that panelling.'

The houses in Bedford Row are Hogarthian in type, tall, symmetrical, with the glamour of better days upon them. The panels in Mr Urquhart's room, though defaced by many coats of paint, were handsomely designed, and over the mantelpiece ran a festoon of flowers and fruit, rather florid for the period, with a ribbon and basket in the centre. If the panel was controlled by a concealed spring, the boss that moved it was probably to be found among this decorative work. Pulling a chair to the fireplace, Miss Murchison ran her fingers quickly over the festoon, pushing and pressing with both hands, while keeping her ear cocked for intruders.

This kind of investigation is easy for experts, but Miss Murchison's knowledge of secret hiding-places was only culled from sensational literature; she could not find the trick of the thing. After nearly a quarter of an hour, she began to despair.

Thump – thump – thump – Mrs Hodges was coming downstairs.

Miss Murchison sprang away from the panelling so hastily that the chair slipped, and she had to thrust hard at the wall to save herself. She jumped down, restored the chair to its place, glanced up – and saw the panel standing wide open.

At first she thought it was a miracle, but soon realised that in slipping she had thrust sideways at the frame of the panel. A small square of woodwork had slipped away sideways, and exposed an inner panel with a keyhole in the middle.

She heard Mrs Hodges in the outer room, but she was too excited to bother about what Mrs Hodges might be thinking.

She pushed a heavy chair across the door, so that nobody could enter without noise and difficulty. In a moment Blindfold Bill's keys were in her hand – how fortunate that she had not returned them! How fortunate, too, that Mr Urquhart had relied on the secrecy of the panel, and had not thought it worth while to fit his cache with a patent lock!

A few moments' quick work with the keys, and the lock turned. She pulled the little door open.

Inside was a bundle of papers. Miss Murchison ran them over – at first quickly – then again, with a puzzled face. Receipts for securities – share certificates – Megatherium Trust – surely the names of those investments were familiar – where had she . . . ?

Suddenly Miss Murchison sat down, feeling quite faint, the bundle of papers in her hand.

She realised now what had happened to Mrs Wrayburn's money, which Norman Urquhart had been handling under that confiding Deed of Trust, and why the matter of the will was so important. Her head whirled. She picked up a sheet of paper from the desk and began jotting down in hurried shorthand the particulars of the various transactions of which these documents were the evidence.

Somebody bumped at the door.

'Are you in here, miss?'

'Just a moment, Mrs Hodges. I think I must have dropped it on the floor in here.'

She gave the big chair a sharp push, effectually closing the door.

She must hurry. Anyway, she had got down enough to convince Lord Peter that Mr Urquhart's affairs needed looking into. She put the papers back into the cupboard, in the exact place from which she had taken them. The will was there, too, she noticed, laid on one side by itself. She peered in. There was something else, tucked away at the back. She thrust her hand in and pulled the mysterious object out. It was a white paper packet, labelled with the name of a foreign chemist. The end had been opened and tucked in again. She pulled the paper apart, and saw that the packet contained about two ounces of a fine white powder.

Next to hidden treasure and mysterious documents, nothing is more full of sensational suggestion than a packet of anonymous white powder. Miss Murchison caught up another sheet of clean paper, tipped a thimbleful of the powder into it, replaced it at the back of the cupboard, and re-locked the door with the skeleton key. With trembling fingers she pushed the panel back into place, taking care to shut it completely, so as to show no betraying dark line.

She rolled the chair away from the door and cried out gaily: 'I've got it, Mrs Hodges!'

'There, now' said Mrs Hodges, appearing in the doorway.

'Just fancy!' said Mrs. Murchison. 'I was looking through my patterns when Mr Urquhart rang, and this one must have stuck to my frock and dropped on the floor in here.'

She held up a small piece of silk triumphantly. She had torn it from the lining of her bag in the course of the afternoon – a proof, if any were needed, of her devotion to her work, for the bag was a good one.

'Dearie me,' said Mrs Hodges. 'What a good thing you found it, wasn't it, miss?'

'I nearly didn't,' said Miss Murchison; 'it was right in this dark corner. Well, I must fly to get there before the shop shuts. Goodnight, Mrs Hodges.'

But long before the accommodating Messrs Bourne & Hollingsworth had closed their doors, Miss Murchison was ringing the second floor bell at 110A Piccadilly.

*　　*　　*

She found a council in progress. There was the Hon Freddy Arbuthnot, looking amiable; Chief Inspector Parker, looking worried; Lord Peter, looking somnolent; and Bunter, who having introduced her, retired to a position on the fringe of the assembly and hovered there looking correct.

'Have you brought us news, Miss Murchison? If so, you have come at the exact right moment to find the eagles gathered together. Mr Arbuthnot, Chief Inspector Parker, Miss Murchison. Now let's all sit down and be happy together. Have you had tea? or will you absorb a spot of something?'

Miss Murchison declined refreshment.

'H'm!' said Wimsey. 'The patient refuses food. Her eyes glitter wildly. The expression is anxious. The lips are parted.

The fingers fumble with the clasp of the bag. The symptoms point to an acute attack of communicativeness. Tell us the worst, Miss Murchison.'

Miss Murchison needed no urging. She told her adventures, and had the pleasure of holding her audience enthralled from the first word to the last. When she finally produced the screw of paper containing the white powder, the sentiments of the company expressed themselves in a round of applause, in which Bunter joined discreetly.

'Are you convinced, Charles?' asked Wimsey.

'I admit that I am heavily shaken,' said Parker. 'Of course, the powder must be analysed –'

'It shall, embodied caution,' said Wimsey. 'Bunter, make ready the rack and thumbscrew. Bunter has been taking lessons in Marsh's test, and performs it to admiration. You know all about it too, Charles, don't you?'

'Enough for a rough test.'

'Carry on then, my children. In the meanwhile, let us sum up our findings.'

Bunter went out and Parker, who had been making entries in a notebook, cleared his throat.

'Well,' he said, 'the matter stands, I take it, like this. You say that Miss Vane is innocent, and you undertake to prove this by bringing a convincing accusation against Norman Urquhart. So far, your evidence against him is almost entirely concerned with motive, bolstered up by proofs of intent to mislead inquiry. You say that your investigations have brought the case against Urquhart to a point at which the police can, and ought to, take it up, and I am inclined to agree with you. I warn you, however, that you still have to establish evidence as to means and opportunity.'

'I know that. Tell us a new one.'

'All right, as long as you know it. Very well. Now Philip Boyes and Norman Urquhart are the only surviving relations of Mrs Wrayburn, or Cremorna Garden, who is rich, and has money to leave. A number of years ago, Mrs Wrayburn put all her affairs into the hands of Urquhart's father, the only member of the family with whom she remained on friendly terms. On his father's death, Norman Urquhart took over those affairs himself, and in 1920, Mrs Wrayburn executed a Deed of Trust, giving him sole authority to handle her property. She also made a will, dividing her property unequally between her two great-nephews. Philip Boyes got all the real estate and £50,000, while Norman Urquhart took whatever was left and was also sole executor. Norman Urquhart, when questioned about this will, deliberately told you an untruth, saying that the bulk of the money was left to him, and even went so far as to produce a document purporting to be a draft of such a will. The pretended date of this draft is subsequent to that of the will discovered by Miss Climpson, but there is no doubt that the draft was drawn out by Urquhart, certainly within the last three years and probably within the last few days. Moreover, the fact that the actual will, though lying in a place accessible to Urquhart, was not destroyed by him, suggests that it was not, in fact, superseded by any subsequent testamentary disposition. By the way, Wimsey, why didn't he simply take the will and destroy it? As the sole surviving heir, he would then inherit without dispute.'

'Perhaps it didn't occur to him. Or there might even be other relatives surviving. How about that uncle in Australia?'

'True. At any rate, he didn't destroy it. In 1925 Mrs Wrayburn became completely paralysed and imbecile, so that there was no possibility of her ever inquiring into the disposition of her estate or making another will.

'About this time, as we know from Mr Arbuthnot, Urquhart took the dangerous step of plunging into speculation. He made mistakes, lost money, plunged more deeply to recover himself, and was involved to a large extent in the great crash of Megatherium Trust, Ltd. He certainly lost far more than he could possibly afford, and we now find, from Miss Murchison's discoveries — of which I must say that I should hate to have to take official notice — that he had been consistently abusing his position as trustee and employing Mrs Wrayburn's money for his private speculations. He deposited her holdings as security for large loans, and embarked the money thus raised in the Megatherium and other wild-cat schemes.

'As long as Mrs Wrayburn lived, he was fairly safe, for he only had to pay to her the sums necessary to keep up her house and establishment. In fact, all the household bills and so on were settled by him as her man of affairs under Power of Attorney, all salaries were paid by him, and, so long as he did this, it was nobody's business to ask what he had done with the capital. But as soon as Mrs Wrayburn died, he would have to account to the other heir, Philip Boyes, for the capital which he had misappropriated.

'Now in 1929, just about the time that Philip Boyes quarrelled with Miss Vane, Mrs Wrayburn had a serious attack of illness and very nearly died. The danger passed, but might recur at any moment. Almost immediately afterwards we find him becoming friendly with Philip Boyes and inviting him to stay at his house. While living with Urquhart, Boyes has three attacks of illness, attributed by his doctor to gastritis, but equally consistent with arsenical poisoning. In June 1929, Philip Boyes goes away to Wales and his health improves.

'While Philip Boyes is absent, Mrs Wrayburn has another alarming attack, and Urquhart hastens up to Windle, possibly with the idea of destroying the will in case the worst happens. It does not happen, and he comes back to London in time to receive Boyes on his return from Wales. That night, Boyes is taken ill with symptoms similar to those of the previous spring, but much more violent. After three days he dies.

'Urquhart is now perfectly safe. As residuary legatee, he will receive, at Mrs Wrayburn's death, all the money bequeathed to Philip Boyes. That is, he will not get it, because he has already taken it and lost it, but he will no longer be called upon to produce it and his fraudulent dealings will not be exposed.

'So far, the evidence as to motive is extremely cogent, and far more convincing than the evidence against Miss Vane.

'But here is your snag, Wimsey. When and how was the poison administered? We know that Miss Vane possessed arsenic and that she could easily have given it to him without witnesses. But Urquhart's only opportunity was at the dinner he shared with Boyes, and if anything in this case is certain, it is that the poison was not administered at that dinner. Everything which Boyes ate or drank was equally eaten and drunk by Urquhart and/or the servants, with the single exception of the Burgundy, which was preserved and analysed and found to be harmless.'

'I know,' said Wimsey, 'but that is what is so suspicious. Did you ever hear of a meal hedged round with such precautions? It's not natural, Charles. There's the sherry, poured out by the maid from the original bottle; the soup, fish and casseroled chicken – so impossible to poison in one portion without poisoning the whole – the omelette, so ostentatiously prepared at table by the hands of the victim – the wine, sealed up and marked – the remnants consumed in the kitchen – you would think the man had gone out of his way to construct a suspicion-proof meal. The wine is the final touch which makes the thing incredible. Do you tell me that at that earliest moment when everybody supposes the illness to be a natural one, and when the affectionate cousin ought to be overwhelmed with anxiety for the sick man, it is natural or believable that an innocent person's mind should fly to accusations of poisoning? If he was innocent himself, then he suspected something. If he did suspect, why didn't he tell the doctor and have the patient's secretions and so on analysed? Why should he ever have thought of protecting himself against accusation when no accusation had been made, unless he knew that an accusation would be well-founded? And then there's the business about the nurse.'

'Exactly. The nurse did have her suspicions.'

'If he knew about them, he ought to have taken steps to refute them in the proper way. But I don't think he did know about them. I was referring to what you told us today. The police have got in touch with the nurse again, Miss Williams, and she tells them that Norman Urquhart took special pains never to be left alone with the patient, and never to give him any food or medicine, even when she herself was present. Doesn't that argue a bad conscience?'

'You won't find any lawyer or jury to believe it, Peter.'

'Yes, but look here, doesn't it strike you as funny? Listen to this, Miss Murchison. One day the nurse was doing something or the other in the room, and she had got the medicine there on the mantelpiece. Something was said about it, and Boyes remarked, "Oh, don't bother, Nurse. Norman can give me my dope." Does Norman say, "Right-ho, old man!" as you or I would? No! He says, "No, I'll leave it to Nurse – I might make a mess of it." Pretty feeble, what?'

'Lots of people are nervous about looking after invalids,' said Miss Murchison.

'Yes, but most people can pour stuff out of a bottle into a

202

glass. Boyes wasn't *in extremis* – he was speaking quite rationally and all that. I say the man was deliberately protecting himself.'

'Possibly,' said Parker, 'but after all, old man, when *did* he administer the poison?'

'Probably not at the dinner at all,' said Miss Murchison. 'As you say, the precautions seem rather obvious. They may have been intended to make people concentrate on the dinner and forget other possibilities. Did he have a whisky when he arrived or before he went out or anything?'

'Alas, he did not. Bunter has been cultivating Hannah Westlock almost to breach of promise point, and she says that she opened the door to Boyes on his arrival, that he went straight upstairs to his room, that Urquhart was out at the time and only came in a quarter of an hour before dinner-time, and that the two met for the first time over the famous glass of sherry in the library. The folding-doors between the library and dining-room were open and Hannah was buzzing round the whole time laying the table, and she is sure that Boyes had the sherry and nothing but the sherry.'

'Not so much as a digestive tablet?'

'Nothing.'

'How about after dinner?'

'When they had finished the omelette, Urquhart said something about coffee. Boyes looked at his watch and said, "No time, old chap; I've got to be getting along to Doughty Street." Urquhart said he would ring up a taxi, and went out to do so. Boyes folded up his napkin, got up, and went into the hall. Hannah followed and helped him on with his coat. The taxi arrived. Boyes got in, and off he went without seeing Urquhart again.'

'It seems to me,' said Miss Murchison, 'that Hannah is an exceedingly important witness for Mr Urquhart's defence. You don't think – I hardly like to suggest it – but you don't think that Bunter is allowing his feelings to overcome his judgement?'

'He says,' replied Lord Peter, 'that he believes Hannah to be a sincerely religious woman. He has sat beside her in chapel and shared her hymn-book.'

'But that may be the merest hypocrisy,' said Miss Murchison, rather warmly, for she was militantly rationalist. 'I don't trust these unctuous people.'

'I didn't offer that as a proof of Hannah's virtue,' said Wimsey, 'but of Bunter's unsusceptibility.'

'But he looks like a deacon himself.'

'You've never seen Bunter off duty,' said Lord Peter, darkly, 'I have, and I can assure you that a hymn-book would be about as softening to his heart as neat whisky to an Anglo-Indian liver. No; if Bunter says Hannah is honest, then she *is* honest.'

'Then that definitely cuts out the drinks and the dinner,' said Miss Murchison, unconvinced, but willing to be open-minded. 'How about the water-bottle in the bedroom?'

'The devil!' cried Wimsey. 'That's one up to you, Miss Murchison. We didn't think of that. The water-bottle – yes – a perfectly fruity idea. You recollect, Charles, that in the Bravo case it was suggested that a disgruntled servant had put tartar emetic in the water-bottle. Oh, Bunter – here you are! Next time you hold Hannah's hand, will you ask her whether Mr Boyes drank any water from his bedroom water-bottle before dinner?'

'Pardon me, my lord, the possibility had already presented itself to my mind.'

'It had?'

'Yes, my lord.'

'Do you never overlook anything, Bunter?'

'I endeavour to give satisfaction, my lord.'

'Well, then, don't talk like Jeeves. It irritates me. What about the water-bottle?'

'I was about to observe, my lord, when this lady arrived, that I had elicited a somewhat peculiar circumstance relating to the water-bottle.'

'Now we're getting somewhere,' said Parker, flattening out a new page of his note-book.

'I would not go so far as to say that, sir. Hannah informed me that she showed Mr Boyes into his bedroom on his arrival and withdrew, as it was her place to do. She had scarcely reached the head of the staircase when Mr Boyes put his head out of the door and recalled her. He then asked her to fill his water-bottle. She was considerably astonished at this request, since she had a perfect recollection of having previously filled it when she put the room in order.'

'Could he have emptied it himself?' asked Parker, eagerly.

'Not into his interior, sir – there had not been time. Nor had the drinking-glass been utilised. Moreover, the bottle was not merely empty, but dry inside. Hannah apologised for the neglect, and immediately rinsed out the bottle and filled it from the tap.'

'Curious,' said Parker. 'But it's quite likely she never filled it at all.'

'Pardon me, sir, Hannah was so much surprised by the episode that she mentioned it to Mrs Pettican, the cook, who said that she distinctly recollected seeing her fill the bottle that morning.'

'Well, then,' said Parker, 'Urquhart or somebody must have emptied it and dried it out. Now, why? What would one naturally do if one found one's water-bottle empty?'

'Ring the bell,' said Wimsey, promptly.

'Or shout for help,' added Parker.

'Or,' said Miss Murchison, 'if one wasn't accustomed to be waited on, one might use the water from the bedroom jug.'

'Ah! . . . of course, Boyes was used to a more or less Bohemian life.'

'But surely,' said Wimsey, 'that's idiotically roundabout. It would be much simpler just to poison the water in the bottle. Why direct attention to the thing by making it more difficult? Besides, you couldn't count on the victim's using the jug-water – and, as a matter of fact, he didn't.'

'And he *was* poisoned,' said Miss Murchison, 'so the poison wasn't either in the jug or the bottle.'

'No – I'm afraid there's nothing to be got out of the jug and bottle department. Hollow, hollow, hollow all delight, Tennyson.'

'All the same,' said Parker, 'that incident convinces me. It's too complete, somehow. Wimsey's right; it's not natural for a defence to be so perfect.'

'My God,' said Wimsey, 'we have convinced Charles Parker. Nothing more is needed. He is more adamantine than any jury.'

'Yes,' said Parker, modestly, 'but I'm more logical, I think. And I'm not being flustered by the Attorney-General. I should feel happier with a little evidence of a more objective kind.'

'You would. You want some real arsenic. Well Bunter, what about it?'

'The apparatus is quite ready, my lord.'

'Very good. Let us go and see if we can give Mr Parker what he wants. Lead and we follow.'

In a small apartment usually devoted to Bunter's photographic work, and furnished with a sink, a bench, and a bunsen burner, stood the apparatus necessary for making a Marsh's test of arsenic. The distilled water was already bubbling in the flask, and Bunter lifted the little glass tube which lay across the flame of the burner.

'You will perceive, my lord,' he observed, 'that the apparatus is free from contamination.'

'I see nothing at all,' said Freddy.

'That, as Sherlock Holmes would say, is what you may expect to see when there is nothing there,' said Wimsey, kindly. 'Charles, you will pass the water and the flask and the tube, old Uncle Tom Cobley and all, as being arsenic-free.'

'I will.'

'Wilt thou love, cherish, and keep her, in sickness or in health – sorry! turned over two pages at once. Where's that powder? Miss Murchison, you identify this sealed envelope as being the one you brought from the office, complete with mysterious white powder from Mr Urquhart's secret hoard?'

'I do.'

'Kiss the book. Thank you. Now then –'

'Wait a sec,' said Parker, 'you haven't tested the envelope separately.'

'That's true. There's always a snag somewhere. I suppose, Miss Murchison, you haven't such a thing as another office envelope about you?'

Miss Murchison blushed, and fumbled in her handbag.

'Well – there's a little note I scribbled this afternoon to a friend –'

'*In* your employer's time, *on* your employer's paper,' said Wimsey. 'Oh, how right Diogenes was when he took his lantern to look for an honest typist! Never mind. Let's have it. Who wills the end, wills the means.'

Miss Murchison extracted the envelope and freed it from the enclosure. Bunter, receiving it respectfully on a developing dish, cut it into small pieces, which he dropped into the flask. The water bubbled brightly, but the little tube still remained stainless from end to end.

'Does something begin to happen soon?' inquired Mr Arbuthnot. 'Because I feel this show's a bit lackin' in pep, what?'

'If you don't sit still I shall take you out,' retorted Wimsey. 'Carry on Bunter. We'll pass the envelope.'

Bunter accordingly opened the second envelope, and delicately dropped the white powder into the wide mouth of the flask. All five heads bent eagerly over the apparatus. And instantly, definitely, magically, a thin silver stain began to form in the tube where the flame impinged upon it. Second by second it spread and darkened to a deep brownish-black ring with a shining metallic centre.

'Oh, lovely, lovely,' said Parker, with professional delight.

'Your lamp's smoking or something,' said Freddy.

'Is that arsenic?' breathed Miss Murchison, gently.

'I hope so,' said Wimsey, gently detaching the tube and holding it up to the light. 'It's either arsenic or antimony.'

'Allow me, my lord. The addition of a small quantity of solute chlorinated lime should decide the question beyond reach of cavil.'

He performed his further test amid an anxious silence. The stain dissolved out and vanished under the bleaching solution.

'Then it is arsenic,' said Parker.

'Oh, yes,' said Wimsey, nonchalantly, 'of course it is arsenic. Didn't I tell you?' His voice wavered a little with suppressed triumph.

'Is that all?' inquired Freddy, disappointed.

'Isn't it enough?' said Miss Murchison.

'Not quite,' said Parker, 'but it's a long way towards it. It proves that Urquhart has arsenic in his possession, and by making an official inquiry in France, we can probably find out whether this packet was already in his possession last June. I notice, by the way, that it is ordinary white arsenious acid, without any mixture of charcoal or indigo, which agrees with what was found at the post-mortem. That's satisfactory, but it would be even more satisfactory if we could provide an opportunity for Urquhart to have administered it. So far, all we have done is to demonstrate clearly that he couldn't have given it to Boyes either before, during, or after dinner, during the period required for the symptoms to develop. I agree that an impossibility so bolstered up by testimony is suspicious in itself, but, to convince a jury, I should prefer something better than a *credo quia impossibile.'*

'Riddle-me-right, and riddle-me-ree,' said Wimsey, imperturbably. 'We've overlooked something, that's all. Probably something quite obvious. Give me the statutory dressing-gown and ounce of shag, and I shall undertake to dispose of this little difficulty for you in a brace of shakes. In the meantime, you will no doubt take steps to secure, in an official and laborious manner, the evidence which our kind friends here have already so ably gathered in by unconventional methods, and will stand by to arrest the right man when the time comes?'

'I will,' said Parker, 'gladly. Apart from all personal considerations, I'd far rather see that oily-haired fellow in the dock than any woman, and if the Force has made a mistake, the sooner it's put right the better for all concerned.'

*   *   *

Wimsey sat late that night in the black-and-primrose library, with the tall folios looking down at him. They represented the world's accumulated hoard of mellow wisdom and poetical beauty, to say nothing of thousands of pounds in cash. But all these counsellors sat mute upon their shelves. Strewn on tables and chair lay the bright scarlet volumes of the *Notable British Trials* – Palmer, Pritchard, Maybrick, Seddon, Armstrong, Madeleine Smith – the great practitioners in arsenic – huddled together with the chief authorities on forensic medicine and toxicology.

The theatre-going crowds surged home in saloon and taxi, the lights shone over the empty width of Piccadilly, the heavy night-lorries rumbled slow and seldom over the black tarmac, the long night waned and the reluctant winter dawn struggled wanly over the piled roofs of London. Bunter, silent and anxious, sat in his kitchen, brewing coffee on the stove and reading the same page of the *British Journal of Photography* over and over again.

At half-past eight the library bell rang.

'My lord?'

'My bath, Bunter.'

'Very good, my lord.'

'And some coffee.'

'Immediately, my lord.'

'And put back all the books except these.'

'Yes, my lord.'

'I know now how it was done.'

'Indeed, my lord? Permit me to offer my respectful congratulations.'

'I've still got to prove it.'

'A secondary consideration, my lord.'

Wimsey yawned. When Bunter returned a minute or two later with the coffee, he was asleep.

Bunter put the books quietly away, and looked with some curiosity at the chosen few left open on the table. They were: *The Trial of Florence Maybrick*; Dixon Mann's *Forensic Medicine and Toxicology*; a book with a German title which Bunter could not read; and A. E. Housman's *A Shropshire Lad*.

Bunter studied these for a few moments, and then slapped his thigh softly.

'Why, of course!' he said under his breath. 'Why, what a mutton-headed set of chumps we've all been!' He touched his master lightly on the shoulder.

'Your coffee, my lord.'

Chapter XXI

'THEN you won't marry me?' said Lord Peter.

The prisoner shook her head.

'No. It wouldn't be fair to you. And besides –'

'Well?'

'I'm frightened of it. One couldn't get away. I'll live with you, if you like, but I won't marry you.'

Her tone was so unutterably dreary that Wimsey could feel no enthusiasm for this handsome offer.

'But that sort of thing doesn't always work,' he expostulated. 'Dash it all, you ought to know – forgive my alluding to it and all that – but it's frightfully inconvenient, and one has as many rows as if one was married.'

'I know that. But you could cut loose any time you wanted to.'

'But I shouldn't want to.'

'Oh, yes, you would. You've got a family and traditions, you know. Caesar's wife and that sort of thing.'

'Blast Caesar's wife! And as for the family traditions – they're on my side, for what they're worth. Anything a Wimsey does is right and Heaven help the person who gets in the way. We've got a damned old family motto about it – "I hold by my Whimsy" – quite right too. I can't say that when I look in the glass I exactly suggest to myself the original Gerald de Wimsey, who bucked about on a cart-horse at the Siege of Acre, but I do jolly well intend to do what I like about marrying. Who's to stop me? They can't eat me. They can't even cut me, if it comes to that. Joke, unintentional, officers, for the use of.'

Harriet laughed.

'No, I suppose they can't cut you. You wouldn't have to slink abroad with your impossible wife and live at obscure

Continental watering-places like people in Victorian novels.'

'Certainly not.'

'People would forget I'd had a lover?'

'My dear child, they're forgetting that kind of thing every day. They're experts at it.'

'And was supposed to have murdered him?'

'And were triumphantly acquitted of having murdered him, however greatly provoked.'

'Well, I won't marry you. If people can forget all that, they can forget we're not married.'

'Oh, yes, *they* could. I couldn't, that's all. We don't seem to be progressing very fast with this conversation. I take it the general idea of living with me does not hopelessly repel you?'

'But this is all so preposterous,' protested the girl. 'How can I say what I should or shouldn't do if I were free and certain of – surviving?'

'Why not? I can imagine what I should do even in the most unlikely circumstances, whereas this really is a dead cert, straight from the stables.'

'I can't,' said Harriet, beginning to wilt. 'Do please stop asking me. I don't know. I can't think. I can't see beyond the – beyond the – beyond the next few weeks. I only want to get out of this and be left alone.'

'All right,' said Wimsey, 'I won't worry you. Not fair. Abusing my privilege and so on. You can't say "Pig" and sweep out, under the circs., so I won't offend again. As a matter of fact I'll sweep out myself, having an appointment – with a manicurist. Nice little girl, but a trifle refained in her vowels. Cheerio!'

*   *   *

The manicurist, who had been discovered by the help of Chief Inspector Parker and his sleuths, was a kitten-faced child with an inviting manner and a shrewd eye. She made no bones about accepting her client's invitation to dine, and showed no surprise when he confidentially murmured that he had a little proposition to put before her. She put her plump elbows on the table, cocked her head at a coy angle, and prepared to sell her honour dear.

As the proposition unfolded itself, her manner underwent an alteration that was most comical. Her eyes lost their rounded innocence, her very hair seemed to grow less fluffy, and her eyebrows puckered in genuine astonishment.

'Why of course I could,' she said finally, 'but whatever do you want them for? Seems funny to me.'

'Call it just a joke,' said Wimsey.

'No.' Her mouth hardened. 'I wouldn't like it. It doesn't make sense, if you see what I mean, it sounds a queer sort of joke, and that kind of thing might get a girl into trouble. I say, it's not one of those, who do they call 'em? – there was a bit about it in Madame Crystal's column last week in *Susie's Snippets* – spells, you know, witchcraft – the occult, that sort of thing? I wouldn't like it if it was to do any harm to anybody.'

'I'm not going to make a waxen image, if that's what you mean. Look here, are you the sort of girl who can keep a secret?'

'Oh, I don't talk. I never was one to let my tongue wag around. I'm not like ordinary girls.'

'No, I thought you weren't. That's why I asked you to come out with me. Well, listen, and I'll tell you.'

He leaned forward and talked. The little painted face upturned to his grew so absorbed and so excited that a bosom friend, dining at a table some way off, grew quite peevish with envy, making sure that darling Mabel was being offered a flat in Paris, a Daimler car, and a thousand-pound necklace, and quarrelled fatally with her own escort in consequence.

'So you see,' said Wimsey, 'it means a lot to me.'

Darling Mabel gave an ecstatic sigh.

'Is that all true? You're not making it up? It's better than any of the talkies.'

'Yes, but you mustn't say one word. You're the only person I've told. You won't give me away to him?'

'Him? He's a stingy pig. Catch me giving him anything. I'm on. I'll do it for you. It'll be a bit difficult, 'cause I'll have to use the scissors, which we don't do as a rule. But I'll manage. You trust me. They won't be big ones, you know. He comes in pretty often, but I'll give you all I get. And I'll fix Fred. He always has Fred. Fred'll do it if I asked him. What'll I do with them when I get them?'

Wimsey drew an envelope from his pocket.

'Sealed up inside this,' he said, impressively, 'there are two little pill-boxes. You mustn't take them out till you get the specimens, because they've been carefully prepared so as to be absolutely chemically clean, if you see what I mean. When you're ready, open the envelope, take out the pill-boxes, put the parings into one and the hair into the other, shut them up at once, put them into a clean envelope, and post them to this address. Get that?'

'Yes.' She stretched out an eager hand.

'Good girl. And not a word.'

'Not – one – word!' She made a gesture of exaggerated caution.

'When's your birthday?'

'Oh, I don't have one. I never grow up.'

'Right; then I can send you an unbirthday present any day in the year. You'd look nice in mink, I think.'

'Mink, I think,' she mocked him. 'Quite a poet, aren't you?'

'You inspire me,' said Wimsey, politely.

Chapter XXII

'I HAVE come round,' said Mr Urquhart, 'in answer to your letter I am greatly interested to hear that you have some fresh information about my unfortunate cousin's death. Of course, I shall be delighted to give you any assistance I can.'

'Thank you,' said Wimsey. 'Do sit down. You have dined, of course? But you will have a cup of coffee. You prefer the Turkish variety, I fancy. My man brews it rather well.'

Mr Urquhart accepted the offer, and complimented Bunter on having achieved the right method of concocting that curiously syrupy brew, so offensive to the average Occidental.

Bunter thanked him gravely for his good opinion, and proffered a box of that equally nauseating mess called Turkish delight which not only gluts the palate and glues the teeth, but also smothers the consumer in a floury cloud of white sugar. Mr Urquhart immediately plugged his mouth with a large lump of it, murmuring indistinctly that it was the genuine Eastern variety. Wimsey, with an austere smile, took a few sips of strong black coffee without sugar or milk, and poured himself out a glass of old brandy. Bunter retired, and Lord Peter, laying a note-book open upon his knee, glanced at the clock and began his narrative.

He recapitulated the circumstances of Philip Boyes's life and death at some length. Mr Urquhart, yawning surreptitiously, ate, drank, and listened.

Wimsey, still with his eye on the clock, then embarked upon the story of Mrs Wrayburn's will.

Mr Urquhart, considerably astonished, set his coffee-cup aside, wiped his sticky fingers upon his handkerchief, and stared.

Presently he said:

'May I ask how you have obtained this very remarkable information?'

Wimsey waved his hand.

'The police,' he said; 'wonderful thing, police organisation. Surprisin' what they find out when they put their minds to it. You're not denying any of it, I presume?'

'I am listening,' said Mr Urquhart, grimly. 'When you have finished this extraordinary statement, I may perhaps discover exactly what it is I have to deny.'

'Oh, yes,' said Wimsey, 'I'll try to make that clear. I'm not a lawyer, of course, but I'm tryin' to be as lucid as I can.'

He droned remorselessly on, and the hands of the clock went round.

'So far as I make it out,' he said, when he had reviewed the whole question of motive, 'it was very much to your interest to get rid of Mr Philip Boyes. And indeed the fellow was in my opinion, a pimple and a wart, and in your place I should have felt much the same about him.'

'And is this the whole of your fantastic accusation?' inquired the solicitor.

'By no means. I am now coming to the point. "Slow but sure" is the motto of yours faithfully. I notice that I have taken up seventy minutes of your valuable time, but believe me, the hour has not been unprofitably spent.'

'Allowing that all this preposterous story were true, which I most emphatically deny,' observed Mr Urquhart, 'I should be greatly interested to know how you imagine that I administered the arsenic. Have you worked out something ingenious for that? Or am I supposed to have suborned my cook and parlourmaid to be my accomplices? A little rash of me, don't you think, and affording remarkable opportunities for blackmail?'

'So rash,' said Wimsey, 'that it is quite out of the question for a man so full of forethought as yourself. The sealing-up of that bottle of Burgundy, for example, argues a mind alive to possibilities – unusually so. In fact, the episode attracted my attention from the start.'

'Indeed?'

'You ask me how and when you administered the poison. It was not before dinner, I think. The thoughtfulness shown in emptying the bedroom water-bottle – oh, no! that point was not

215

missed – the care displayed in meeting your cousin before a witness and never being left alone with him – I think that rules out the period before dinner.'

'I should think it might.'

'The sherry,' pursued Wimsey, thoughtfully. 'It was a new bottle, freshly decanted. The disappearance of the remains might be commented on. I fancy we can absolve the sherry.'

Mr Urquhart bowed ironically.

'The soup – it was shared by the cook and parlourmaid and they survived. I am inclined to pass the soup, and the same thing applies to the fish. It would be easy to poison a portion of fish, but it would involve the co-operation of Hannah Westlock, and that conflicts with my theory. A theory is a sacred thing to me, Mr Urquhart – almost a what d'you call it – a dogma.'

'An unsafe attitude of mind,' remarked the lawyer, 'but in the circumstances I will not quarrel with it.'

'Besides,' said Wimsey, 'if the poison had been given in the soup or fish, it might have started to work before Philip – I may call him so I hope? – had left the house. We come to the casserole. Mrs Pettican and Hannah Westlock can give the casserole a clean bill of health, I fancy. And, by the way, from the description it must have been most delicious. I speak as a man with some considerable experience in gastronomic matters, Mr Urquhart.'

'I am well aware of it,' said Mr Urquhart, politely.

'And now there remains only the omelette. A most admirable thing when well made and eaten – that is so important – eaten immediately. A charming idea to have the eggs and sugar brought to the table and prepared and cooked on the spot. By the way, I take it there was no omelette left over for the kitchen? No, no! One does not let a good thing like that go out half-eaten. Much better that the good cook should make a fine, fresh omelette for herself and her colleague. Nobody but yourself and Philip partook of the omelette, I am sure.'

'Quite so,' said Mr Urquhart, 'I need not trouble to deny it. But you will bear in mind that I did partake of it, without ill-effects. And, moreover, that my cousin made it himself.'

'So he did. Four eggs, if I remember rightly, with sugar and jam from what I may call the common stock. No – there would be nothing wrong with the sugar or the jam. Er – I believe I am right in saying that one of the eggs was cracked when it came to table?'

'Possibly. I do not remember.'

'No? Well, you are not on oath. But Hannah Westlock remembers that when you brought the eggs in – you purchased them yourself, you know, Mr Urquhart – you mentioned that one was cracked and particularly desired that it should be used for the omelette. In fact, you yourself laid it in the bowl for that purpose.'

'What about it?' asked Mr Urquhart, perhaps a trifle less easily than before.

'It is not very difficult to introduce powdered arsenic into a cracked egg,' said Wimsey. 'I have made the experiment myself with a small glass tube. Perhaps a small funnel would be even easier. Arsenic is a fairly heavy substance – seven or eight grains will go into a teaspoon. It collects at one end of the egg, and any traces on the exterior of the shell can be readily wiped off. Liquid arsenic could be poured in still more easily, of course, but for a particular reason I made my experiment with the ordinary white powder. It is fairly soluble.'

Mr Urquhart had taken a cigar from his case, and was making rather a business of lighting it.

'Do you suggest,' he inquired, 'that in the whisking together of four eggs, one particular poisoned egg was somehow kept miraculously separated from the rest and deposited with its load of arsenic at one end of the omelette only? Or that my cousin deliberately helped himself to the poisoned end and left the rest to me?'

'Not at all, not at all,' said Wimsey. 'I suggest merely that the arsenic was in the omelette and came there by way of the egg.'

Mr Urquhart threw his match into the fireplace.

'There seem to be some flaws in your theory, as well as in the egg.'

'I haven't finished the theory yet. My next bit of it is built up from very trifling indications. Let me enumerate them. Your disinclination to drink at dinner, your complexion, a few nail-parings, a snipping or so from your very well-kept hair – I put these together, add a packet of white arsenic from the

217

secret cupboard in your office, rub the hands a little – so – and produce – hemp, Mr Urquhart, hemp.'

He sketched the shape of a noose lightly in the air.

'I don't understand you,' said the solicitor, hoarsely.

'Oh, *you* know,' said Wimsey. 'Hemp – what they make ropes of. Great stuff, hemp. Yes, well, about this arsenic. As you know, it's not good for people in a general way, but there are some people – those tiresome peasants in Syria one hears so much about – who are supposed to eat it for fun. It improves their wind, so they say, and clears their complexions, and makes their hair sleek, and they give it to their horses for the same reasons; bar the complexion, that is, because a horse hasn't much complexion, but you know what I mean. Then there was that horrid man Maybrick – he used to take it, or so they say. Anyhow, it's well known that some people take it and manage to put away large dollops after a bit of practice – enough to kill any ordinary person. But you know all this.'

'This is the first time I've heard of such a thing.'

'Where *do* you expect to go to? Never mind. We'll pretend this is all new to you. Well, some fellow – I've forgotten his name,[1] but it's all in Dixon Mann – wondered how the dodge was worked, and he got going on some dogs and things and he dosed 'em and killed a lot of 'em I daresay, and in the end he found that whereas liquid arsenic was dealt with by the kidneys and was uncommonly bad for the system, solid arsenic could be given day by day, a little bigger dose each time, so that in time the doings – what an old lady I knew in Norfolk called "the tubes" – got used to it and could push it along without taking any notice of it, so to speak. I read a book somewhere which said it was all done by leucocytes – those jolly little white corpuscles, don't you know – which sort of got round the stuff and bustled it along so that it couldn't do any harm. At all events, the point is that if you go on taking solid arsenic for a good long time – say a year or so – you establish a what-not, an immunity, and can take six or seven grains at a time without so much as a touch of indi-jaggers.'

'Very interesting,' said Mr Urquhart.

'Apparently those beastly Syrian peasants do it that way, and they're very careful not to drink for two hours or there-

[1] Valetta.

abouts after taking it, for fear it should all get washed into the kidneys and turn poisonous on 'em. I'm not bein' very technical, I'm afraid, but that's the gist of it. Well, it occurred to me, don't you see, old horse, that if you'd had the bright idea to immunise yourself first, you could easily have shared a jolly old arsenical omelette with a friend. It would kill him and it wouldn't hurt you.'

'I see.'

The solicitor licked his lips.

'Well, as I say, you have a nice clear complexion – except that I notice the arsenic has pigmented the skin here and there (it does sometimes), and you've got the sleek hair and so on, and I noticed you were careful not to drink at dinner, and I said to myself, "Peter, my bright lad, what about it?" And when they found a packet of white arsenic in your cupboard – never mind how for the moment! – I said, "Hullo, hullo, how long has this been going on?" Your handy foreign chemist has told the police two years – is that right? About the time of the Megatherium crash that would be, wouldn't it? All right, don't tell me if you don't want to. Then we got hold of some bits of your hair and nails, and lo and behold! they were bung-full of arsenic. And we said "What-ho!" So that's why I asked you to come along and have a chat with me. I thought you might like to offer some sort of suggestion, don't you know.'

'I can only suggest,' said Urquhart, with a ghastly face but a strictly professional manner, that you should be careful before you communicate this ludicrous theory to anybody. What you and the police – whom, frankly, I believe to be capable of anything – have been planting on my premises I do not know, but to give out that I am addicted to drug-taking habits is slander and criminal. It is quite true that I have for some time been taking a medicine which contains slight traces of arsenic – Dr Grainger can furnish the prescription – and that may very likely have left a deposit in my skin and hair, but, further than that, there is no foundation for this monstrous accusation.'

'None?'

'None.'

'Then how is it,' asked Wimsey, coolly, but with something menacing in his rigidly controlled voice, 'how is it that you have this evening consumed, without apparent effect, a dose of arsenic sufficient to kill two or three ordinary people? That disgusting sweetmeat on which you have been gorging yourself in, I may say, a manner wholly unsuited to your age and position, is smothered in white arsenic. You ate it, God forgive you, an hour and a half ago. If arsenic can harm you, you should have been rolling about in agonies for the last hour.'

'You devil!'

'Couldn't you try to get up a few symptoms?' said Wimsey, sarcastically. 'Shall I bring you a basin? Or fetch the doctor? Does your throat burn? Is your inside convulsed with agony? It is rather late in the day, but with a little goodwill you could surely produce *some* display of feeling, even now.'

'You are lying. You wouldn't dare to do such a thing! It would be murder.'

'Not in this case, I fancy. But I am willing to wait and see.'

Urquhart stared at him. Wimsey got out of his chair in a single swift movement and stood over him.

'I wouldn't use violence if I were you. Let the poisoner stick to his bottle. Besides, I am armed. Pardon the melodrama. Are you going to be sick or not?'

'You're mad.'

'Don't say that. Come, man – pull yourself together. Have a shot at it. Shall I show you the bathroom?'

'I'm ill.'

'Of course; but your tone is not convincing. Through the door, along the passage, and third on the left.'

The lawyer stumbled out. Wimsey returned to the library and rang the bell.

'I think, Bunter, Mr Parker may require some assistance in the bathroom.'

'Very good, my lord.'

Bunter departed, and Wimsey waited. Presently there were sounds of a scuffle in the distance. A group appeared at the door – Urquhart, very white, his hair and clothes disordered, flanked by Parker and Bunter, who held him firmly by the arms.

'Was he sick?' asked Wimsey, with interest.

'No, he wasn't,' said Parker, grimly, snapping the handcuffs on his prey. 'He cursed you fluently for five minutes, then tried to get out of the window, saw it was a three-storey drop, charged in through the dressing-room door, and ran straight into me. Now don't struggle, my lad; you'll only hurt yourself.'

'And he still doesn't know whether he's poisoned or not?'

'He doesn't seem to think he is. At any rate, he made no effort about it. His one idea was to hop it.'

'That's feeble,' said Wimsey; 'if I wanted people to think I'd been poisoned I'd put up a better show than that.'

'Stop talking, for God's sake,' said the prisoner. 'You've got me by a vile, damnable trick. Isn't that enough? You can shut up about it.'

'Oh,' said Parker, 'we've got you, have we? Well, warned you not to talk, and if you *will* do it, it's not my fault. By the way, Peter, I don't suppose you did actually poison him, did you? It doesn't seem to have hurt him, but it'll affect the doctor's report.'

'No, I didn't, as a matter of fact,' said Wimsey. 'I only wanted to see how he'd react to the suggestion. Well, cheerio! I can leave it to you now.'

'We'll look after him,' said Parker. 'But you might let Bunter ring up a taxi.'

When the prisoner and his escort had departed, Wimsey turned thoughtfully to Bunter, glass in hand.

'*Mithridates he died old*, says the poet. But I doubt it, Bunter. In this case I very much doubt it.'

Chapter XXIII

THERE were gold chrysanthemums on the judge's bench: they looked like burning banners.

The prisoner, too, had a look in her eyes that was a challenge to the crowded court, as the clerk read the indictment. The judge, a plump, elderly man with an eighteenth-century face, looked expectantly at the Attorney-General.

'My lord, I am instructed that the Crown offers no evidence against this prisoner.'

The gasp that went round the room sounded like the rustle of trees in a rising wind.

'Do I understand that the charge against the prisoner is withdrawn?'

'Those are my instructions, my lord.'

'In that case,' said the judge, impassively, turning to the jury, 'there is nothing left for you but to return a verdict of "Not Guilty". Usher, keep those people quiet in the gallery.'

'One moment, my lord.' Sir Impey Biggs rose up, large and majestic.

'On my client's behalf – on Miss Vane's behalf, my lord, I beg your indulgence for a few words. A charge has been brought against her, my lord, the very awful charge of murder, and I should like it to be made clear, my lord, that my client leaves this court without a stain upon her character. As I am informed, my lord, this is not a case of the charge being withdrawn in default of evidence. I understand, my lord that further information has come to the police which definitely proves the entire innocence of my client. I also understand, my lord, that a further arrest has been made and that an inquiry will follow, my lord, in due course. My lord, this lady must go forth into the world acquitted, not only at this bar, but at the bar of public opinion. Any ambiguity would be intolerable, and I am sure, my lord, that I have the support of the learned Attorney-General for what I say.'

'By all means,' said the Attorney. 'I am instructed to say, my lord, that in withdrawing the charge against the prisoner, the Crown proceeds from complete conviction of her absolute innocence.'

'I am very glad to hear it,' said the judge. 'Prisoner at the bar, the Crown, by unreservedly withdrawing this dreadful charge against you, has demonstrated your innocence in the clearest possible way. After this, nobody will be able to suppose that the slightest imputation rests upon you, and I most heartily congratulate you on this very satisfactory ending to your long ordeal. Now please – I sympathise very much with the people who are cheering, but this is not a theatre or a football match, and if they are not quiet, they will have to be put out. Members of the jury, do you find the prisoner "Guilty" or "Not Guilty"?'

'Not guilty, my lord.'

'Very good. The prisoner is discharged without a stain upon her character. Next case.'

So ended, sensational to the last, one of the most sensational murder trials of the century.

*   *   *

Harriet Vane, a free woman, found Eiluned Price and Sylvia Marriot waiting for her as she descended the stairs.

'Darling!' said Sylvia.

'Three loud cheers!' said Eiluned.

Harriet greeted them a little vaguely.

'Where is Lord Peter Wimsey?' she inquired. 'I must thank him.'

'You won't,' said Eiluned, bluntly. 'I saw him drive off the moment the verdict was given.'

'Oh!' said Miss Vane.

'He'll come and see you,' said Sylvia.

'No, he won't,' said Eiluned.

'Why not?' said Sylvia.

'Too decent,' said Eiluned.

'I'm afraid you're right,' said Harriet.

223

'I like that young man,' said Eiluned. 'You needn't grin. I do like him. He's not going to do the King Cophetua stunt, and I take off my hat to him. If you want him, you'll have to send for him.'

'I won't do that,' said Harriet.

'Oh, yes, you will,' said Sylvia. 'I was right about who did the murder, and I'm going to be right about this.'

* * *

Lord Peter Wimsey went down to Duke's Denver that same evening. He found the family in a state of perturbation, all except the Dowager, who sat placidly making a rug in the midst of the uproar.

'Look here, Peter,' said the Duke, 'you're the only person with any influence over Mary. You've got to do something. She wants to marry your policeman friend.'

'I know,' said Wimsey. 'Why shouldn't she?'

'It's ridiculous,' said the Duke.

'Not at all,' said Lord Peter. 'Charles is one of the best.'

'Very likely,' said the Duke, 'but Mary can't marry a policeman.'

'Now, look here,' said Wimsey, tucking his sister's arm in his, 'you leave Polly alone. Charles made a bit of a mistake at the beginning of this murder case, but he doesn't make many, and one of these days he'll be a big man, with a title, I shouldn't wonder, and everything handsome about him. If you want to have a row with somebody, have it with me.'

'My God!' said the Duke, 'you're not going to marry a policewoman?'

'Not quite,' said Wimsey. 'I intend to marry the prisoner.'

'What?' said the Duke. 'Good Lord, what what?'

'If she'll have me,' said Lord Peter Wimsey.